Re-creati

For the first time in the t_____
stroyer series, this book _____ _ _____ ____ ___ "by
Richard Sapir and Warren Murphy."

Dick Sapir, my friend and partner, died twenty years ago,
and in the years since then I've worked to preserve Dick's
name in connection with the series.

But time does move on. The new byline on this book
credits James Mullaney as coauthor. Jim is a talented
young writer who has worked with me on Destroyer books
for a number of years, and I know his energy and skill will
help move The New Destroyer series into a more ener-
getic day.

Dick Sapir was and is irreplaceable. The new byline is
simply a long overdue acknowledgment of the outstanding
work Jim Mullaney has done and will continue to do.

I know Dick Sapir would have approved.

Warren Murphy
April 2007

And just to allay any concerns, our intention with The New
Destroyer is not to reinvent the wheel but to harken back to
Warren and Dick's old Destroyers. Many fans have noted
in recent years that the ground underfoot had gotten a little
rocky, so we've decided to smooth it out a little. In the new
books you might notice a lack of references to characters
and situations from the last dozen-or-so books. That's because as far as we scribblers (as well as Remo, Chiun, and
Smitty) are concerned, they never happened. A clean slate,
a fresh start.

With luck, the good Lord willing, and the wind at our
backs, you'll be stuck with us for a while. So on to bidness.

And to my truck driver Dad who got me started on this

road when he brought home those first Destroyers thirty years ago: I got in the truck and drove.

Jim Mullaney
April 2007

THE NEW DESTROYER:
GUARDIAN ANGEL

Warren Murphy and James Mullaney

TOR®

A TOM DOHERTY ASSOCIATES BOOK
NEW YORK

This is a work of fiction. All of the characters, organizations, and events portrayed in this novel are either products of the author's imagination or are used fictitiously.

THE NEW DESTROYER: GUARDIAN ANGEL

Copyright © 2007 by Warren Murphy

A Tor Book
Published by Tom Doherty Associates, LLC
175 Fifth Avenue
New York, NY 10010

www.tor.com

Tor® is a registered trademark of Tom Doherty Associates, LLC.

ISBN-13: 978-0-765-35759-5
ISBN-10: 0-765-35759-3

First Edition: May 2007

Printed in the United States of America

0 9 8 7 6 5 4 3 2 1

Many people—fans and friends and readers and correspondents and Webmasters—are responsible for where we are right now, ushering in a new era of The Destroyer. This book is dedicated with the greatest respect, love, and admiration to all of the folks who have stuck with us through the fat, and the lean, and the sometimes anorexic times.

Special thanks to Jerry Welch and Donna Courtois of www.destroyerclub.com, as well as Cam Bailey, Dale Barkman, and Rick Drew, who have some pretty nifty Destroyer Web sites of their own. Also to Brian Murphy, Mark Mullaney, and Pinhead.

For www.warrenmurphy.com, where one of us can be reached.

For www.jamesmullaney.com, where the other one can.

Special thanks to Dick Sapir, friend and inspiration. We're still at it. Extra special thanks to the greatest mom on earth, Mrs. Kathleen Mullaney. And, once more, for the Glorious House of Sinanju, email: housinan@aol.com

And no squids. We promise.

THE NEW DESTROYER:
GUARDIAN ANGEL

Rob Scott stared up at the cold night stars, scat-
tered like sparkling grains of sand above the vast New
Mexico desert, and for the first time in his thirty-three
years of life fully appreciated the sheer, mind-numbing
boredom of the vastness of creation.

The light of those stars had taken millions of years to
reach Rob Scott's upturned face and he felt as if he had
been waiting out in the desert all that time. Of course, he
had not been in New Mexico for millions of years—only
five hot days and four long nights—but the desert had a
way of warping one's sense of time.

To while away the incredible tedium of the late night
hours, Rob thought about counting the stars. But he had
tried that the previous night and had lost count as they
slowly slipped behind the horizon and the desert morning
bleached them from the sky.

He had brought his iPod with him and could have listened to his favorite Springsteen music, but on this night, the last of his life, he was too bored even for that.

Maybe the sky was too clear, too unobstructed. Back home in Minneapolis it was impossible to see the sky from horizon to horizon. Here though, with the great panoply of creation spread out before him, Rob, for the first time in his life, was able to see not only himself, but his planet earth, in contrast with the vastness of the universe. The desert had a way of doing that too and for the first time in his life Rob realized that he was just an insignificant speck standing on yet another insignificant speck.

"You guys ever wonder why we're here?" Rob asked.

His brief moment of introspection was lost on his companions and there was a grunt at his elbow. "Somebody's gotta keep half the population of Mexico from sneaking in here. Government sure as hell isn't interested."

The man who spoke was seated before a small computer monitor. His face was bathed in a soft green glow.

There was only one other man standing out there in the desert with Rob Scott, but he knew that five miles distant in either direction was another three-man group. Another three were stationed five miles beyond that, and so on, thirty-three men snaking out fifty miles across the desert. Stationed all along that fifty-mile stretch, straight as the crow flies, was various equipment: sound and motion detectors, as well as night vision cameras on tripods. Nothing moved in the desert without someone in that fifty-mile stretch knowing about it.

All the men were members of the Civilian Border Patrol, all unpaid volunteers, all of whom had signed up to track the movement of illegal aliens across the border.

So far that week, along their little fifty-mile strip, the CBP had spotted one hundred and forty-seven illegals sneaking in from Mexico.

Rob and the rest of the CBP could do nothing to stop them. They could only relay the information to authorities and hope that the lawbreakers were picked up by the Feds somewhere along the line. But out of the one hundred and forty-seven spotted by Rob's cohorts only two had been apprehended and were awaiting repatriation. For Rob, it was a disheartening statistic. It was as if, back in Washington, D.C., nobody in the government really cared.

But, dammit, Washington might not care but out in the heartland, real Americans did. These days there were a bunch of groups doing the same work as the CBP. You couldn't swing a dead rattlesnake without slapping some volunteer in the back of the head. Rob's group was one of the better financed, backed by the resources of Worthington International, Inc. But despite the generous financial backing they received in the form of food, supplies and equipment, even the CBP's track record was dismal.

Two catches in five days. Spot, report, and then be ignored.

Rob knew that even the two they had helped apprehend would simply be returned to the Mexican side of the border. And then they would attempt the crossing again, and next time would more than likely succeed. After all, with five hundred thousand illegals estimated to be sneaking into the country annually, the odds were in their favor.

Rob had taken some vacation time from his insurance agency to help out with the CBP. That was how committed he was to the cause. And, truth be told, he had thought that catching illegals would be exciting. He knew it was important. Instead, after less than a week in the desert, he found it every bit as tedious and unfulfilling as his work behind a desk back in Minneapolis.

A throat cleared nearby. When Rob glanced down from contemplating the heavens, he saw that the man at the monitor had shifted forward on his little folding stool. His finger, cast in an eerie green glow, tapped the screen.

"Beaners at ten o'clock," the man said softly and giggled.

The Civilian Border Patrol had members as old as

seventy-eight and as young as nineteen. In its ranks were whites, blacks, and even some people of Mexican ancestry. With a group so diverse there were bound to be a few racist idiots, but thankfully they were few and far between.

Most of the CBP volunteers were men legitimately concerned about the nation's porous borders. For those like Rob Scott it had nothing to do with cheap labor or lost jobs. It was not a coincidence that these groups had formed after 9/11. Rob had an image of two burning buildings forever emblazoned in his memory.

Rob Scott was worried about who—or what—might someday sneak across the Mexican border into the U.S.

On the monitor screen, three . . . four . . . no, five bright blobs were making their way toward Rob's camp. The monitors picked up the heat cast by warm bodies in the chill desert night. The group on the screen moved tightly together.

"Wish I had my M16 here," the man at the screen said, giggling again, and then sighed wistfully. "Look at 'em cluster. I could kack those wetbacks easy before they got within a hundred miles of the nearest welfare office."

"Shut up, Eric," Rob said and reached for the camp walkie-talkie.

They had strict instructions not to approach, not to impede. If the illegals came within five feet of them, Rob and the others were to step aside and let them pass, like doormen politely ushering the lawbreakers into a nation that had set out the good china dinnerware in anticipation of their arrival.

Rob was not without compassion. He certainly didn't blame these men and women for trying to sneak into the United States. A vacation trip to Mexico back in his college days had left him stunned at the poverty that existed just off America's back porch. It was only the luck of the draw that had placed him at birth on this side of the border, and Rob was thankful every day for it. But none of that made a wrong thing right and none of it erased Rob's security concerns.

Rob was about to report the sighting when something strange happened. The blobs on the screen stopped moving.

Rob lowered the walkie-talkie. "What's happening?" he asked. "Why have they stopped?"

The man named Eric shrugged. "Beats me. If they were bending over I'd say they were picking lettuce. Maybe one of them just plopped out another baby." The broad smile on Eric's face lasted only a few brief seconds.

There was a bright flash on the monitor screen. A split second later, the monitor erupted in a burst of sparks and flying shards of glass. Rob heard the report of the first gunshot only after the bullet had passed through the monitor and into the grinning face of Eric Bozeman Collins.

Eric was flung backward off his stool, a gaping hole where his nose had been. Rob Scott could barely see him. His vision was blurred by a splash of brilliant white, the result of the monitor flash. Blinking away stars, still in shock, Rob was only startled to action by the second shot.

The gunshot cracked like thunder in the clear desert night.

Rob threw himself to the ground. The walkie-talkie fell out of his hand and slid away in the dirt.

"What are they . . . they're shooting at us!" Rob cried to the third member of their small group.

His vision was clearing. He saw that the third man—a produce manager from a Wyoming grocery store—had dropped to the ground as well. Rob crawled over to him.

"What are we going to do?"

The man didn't answer. Frantically, Rob shook the man's shoulder. His hand came back damp and sticky.

The second shot had been clean as well. A bull's-eye dead center in the man's heart.

Rob heard voices nearby. Hushed, but closing in.

He took in a hiss of breath. Night vision goggles. The

CBP had them. These strangers who came out of the night and hunted unarmed, apparently for sport, must have had similar equipment. That's how they had found Rob's CBP camp, that's why the only two shots they had fired had managed to find their intended targets. Which meant that they could more than likely see Rob as well.

The equipment was partially blocking him from the gang that was somewhere out there. Maybe, he thought hopefully, they could not fire off a third clean shot.

There was a chance. Rob made a best guess where the men must be by now and, keeping the tents between him and his invisible stalkers, he began crawling on all fours in the opposite direction. As he crawled, his hand landed on a small, square object.

The walkie-talkie. He snatched it up, stuffing it in the pocket of his fatigue jacket.

His eyes were clear now. Starlight illuminated the ground an ethereal blue.

Fifteen yards along, the sand thinned and his hands started to scrape across rock. A dark strip stretched out in either direction before him. Rob tumbled over the edge of the old dried-out riverbed. Rocks and sand slid with him to the bottom. His feet went out from under him and he hit hard on his side, smashing his elbow on a sharp boulder. He nearly cried out in pain but swallowed the sound.

Scrambling upright, he pressed his back hard against the dead river bank. With shaking hands he fumbled the walkie-talkie from his pocket. He had barely brought it to his face when he heard a noise up above. The scuffing of someone's foot.

Pausing, holding his breath, hand clenched white around the walkie-talkie, Rob listened intently.

The desert breeze had stilled. Far in the distance, a lone coyote howled at the heavens. No other sound.

Maybe it was his imagination. Maybe these maniacs—whoever they were—had skulked off into the night. Rob heard no one talking, and there had been no gunshots as he crawled away. Maybe the nightmare had passed him by.

The vans that had brought them all out here had deposited men and cargo along the fifty-mile stretch. Rob knew that the vans were parked at a camp miles away and men drove the circuit daily, passing out food and water and cleaning and checking equipment. His two partners were dead, but maybe when the vans arrived in the morning they would find Rob Scott safe and sound. And he would get in one of them, steal it if he had to, and drive the hell out of this frightening, lonely place that forced a man to contemplate his own life and then on a whim and with a sniper's bullet, cruelly ended it.

Still no sound. The killers had left.

Rob brought the walkie-talkie back to his lips.

"Hello! Hello!" he whispered frantically. "Someone out there's shooting at us. I think they're gone now. But Eric and Phil are dead. My God, they're dead. I mean, they just came up out of nowhere and shot them dead. Someone . . . you'd better get the police here." He suddenly realized they would not know who he was, and remembered the protocol for reporting in. It seemed ridiculous now. Civilians playing at being soldiers. "This is Rob Scott, at checkpoint four. Please, you've . . . just send help, please."

He took his finger off the button. The box in his hand immediately squawked to life. Someone had been talking back while he was pleading for help.

". . . donde esta el bastardo . . ."

Rob threw the walkie-talkie as if it were a scorpion. It cracked on a rock.

Above his head, a sharp sound. A human grunt. Rob knew that this time he was not mistaken.

On all fours once more he began a desperate crawl down the dried-up riverbed.

Behind him, a second grunt became a shout. Words were called out in Spanish. Someone laughed.

At his back, Rob heard boots scraping and rocks falling.

They were in the arroyo with him. No hiding any longer. They knew where he was.

Rob scrambled to his feet and began sprinting. His toe caught a rock and he went down on his face. A sharp stone gashed his chin, slicing to bone. He clambered back to his feet and resumed his mad dash for life.

The bullet that took him off his feet a moment later did not hurt as much as he feared it would. It was like a hard punch to the shoulder that lifted him up and spun him around.

And then he was down once more, slamming to his back onto the dust and rock of the dead river.

And there were the stars above him once more. But the universe no longer seemed like a cold, vast nothingness. Somehow that sea of infinite blackness and those same twinkling little lights that had so recently forced unwelcome and dispiriting introspection upon Rob Scott now seemed warm and inviting, welcoming him home.

When the shadow fell over him, blocking the stars, he scarcely registered it.

There was a man in a uniform. The man had Mexican features. But such terrestrial matters held little interest for Rob Scott any longer. And when the rifle aimed at his forehead, Rob did not see an empty blackness in the barrel that was darker than the New Mexico desert sky.

And then there was a flash, like the first burst of Creation itself, and Rob Scott knew nothing more.

Mitch Lansing was steering his big RV down the long stretch of unmarked blacktop and trying to tune out his wife's incessant squawking.

"We're lost," insisted Dottie Lansing from the passenger seat. She was half hidden behind a map of New Mexico. The map was rolled out on her lap, bent up over the dashboard and wrapped around on both sides of her, blocking all but Dottie's pudgy fingers and kneecaps. She rattled the map. "I hate this. So big. Why do they make these things so darned big?" she complained.

From somewhere under the unfurled map, Dottie's toy Pekinese yipped incessantly, its barking like an ice pick in Mitch's ear.

Mitch had bought the map back in Omaha, back when he still thought it would be a good idea to spend his retirement traveling the country with his wife. Maybe it would not have been so bad, maybe he could even have stood Pookie's barking, if Dottie did not seem to insist that unity, togetherness and family values demanded that if he were going to drive, she would have to be the navigator. The problem with that was that Dottie could not read a map.

She couldn't even read the map that came on the puzzle-page children's placemat at the diner back down the road. At breakfast a few dozen miles back, before she had gotten them lost again, Dottie had grabbed a pencil and tried to solve the map puzzle on the placemat but was unable to find Yogi Bear safe passage to his cave. Instead, Dottie's pencil had led Yogi straight into an alligator pit, and now Dottie's real-life map skills had led them to an abandoned stretch of highway out in the middle of nowhere.

"I'm going to turn around," Mitch intoned. "Don't say a word."

As Mitch slowed the RV, Dottie wadded up the map. She was sure that there was a conspiracy to make all maps impossible to refold along the original lines, and so when she was done with one, it was about an inch thick and could never be opened flat again.

"What's that, dear?" Dottie asked as she attempted to jam the map into the overflowing glove compartment. She was looking out the broad windshield.

Mitch had spotted the vans before his wife. There was no way to miss them. In the bland expanse of the New

Mexico desert, bisected by the lonely, two-lane strip of asphalt, the pair of vans parked at the shoulder of the road were a godsend to a couple of lost, elderly tourists.

"Maybe they can get us back to the interstate," Mitch said. He pulled the RV behind the second van.

When Dottie opened the door, Pookie bounded out into the hot sand. Mitch was glad to stretch his legs.

There were men around the vans. Mitch and Dottie had seen them as they drove closer. But these men didn't seem bothered by the new arrivals. In fact, they must have been on some sort of morning siesta, because they didn't move at all, even when Mitch called to them. They just sat in the shade of the vans, a dozen of them in all, heads bent over their chests.

For some reason, Pookie stayed back near the RV. That was odd. Usually Mitch had to keep his wife's dog from nipping the fingers of anyone who made the mistake of trying to pet it. But for once, Pookie didn't yip, didn't snap. Oddly, the annoying little dog stayed in the shadow of the RV's wheel. A low growl rose from its throat.

"Excuse me," Mitch said, stopping above the nearest seated man. "We must have taken a wrong turn back there. Can you aim us back toward 285?"

The man did not answer. None of them did. There were a lot of flies buzzing around the area. Mitch waved at them with his hands. Pookie growled again, and for the first time, Mitch thought something might be wrong.

Tentatively, he reached down to touch the man's shoulder. And then, what with Dottie screaming and Pookie running back inside the RV and barking like mad from his perch on the dashboard, Mitch wasn't quite sure exactly what happened next.

He remembered taking out his cell phone. He remembered that distinctly, because he thought he'd broken it the first time he dropped it from his shaking hands. He remembered the flashing lights of the state cruiser; then more lights. He remembered an ambulance, and someone injecting something into the arm of his hysterical wife. He remembered the police being very interested in some words that had been spray-painted across the sides of the two vans. The words were green, and stood out in sharp contrast to the white vans.

Mostly, though, he remembered the hole in the dead man's forehead; remembered those awful glassy eyes staring vacantly into space. When the body fell onto the road, the man's hat had fallen off, revealing a gaping wound in the back of the head. The flies had gotten into the mottled hair and blood.

The sale of the Lansings' RV—"barely used, motivated sellers"—would be a little-noted back page ad in the auto section of their Omaha home paper. But the deaths of Rob Scott and eleven more Civilian Border Patrol volunteers would become national news and precipitate a political crisis unlike any the United States had seen since 1836.

The first reports out of New Mexico were police chatter, which soon filtered up to the FBI and Homeland Security. As the reports split off and multiplied, zipping from agency to agency, no one detected the detour they took to a corner office in an ivy-covered brick building in Rye, New York, on the shore of Long Island Sound.

A pair of glasses was directed at the data as it flowed across a computer screen. Behind spotless lenses, sharp gray eyes read the report with frowning concern.

Dr. Harold W. Smith, director of CURE, America's most secret crime fighting agency, had an unerring ability to recognize the beginnings of a crisis. And he knew he was looking at one right now.

He read the report again, making certain he had not gotten anything wrong. Of course, he hadn't. It was more of a hope than a belief that he could have been mistaken.

The border issue had become a tense one in recent years. And even though Smith kept himself totally free of politi-

cal opinion, he knew the politicians had done with the issue what politicians generally do: Instead of solving the
problem, they had tried to milk it for every last ounce of
Election Day benefit they could squeeze from it. And now
a dozen men, a dozen members of a well-meaning volunteer border patrol group, had been killed.

And Smith knew, deep in his soul, that it was not going
to stop with those deaths. The killers had not been satisfied
with just killing. Like artists, they had signed their work.

The words that had been painted on the sides of the vans
read, "¡Viva Mexico! ¡Viva Santa Anna!"

Smith leaned back in his chair.

The words were a taunt; that much was certain. That
Santa Anna, the nineteenth-century Mexican general, was
mentioned at all might just have been someone's idea of a
sick joke. Nevertheless, stopping it now before it mush-
roomed out of control . . . that was the kind of work that
CURE had been created to do.

But how? How could he do it this time?

The two men he had trusted for years to solve such matters had not been much help in recent months. One spent
most of his time ripping ringing phones out of walls and
ignoring telegrams. As for the other, Smith wasn't even
sure where he was.

And now America needed him. More than ever.

His name was Remo and he was home.

After a long time lost in the wilderness he was now finally, blessedly and at last, home.

Unfortunately for Remo, what should have been a time of great rejoicing in his personal journey had been spoiled by hidden forces seemingly determined to stamp out any trace of happiness in his life.

Remo didn't like cop killers. He did not like cop killers who were media darlings. And he particularly did not like media-darling cop killers who were foisted on him while he was trying to learn about lions. This and other dark thoughts did pass through the mind of Remo Williams as he drifted through the parking lot of the State Correctional Institution in southwestern Pennsylvania.

It was a little after 12:30 a.m. A small crowd was clustered up ahead. A group of men and women huddled together to ward off the post-midnight chill. A dozen tiny flames flickered in the dark, but the fires were not to fight the cold. The little flames danced at the tips of skinny white candles held in shivering fingers.

The candlelight vigil was a nightly event. Although the crowds were rarely very large, they were always there. People traveled from all over the country to participate. Some stayed on for a few days, others for a few weeks. The crowds grew dramatically in size whenever there were TV cameras present. And if it was network television, the celebrities would come, like cockroaches drawn to the molding grime under a refrigerator. A BBC documentary crew had been there for two days the previous week. Several celebrities had shown up then, including an actor who had played the president of the United States for a few years on a popular television drama and a movie actor who was famous for playing a cop in a series of films during the eighties and nineties. But the celebrities had left the instant the TV cameras had gone, and so the only ones now present were the nobodies who were charged with keeping the faith in that long, undramatic down-time that came between *20/20* segments and *60 Minutes* interviews.

Remo saw that the faces were a mix of young and old. Several of the protesters wore T-shirts, which were pulled over their lumpy spring jackets. The shirts read "Free Barak." None in the small group looked like the kind of person who would support the cold-blooded murder of police officers. Yet their T-shirts told a different story.

Remo drifted along at the edge of the crowd; always at the periphery, never a part of the group.

In a nation as big as the United States, it was understandable that there would be great diversity of opinion on all subjects under the sun. But it seemed to Remo that the one thing everyone should have been able to agree upon was that the murder of the men and women who daily put their lives on the line to keep the peace was a bad thing. Sadly, however, to Remo, who knew a thing or two about the difficulties of being a police officer, such was not the case.

Remo knew that others did not share his view. He saw some of them among the flickering candles as he skirted the crowd and headed for the high prison walls.

There was a small police presence. Protection for the protesters. That the police were there to defend men and women who had gathered in support of a convicted cop killer was an irony lost on the people carrying the candles.

The police did not notice Remo. Amid the parking lot lights, tower searchlights and flickering candle flames, Remo somehow managed to remain in the dark areas just outside the field of vision of the uniformed men.

As he approached the high outer fence, a soft hymn rose at Remo's back. The crowd had begun to sing.

"We shall overco-o-ome," the protesters warbled.

Although one could have guessed their thoughts, the police who rimmed the roped-off protest area remained stone-faced. When the singing started, one officer thought he heard a voice behind him, from the direction of the prison. He could have sworn the cold voice had said, "Start with overcoming your ignorance." But when he turned to see if someone had somehow slipped past him, all he saw was a tall fence wrapped in razor wire and a high prison wall. He returned his gaze to the protesters whose position on the murder of police officers he could not stomach, but whom he had sworn to protect nonetheless.

The man for whom the midnight crowd sang nightly hymns was not near enough to hear the soft voices caroling on his behalf. Buried in the depths of the prison, in a medium-sized cell at the end of death row, Prisoner #41602BB was sleeping the sleep of the blissfully oblivious.

If Barak Wallace had heard the singers, he might have reacted as one would react to a cat meowing too loudly on a backyard fence.

But he did not hear them, and so this night had passed like all the rest of the nights he had spent in his fifteen years as a guest of the state of Pennsylvania. Everything was oppressively ordinary, right up until he felt someone toe him in the ribs.

"Wakey-wakey," a voice whispered in the dark.

Barak squeezed open his eyes. There was someone standing above his cot. A stranger wearing a black T-shirt, chinos, and an unkind expression.

"You've got a busy night ahead of you, sweetheart," Remo said.

There were pictures all around the cell, photographs of Barak and some of his more famous supporters. Remo saw one of an actor from a 1970s sitcom. The man had played a gruff television news producer with a heart of gold. In real life, the man was an elderly actor with a brain of oatmeal. In the photo, the portly actor had his arm around Barak and was grinning broadly for the camera. Barak was not smiling. In not one of the many pictures on all four walls of the cell was Barak smiling. Barak did not smile. There were too many Big Things wrong with America for Barak to smile. Things such as institutional racism, wrongful incarceration and the death penalty for convicted murderers of police officers.

Barak could now add something new to that list: smartasses who came into your cell and woke you in the middle of the night when you had a big interview scheduled the next day on public television.

"Who the hell are you?" Barak growled.

"How about Jacob Marley?"

"Huh?"

"Never mind. Let's just say that I'm the spirit of a murdered cop," Remo said. "Come to warn you to repent of your wicked ways."

Under the circumstances it would have been easy to imagine that Remo was some sort of otherworldly specter. It was never completely dark in the cell. The wan prison light that entered from beyond the cell bars cast the room in bluish white and the light that washed over Remo's face revealed a man of indeterminate age, with high cheekbones and short, dark hair. It was the eyes that made him appear ghostly. Remo's eyes were set so deep in his face, all that could be seen in the semi-darkness of the cell was twin smears of limitless blackness. It looked like the face of a dead man. As he moved about the cell, he made not a sound, as if he floated a millimeter above the concrete floor.

On his cot, Barak seemed undisturbed by what, in the eeriness of this midnight hour, he might justifiably have mistaken for an animated corpse hovering above him. This was mostly because Barak's eyes were once more closed.

"Get outta here," Barak grunted from his cot. "I need my sleep." His mouth dropped open wide and he yawned with what seemed like his entire head. "I got my rights," he added when he was through yawning. "Violation . . . lawsuit. . . ." He yawned again. "Sue your ass . . . sue whole prison. . . . Aw, just get out, man, huh? I got Charlie Rose coming in the morning." He stuffed his head beneath his feather pillow, the better to contemplate sugarplum fairies and his cherished constitutional rights.

"I know," Remo said. "I saw the commercial for your big interview on TV tonight. That's why I'm here."

"No autographs," Barak's muffled voice insisted. "You a guard? Well, get back to guarding the way you're supposed to and let me get some sleep." The prisoner fell silent.

Remo reached down, took hold of the metal frame of the cot and lifted. The cot was bolted to the floor and there was a painful sound of tearing metal. Somehow all twelve bolts twisted free of their moorings, and Remo lifted cot and contents from the floor. He held the cot perfectly steady, perfectly parallel to the cell floor.

The demonstration was wasted.

"Zzzzzzz," said Barak Wallace from his floating bed.

"Some people sleep through all the best parts," Remo said and dumped the sleeping convict onto the floor of the cell.

"Wha . . . wha . . . wha . . . the . . . ?" Barak said.

But he was still only half awake and Remo decided to help him chase away the sleep bunnies. He did this by stuffing Barak's head in the toilet.

"Rise and shine, sleepyhead."

Barak lay spluttering on the floor of the cell. Fully awake now, blinking water from his eyes, he began to consider the possibility that this midnight visitor might not be the type of prison guard he was used to.

Since he had been arrested for murdering two Philadelphia policemen back in the early 1990s, Barak had become accustomed to being treated well. The police who had arrested him were nicer than they wanted to be, mostly out of fear that Barak would be freed if he could make the case that his treatment at the hands of a vengeful Philly police department had been less than elegant. The attorneys on both sides had been nice, the courtroom had been civil, the audience had been attentive. The case got national attention. Out on the streets, Barak had learned how to work a crowd and he soon found himself a devoted following among the sort of people who believed that every prisoner in the United States was a political prisoner, and every crime against authority was a blow against American fascism. Colleges, mostly in the Ivy League, invited him to give commencement speeches. A suburb of Paris had named a street in his honor.

Even in prison, Barak's growing fame made him a celebrity among his fellow inmates. The fact was, despite all he had been through, from trial to death row, Barak had never once feared for his life—until this night, when he found himself wiping toilet water from his face and finally staring up into eyes that he suddenly realized could have belonged to Death himself.

Barak started to scream for help but before a sound had passed his lips, Remo touched him on the side of the throat and Barak could summon only a feeble squeak. When he was able to speak again, his voice was a barely audible whisper.

"You are a guard, ain't you?"

The thin young man with the dead eyes apparently heard Barak well enough.

Remo shook his head. "Never a guard," he said. "But in my first life, back before I was killed the first time, I was a cop."

Barak still knelt on the floor. His spine went rigid.

"Cop, huh? You, uh, ain't one for holding grudges or nothing like that, are you?" The convict smiled weakly.

"Me? Come on. Do I look like the type who'd hold a grudge?" Remo grabbed Barak by the scruff of the neck and lifted him to his feet.

The next few minutes seemed to take place in some strange, otherworldly dream. Maybe Barak was dreaming. It would explain how the white dude, whose wrists Barak noted were unusually thick, was able to do the things he did.

Barak and the stranger passed through the cell door like ghosts. The barred door was not open, then it seemed suddenly to be, but when Barak looked back he was on the outside of the cell and the door was closed once more.

Remo held the cop killer at arm's length, as if he were a dog owner at the park and Barak were a bag of fresh poo.

They drifted down hallways, through doors, past guards who seemed not to notice the ghosts in their midst. Barak was scarcely given time to be amazed by Remo's apparent ability to travel through a well-guarded prison undetected

before they were outside. More guards, a wall, a fence and
Barak Wallace was breathing free air for the first time in
fifteen long years.

In the distance he could hear the sound of singing. His
choir of supporters was somewhere beyond a bend in the
high wall. Barak's fear began to lift. Maybe this dude with
the dead eyes was on his team after all.

"Hey, thanks, man," Barak said. "It was taking forever to
get my butt outta there."

Remo said nothing. They drifted through a side parking
lot and off prison grounds.

"You can put me down now."

Barak wriggled at the end of Remo's outstretched arm.
He weighed one hundred and seventy pounds but Remo was
holding him out like a shield, arm slightly bent at the elbow,
his face showing nothing more than bland disinterest.

Barak shook harder, trying to jar himself free.

"Put me down," he demanded.

"Stop wiggling. You're gonna get toilet water on me."

Dangling from Remo's outstretched hand, Barak's
shoulders sank. "You're not letting me go, are you?"

"In case I didn't tell you, I am the Ghost of Victims Past,"
Remo said. "Letting you go isn't in my job description."

"Wait. I thought you said back in my cell you were the
spirit of a murdered cop."

"What are you, the court stenographer? Work with me
here."

They found Remo's rental car parked at the curb of a
side road. Barak was tossed into the passenger seat and
tried grabbing for the door. Before he reached the handle,
though, Remo did something to Barak's wrists. It was like
the gentle touch to Barak's throat, but this time there was
more than simply frustration at not being able to cry out.
This time there was pain.

It was blinding fire. His hands burned like the heart of
an inferno. His eyes flashed white with shock.

And as quickly as it came, it was gone.

Barak gulped air.

"That's what you get if you don't behave," Remo said.

Barak vowed that he would behave. He had always been a model prisoner. Everyone said so. But he would do much better now. He promised his kidnapper that he would be a better captive than he had ever been a prisoner. He did this while offering a small token of respect to his captor, just to prove how much he loved the wonderful kidnapper who could deliver such horrific pain with scarcely a touch.

"Stop kissing my feet," Remo said, pushing the man's face away with his foot. "Your hair is dripping ass water on my shoes."

They drove out into the country. Barak wasn't quite sure how far they had gone. He only knew where they were going when they passed through a pair of open gates bearing the wrought iron legend, "Evergreen Cemetery."

Whatever town it was in, the people were still trusting enough to not lock the place up at night. Remo drove along the narrow graveyard roads, finally stopping on a small hill in a newer section of the century-old cemetery.

"You know why we're here," Remo said.

Barak shrugged. "I don't know. Why here? Place gives me the creeps. I don't like dead people."

"Then why'd you go into manufacturing them? Get out."

Out of the car, they climbed to the top of the hill. Barak slipped on the damp grass and stumbled in the dark. Remo hauled him to his feet.

"Let's get a move on," he said. "The Ghost of Victims Past doesn't have all night." As they walked, he fished something from his pocket. "I am here to get you to repent of past deeds."

"I'm innocent."

"Jury didn't think so. Neither does anyone with more than two working brain cells."

Remo handed the killer the item he had pulled from his pocket. It was one of the candles from the prison vigil service. Remo had filched it on his way past the crowd.

Barak saw Remo reach toward the wick. It looked as if he merely rubbed his fingers together. There was no match but suddenly, there was a tiny flash and the wick flamed to life.

They were standing above a grave. Remo pointed to the headstone. In the flickering light, it read, "Daniel Fitzwater, loving husband, father and son, Guardian of the People." Below were the dates of birth and death.

Barak recognized the last date, as well as the name on the headstone. He had heard them enough at his trial. Patrolman Dan Fitzwater was one of the two police officers he had driven his car over in a Philadelphia alley fifteen years before. Fitzwater had not died from the initial impact. Barak had gotten out of his car to check, found the patrolman still breathing, and had gotten back behind the wheel and slowly backed his car back over the chest of the injured police officer.

Remo's eyes were narrowed. He studied the face of the convicted murderer.

"You feel anything?" he asked.

Barak looked at the grave. Six feet below, sealed in a mahogany casket was the rotting corpse of a man he had deliberately lured into an alley with a bogus 911 call. A man who had apparently been loved by a wife, children and parents, if his headstone was to be believed.

"I'm cold," Barak said.

Remo's voice was colder. "That's it?"

"What do you want me to say?" Barak asked.

Despite himself, he could feel the hostility swelling. He did not know what this man—if he indeed was a man and not a ghost—expected of him. But he was not used to this sort of treatment, that was for damned sure.

"No guilt?" Remo asked. "No remorse? No nothing?"

Barak thought a little as he stared down at the grave. "I'm a little annoyed at all this," he ventured quietly.

He did not recognize the slight relaxation of the muscles around Remo's mouth and eyes.

Remo was thinking that annoyance wasn't much, but maybe it was a start, a step down the road toward normal human emotions. And besides, he understood annoyance.

For the past few years, Remo had spent a lot of time out of the country. He had just gotten back the previous afternoon, back to his condominium in Connecticut, back to the life that he had put on hold. And once back, all he had wanted to do was unwind. To that end he had been minding his own business earlier that evening, vegging out in front of the TV, watching a PBS documentary about the lions of the Serengeti, and thinking how truly inadequate television cameras were for capturing the amazing beauty of the real-life African plains. That was when the commercial had come on for the special live interview with Barak Wallace.

Talk about annoyance. Remo could not believe the man was still around and the way the program was being hyped one would have thought PBS had snagged the first interview with Jesus Christ on Judgment Day.

So this was the country that Remo had come back to. He had spent little time in the U.S. these past three years and perhaps he had been hoping that in his absence things had changed for the better. But nothing had changed. It was still up to Remo Williams to take out the garbage.

Remo had been telling the truth to Barak. At one time, although it seemed now a million years ago, Remo had been a police officer. A simple, idealistic beat cop. These days he felt little connection to that ancient life, except for a deep, inescapable stirring of emotion for a fellow cop who had been killed in the line of duty.

In any interview Remo had ever seen, Barak Wallace had expressed zero sympathy for the men he had murdered. But now, standing over the grave of one of his two victims, the cold-blooded killer was annoyed.

If Barak was annoyed with himself, that could be the beginning of basic human understanding for what he had done. And from that might come sympathy for his victims. And from that, maybe an actual human being could finally emerge from whatever dark chamber it had been lurking in within the frozen heart of Barak Wallace. And then maybe Remo would see that things in this world could change for the better.

"Annoyance is okay," Remo said.

And then Barak spoke and burst the bubble of Remo's short-lived optimism.

"Damn right I'm annoyed. Bastard got my license plate and called it in from his belt walkie-talkie," Barak complained. "If I only threw it in reverse and backed over him right away 'stead of getting out and checking to see he was dead, I wouldna been caught."

For good measure, he spat on the dead man's grave.

Barak felt a hand like a vise clamp onto the back of his neck. The butterflies in his stomach swirled as he was twirled around, the grave of Patrolman Fitzwater to his back.

"Say goodbye to the Ghost of Victims Past."

Remo bowled the murderer down the hill toward the car, making sure that he bounced off a few large grave markers along the way.

Their next stop was a small Cape Cod at the edge of the same little town.

Again, Barak felt the same floating sensation he had felt back at prison. Doors opened and closed as if by magic. A blinking door alarm failed to go off as they entered. The red light of a motion detector seemed unconcerned by their presence as they glided like specters down a carpeted hallway.

Barak found himself standing at the bedside of a thin,

pale woman. She was in her early forties, although she looked a good ten years older.

The woman was sleeping.

Remo touched the woman on the forehead.

"It's okay," he said softly once he withdrew his hand. "She won't wake up for the time being."

"Oh," Barak said. "Okay." He glanced from Remo to the sleeping woman, then back again. "We gonna do her?"

Remo smacked him in the back of the head. Then he remembered where that head had recently been and wiped his palm clean on the back of Barak's pajama top.

"Remember what I told you in the car. I'm the Ghost of Victims Present now."

Barak Wallace was no dummy. He had problems with authority, sure, and particularly with police, whom he saw as the corrupt enforcers of a corrupt system. But he had been in prison for fifteen years now, and there was no way that he could have any present victims, not counting any unfortunate, uninitiated soul who during that time had happened to stumble across one of his television hagiographies.

"No way," Barak insisted. "Present is now, and I didn't do nothing to her."

Wordlessly, Remo reached for a picture on the woman's nightstand. He handed it to Barak. In the glow of a night-light, the prisoner saw it was a wedding photograph.

He looked up from the picture, peering more carefully at the sleeping woman. It was Patrolman Fitzwater's widow.

Something glinted in the light. A single tear rolled down the woman's face, a face older than her years, a face lined with pain. Daniel Fitzwater's widow was crying in her sleep.

Remo looked for a sign of humanity on Barak's face. This time the murderer understood what was expected of him and he tried hard to fake sincerity.

"Bad," Barak said. He shook his head sadly, closing his eyes. "This poor woman an' what I done to her. I feel real bad about all this. Wish I hadn'ta killed them cops now. Boy, am I ever sorry for that." Head still downturned, eyes still closed, he kept one eye squinted shut and opened the other a sliver, looking at Remo without raising his head.

Remo glared back.

"Save the bulldookey for Wolf Blitzer," Remo said. "You've got one more chance this night to repent."

Collaring Barak Wallace, Remo dragged the thus-far unrepentant murderer from the home of his victim's widow.

Their final stop was a small park in Philadelphia where they stood in front of a modest granite monument to which was affixed a bronze plaque. On the plaque was the name Daniel Fitzwater, as well as the other patrolman Barak Wallace had murdered all those years before. The simple engraving on the plaque ended with the words, "Two men who gave their lives in service to the community they loved."

Remo allowed Barak a few moments to read the plaque.

"When I was a cop," Remo began once he was sure Barak had absorbed the words before them, "I had only one really bad day. It was my last day as a cop. They found a pusher dead in an alley with my badge in his hand. I told everyone it was a frame, but nobody listened. I was a good cop, but it didn't matter. I got the chair for that."

Barak's eyes opened wide. Could it be? Was this stranger really a ghost after all?

"The chair didn't work," Remo said. "But the world thought it did. When I woke up I found out why I'd been framed. See, there's a secret organization called CURE that was set up to fight crime outside the confines of the Constitution. We break the law in order to save the country. I was bamboozled into all this by the tight-ass who runs the show. I kill the bad guys who prey on everybody else. Although, actually, I've kind of been mostly on sabbatical these past couple of years."

"So what does all this have to do with me?" Barak asked.

"What it has to do with you, Mr. Impatient, is that I was an innocent good cop who was killed for what I didn't do, and you're a guilty murderer who killed two good cops, and you're getting booked on *Inside Edition*. You're not getting punished for your crimes. Hell, you're living the high life you never could have lived on the outside. That seems like exactly the sort of thing we're in business for."

And when Remo smiled, Barak Wallace felt his stomach turn to water.

"You gonna kill me?" Barak asked.

"Maybe," Remo said. "Okay, probably," he amended. "But I'm a fair guy. And remember, now I'm the Ghost of Victims Yet To Be. Someday some idiots on some future parole board will take that 'Free Barak' T-shirt crapola to heart and let you out. I don't see that you've repented of your evil ways, so you'll probably just kill again. But maybe I'm wrong. So prove it. Prove to me in ten words or less that you're sorry for your past sins, and maybe I'll show leniency. Maybe I'll bring you back to that prison cell, where you can rot for the rest of your miserable life, just so long as you don't do any more interviews. Okay, go. Ten words."

Remo pointed at Barak. Barak jumped.

"Oh," the murderer said. He licked his lips. His mind raced. "Okay. Wait. Do these count toward my ten words?"

"Eight . . . nine . . . ten," Remo said. "Everything counts. Goodbye."

Barak did not see the hand that stopped his heart. He felt only a great pressure over his sternum, as if someone had dropped a thousand-pound weight on his chest. Then he felt his stopped heart beat one last time, but it seemed to forget how to properly do its job. This time it didn't stop inflating, and the pressure was even greater than before, and the pain was worse than anything he had ever experienced in his entire life, and then the pain was gone because pain was something only living organisms could feel and Barak Wallace had stopped feeling pain the instant his heart exploded in his chest like an overfilled water balloon.

The dead killer flopped forward across the monument to the men he had murdered in cold blood.

Remo looked down on the dead man. When the body was found the next day, there would be cries of outrage around the country. There would be rallies and parades. The usual crowd would gather for the funeral, and the usual fingers would point in the usual directions. It would look like a state funeral. Even a former American president would attend. Missing from the coverage would be any serious mention of what had landed Barak in prison in the first place.

But none of that would matter, because justice had finally been served, and maybe now a woman who still slept alone after fifteen years would no longer cry to herself in the dark heart of the lonely night.

Standing above the body, former beat cop Remo Williams smiled. "It's good to be back," he said. "I love America."

Whistling to himself, hands thrust deep in his pockets, Remo strolled off into the darkness.

Although he heard the engine coming up the hill, he refused to allow it to intrude on his meditation. The same was true for the car stopping in the driveway, the car door slamming and the key turning in the house lock. All of these noises, right up to the clodhopper-stomping feet that banged through the front hallway, were gross violations of common courtesy. But he would not complain.

Only when the braying jackass voice echoed across the living room did the old man finally, reluctantly, open his eyes.

Chiun, Reigning Master Emeritus of the House of Sinanju, the most lethal house of assassins ever to grace the face of the planet, regarded the intruder through hooded, hazel eyes.

"Oh, dear me," the old Korean said, feigning alarm. Slender fingers covered his heart. "A stranger come to molest a poor elderly innocent. I have heard of this growing wave of crime that is sweeping the nation. Woe to me. I am to be a statistic on the television news."

He was seated cross-legged on the floor. Brilliant morning sunlight cascaded through the east-facing picture window, suffusing his wizened form in a warm yellow glow.

"Hah-hah," said Remo Williams, who stood across the room from his mentor. "That joke is as big a gut-buster today as it was the fifty-seven times you used it yesterday."

A 32-inch television played silently at the Master of Sinanju's back. The "eye" graphic in the corner of the screen identified it as Teleluna, the Spanish language channel. Chiun enjoyed watching Mexican soap operas, but today the usual broadcast schedule had been interrupted.

On the screen, a huge crowd had gathered, in Las Cruces, New Mexico, if the caption was to be believed. But when the cameras cut to close-up images of the crowds, Remo saw that the flags being waved were not American flags. Chiun had muted the sound. Not that it would have mattered if he hadn't. Remo did not speak Spanish.

"What's going on?" Remo asked, nodding to the TV.

The remote control was on the carpet near the old Asian's knee. A delicate hand snaked out, tapping the power button. The rally collapsed into an angry white dot.

"What always goes on in this nation of fools? Ugliness and shouting. More intrusions on a poor old man who has been abandoned to the wolves."

"Pity the wolves," Remo said.

Chiun wore a gold kimono, trimmed with black. Craning his wattled neck from his collar, he resembled a baby bird at feeding time.

The Korean's head was bald, save twin tufts of yellowing white hair above his shell-like ears. He tipped his head to one side. His hazel eyes were clear, belying his age. Hooded lids narrowed, as if touched by distant memory.

"Do I know you? You seem familiar and one does not

easily forget such big-nosed ugliness." He snapped his fingers. "Yes! You are the man who cleans the rain gutters. Welcome. There is a ladder in the garage. It was abandoned, along with me, by my son, long departed. But you probably will not need it. With those monkey-like arms you can swing up on your own."

"Knock it off, Little Father. I was away for a long time and now I'm back. Deal with it."

"Oh," Chiun said, voice sinking in deep disappointment. "Well, forgive me for not knowing your face, Remo. It has been so long since I have seen it."

"I was here yesterday," Remo said. "That was me you were slamming all those doors on, remember?"

"If I do, I probably blotted out the memory. It has become a pastime of mine. I have spent many an hour these past many months blotting out memories of you. Unfortunately every time I believe I have finally been successful erasing you from my memory, you stick your bulbous white nose back in my front door. . . ."

"Our front door," Remo corrected.

"My front door," Chiun corrected the correction. "And when you and your nose come back, all the memories, all the pain and humiliation, all the degradation and ingratitude, all the thousand cuts my innocent soul has been forced to endure at your wicked hands return with the force of a typhoon wind, and I am forced to start blotting again."

"Awwwww, poor Chiun."

"This time I had successfully erased as far back as the last time you showed me kindness and gratitude. You remember that afternoon, Remo, don't you? It was back in 1972. I think you were drunk."

"I'm drunk on life, Little Father," Remo said. "I told you yesterday that I'm back."

Chiun's eyelids fluttered shut. "Be still my heart."

"Whatever," Remo said. "But back for real. My bidness in Africa is over for now. I'm back in the land of the free

and the home of the brave. Now you can sit there and
grumble or you can join me in the kitchen for breakfast.
I'm thinking something brown, grainy and rice-like."

Chiun, annoyed that Remo could so cavalierly brush
aside not only the neglect he had subjected Chiun to, but
that he could sweep away as well Chiun's justifiable com-
plaints about all that neglect, rose to his feet like a puff of
indignant steam and marched into the kitchen after Remo.

"The world does not revolve around you," he said.

Remo was filling a pot with water. "Nope. If it did, I
could turn the volume down."

"The Master is not some peripheral character with a
walk-on role in the life of the magnificent Remo Williams.
You could not tie your shoes without me."

"I wear loafers."

"See? See?" Chiun's voice rose excitedly. "No more.
You think you can just march in here and announce that
you are back. Well, I am back too." His arms crossed
sharply over his puffed-out chest.

"Good. Back together. Like Martin and Lewis."

The truth was Remo was ready to get back to normal.
His life had taken some strange turns in the past few years
and at some point he would talk about it, he supposed, but
right now Chiun did not appear to be in any mood to listen.
The old constantly-complaining status quo would have to
do for a while.

"Fine," Chiun said.

"Fine," Remo said.

"Fine-fine," Chiun said. "So we agree to put your elder
abuse behind us, and that I am back in charge."

Remo had set the pot on the stove and turned up the gas.
He turned a dull eye on his teacher. "When have you ever
not been in charge?"

That simple statement of absolute, unvarnished truth
brought a moment of silence into the room.

The problem had come with Remo's ascendance a few

years before to Reigning Master of the House of Sinanju. To Remo, it was nothing more than a label although Chiun had seen Remo's easy acceptance of the honorific as an affront.

But for Remo, it was just a title. In his mind, the true Master of Sinanju would always be Chiun.

Chiun was the expert on languages. Remo knew only English and Korean, and maybe a few gutter oaths in a handful of other foreign tongues. Where undiplomatic Remo was more apt to punch most foreign leaders in the throat rather than to display the necessary obsequiousness that station and custom demanded, Chiun knew the proper protocol for greeting the heads of every civilization in the past five thousand years, including hundreds that had vanished beneath the sands of time.

And Chiun would not let Remo within a country mile of anything resembling contract negotiations with any employer. In fact, just before Remo's ascendance to Reigning Masterhood, Chiun had made certain to sign an extra-long contract with option years built in. A new contract would not come up for some time, and when it did Remo had no illusions about who would be doing the wheeling and dealing.

Most important of all in their arrangement were the histories of Sinanju. Chiun had shared much with his pupil, but he had forever alluded to "special histories" that Remo had yet to see. Remo would have thought that Chiun was yanking his chain and that these other histories did not exist, but then, perhaps, a crisis would arise and the resolution to it would be found in these hidden Masters' scrolls. Wherever Chiun had them hidden, he was not telling, and Remo doubted that he would be seeing them for a great many years to come.

The truth was, while technically Reigning Master, it was a title-on-paper that Remo had not yet found need to use, and which would probably only get pulled out in the rarest circumstances. Remo was really, truly fine with that, and he said so. Chiun doubted Remo's veracity and said so. Remo said Chiun could doubt him until the cows came home, but he was telling the truth and if Chiun didn't like it, Chiun could kindly blow it out his butt. Chiun had called Remo a vulgarian white who was given everything and appreciated nothing, but then had harrumphed grudging acceptance.

The moment of truthful silence lingered and Chiun sank to the floor before a low taboret while Remo set out bowls for their rice.

"Do not overcook my breakfast," Chiun commanded. "And where are my chopsticks? Unlike some, I am not a chimpanzee who eats with his fingers."

"Coming right up, Little Father."

Chiun allowed a thin smile of satisfaction when his favorite chopsticks were delivered to his placemat.

The water boiled. Remo added the rice.

"Smith wants to talk to you," the old Asian announced suddenly.

"More al-Khobar?" Remo asked. He tapped the wooden stirring spoon on the edge of the pot.

There had not been many assignments in recent months. Most had involved Remo and Chiun rooting out and eliminating cells of terrorists, most of them part of the al-Khobar terror network. It had not been challenging work, but had given Remo freedom to go off on his own.

"I do not know. He sent a runner to deliver the news."

"Howard?" This was Mark Howard, the only assistant that Harold W. Smith would allow himself at CURE.

"No, not the prince. This was some short pants-wearing cretin from something called FexEd."

Remo shot his teacher a glance. "Is there a FedEx body rotting in the rosebushes because he interrupted your television show?"

"Of course not," Chiun said. "I would not litter my own neighborhood. Especially with an absentee son who complains about picking up every little bit of trash and does not even clean out the rain gutters when he is here."

"Don't start again. Please. What did Smitty want me for?"

"Who knows? Some silly white nonsense he claims is an end-of-the-world crisis. I fear that his focus on maniacs who fly planes into buildings has passed as well, and Mad Harold is back to his old lunatic ways." He cocked his head toward the other room. "Whatever it is he wants, you may ask him yourself."

And even as he spoke there was a sharp rap of knuckles at the front door.

"After," Chiun said, tapping the edge of his bowl, "you have finished serving my breakfast."

A minute later, once Remo had ladled a generous spoonful of rice into the Master of Sinanju's bowl, he opened the front door to see a familiar gaunt face, lined with its usual familiar anxiety. Wordlessly, the man hustled past Remo into the foyer.

"Hiya, Smitty," Remo said.

Dr. Harold W. Smith had never been one to linger on pleasantries, and this morning was no exception.

"I knew you were back the moment I saw the news this morning," Smith said. "I assume you had a hand in the elimination of Barak Wallace?"

"Both hands actually," Remo said, waving them in front of Smith's face.

Smith's expression made it appear as if someone had poured battery acid over his morning Maypo.

The director of CURE was tall and thin. Although it had been some time since he had left middle age behind him, his determination and devotion to duty had not permitted him to slow his stride. There was always too much that needed to be done.

Smith was shaded in tones of gray. Even his skin seemed

color-coordinated with his three-piece gray suit. The only
dash of color was the green-striped Dartmouth tie which
Smith drew up to his Adam's apple like a noose.

When the protruding Adam's apple bobbed in disapproval, the tie jumped in sympathetic displeasure.

"That was not a CURE assignment," Smith complained.

"Consider it a 'welcome home' freebie."

"Bite your tongue," a disembodied voice called in Korean from the kitchen.

An instant later the Master of Sinanju was flouncing into
the room.

"Hail to thee, O Emperor Smith, whose voice is nectar to
these parched and aged ears, and a glimpse of whose be-
atific visage sends unworthy hearts soaring. Your outward
regality is eclipsed only by your great wisdom; a wisdom
daily demonstrated by permitting us to humbly serve in your
employ. For an emperor rules best who hires only the best,
and we modestly submit that we are proof of your great wisdom. Sinanju stands ready to do your bidding and, as a mark
of the professionals you in your wisdom have retained, we
would not dream of insulting you with talk of 'freebies.'"

Chiun offered a bow to Smith.

"Er, thank you, Master Chiun," Smith said uncomfort-
ably. He found a hard wooden chair and sat down, tucking
his battered leather briefcase between his heels.

As Smith settled in, Chiun hissed to Remo in Korean, "I
know you have been out of this madman's realm these past
months, but do not stick your foot in your mouth the moment you return." In English, to Smith, he said, "Our customers are always satisfied." He winked.

Smith, who detested the killing that he was forced to order in service to the nation he had sworn to protect, could
not tell the Master of Sinanju that he was never satisfied.
The function Remo and Chiun performed for CURE was
absolutely necessary, and they did it with unsurpassed,
even otherworldly skill, but it was onerous work that could

not help but trouble Smith to the very core of his being. Until all lawlessness ceased and America was safe from her enemies, a goal that harsh reality dictated could never be achieved, Dr. Harold W. Smith would never be truly satisfied.

Smith allowed another thank you to the Master of Sinanju and quickly turned his attention to Remo.

"Have you heard of the incident two days ago with a group calling itself the CBP?"

Remo sank cross-legged to the floor. Chiun sank down beside him, kimono settling to his bony knees like a delicately settling parachute.

"Sure I have," Remo said. "That's the Corporation for Public Broadcasting. They ruin good lion documentaries with ads for interviews with cop killers."

Smith shook his head. "That is the C . . . P . . . B. The CBP is the Civilian Border Patrol."

Smith went on to tell him about the dozen bodies that had been discovered in New Mexico, as well as the graffiti that had been painted on the CBP vans.

"What were these numbnuts doing out in the desert in the first place?" Remo asked.

"There's a lot of them, Remo. A lot of privately-funded groups that have taken it upon themselves to patrol the border between Mexico and the United States."

"So they're vigilantes."

"Not in the strictest sense of the word, no. They don't assume any authority to stop anyone who is crossing illegally. For the most part it seems they merely wish to call attention to the issue. Until this week there have been no violent clashes between them and any of the illegal immigrants they have tracked. In fact, they have been setting up in the desert around Las Cruces for several years now, and there have been no confrontations of any kind."

"Las Cruces?" Remo said. "Wait a minute. I think there was something on TV about all this this morning."

Smith nodded, his expression one of pinched concern. "After the CBP murders, advocacy groups fearing a backlash sprang into action. Apparently the Spanish-language channels have been helping get their message out. There have been demonstrations this morning in five major U.S. cities, as well as one in Las Cruces near the Mexican border."

"Wait a minute," Remo said. "Advocacy groups. Advocacy of what?"

"Well, they seem mostly to advocate open borders. Let everybody cross and don't send anyone back."

"Well, that's just stupid," Remo said. "Doesn't the government do anything about this?"

"They talk," Smith said. "It's our democracy."

"That is the part that is stupid," Chiun said in Korean. "Democracy. When we help Smith ascend the throne, we will put an end to this lunacy."

Remo nodded and turned back to Smith. "So why us? What can we do?"

"The fly in the ointment, Remo, is that these rallies are not as spontaneous as their supporters claim. The CURE computers spotted it. The rallies are too rapidly organized for there not to be a larger hand involved. Now with these dozen CBP deaths, it seems that someone has decided to take things a step further . . . a dangerous step."

"Any ideas? Who? What?"

Smith shook his head in frustration. "I wish we knew. One can assume the cryptic messages left with the CBP bodies have some bearing on things."

" 'Viva Santa Anna' isn't much to go on, Smitty."

"But a Mexican general who fought the United States a hundred and sixty years ago is obviously just a symbol to rally behind."

"He was barely a symbol one hundred and sixty years ago," the Master of Sinanju interjected. "Even as a soldier, he was less than useless."

"I take it the House of Sinanju met up with Santa Anna at some point?" Remo asked his teacher.

Chiun waved a vague hand. "A Master of Sinanju may have crossed paths with him. Obviously, the fool failed to retain our services. And look what happened to him. He lost his leg in battle. To the French of all people. Santa Anna was a cheapskate who was unable to see the big picture. He died penniless." The old Korean stroked his thread of beard thoughtfully. "Still, I understand the French general was happy. With three legs, even one of them borrowed, he could retreat that much faster."

"Start with the CBP," Smith told Remo. "Perhaps you can track up from there. It is headed, incidentally, by Prescott Worthington."

"Why do I know that name?" Remo asked.

"For much of the twentieth century, the Worthingtons were one of the wealthiest families in the world," Smith explained. "Their fortune was made in the cattle, railroads, telegraph and the steel industry. For many years the Worthington name was the leader in home electronics."

Remo snapped his fingers. "That's it." He pointed across the room to the VCR where the name "Worthington" was written in script in the right hand corner. "And I think they did our microwave, too."

"An evil contraption," the Master of Sinanju said. "If one cannot wait for the tea water to boil properly, one should not drink it at all. When we meet this Worthlesston, Remo, remind me to mention that he should cease production of those microwave things at once."

"I doubt that you will meet him," Smith said. "Besides, a Japanese company bought Worthington Electronics back in the 1980s and moved all production to Osaka. They keep the brand name, but that's all. Truth is the Worthington family empire has seen better days."

"So their old blue blood is in the red? But he's still got

money to spend on volunteer armies? Cry me a river of tears, Smitty."

"Worthington is hardly a pauper, Remo," Smith said. "He is still one of the wealthiest men in the country. And, as I said, you needn't even bother with him. He only funds the Civilian Border Patrol. The group has an office in Albuquerque. Start there. Find out if anyone in that group has a clue who might be behind the massacre. So far, the regular law enforcement people have come up empty."

"Sure," Remo said. "It's a pleasure to be back to work in the good old U.S. of A."

"I won't beat around the bush, Remo. This one frightens me. It has the potential for turning into something very large and very ugly."

Smith rose from his chair, bowed politely to the Master of Sinanju, gathered up his briefcase and headed for the door, where he paused.

"I suppose, Remo, that you are still not going to tell me why you have spent so much time in Africa these past three years?"

"It'd just give you ulcers, Smitty."

"I've already got ulcers."

"It would give your ulcers ulcers. Let's all just be happy that I'm home."

Chiun laughed derisively.

Smith seemed to want to press the issue but the acid churning in his stomach caused him to hesitate. Remo was probably right. As far as Remo and Chiun were concerned, there were some things that he was probably better off not knowing.

"Stay in touch, though. Please. I'm worried about this one," the CURE director said crisply. The thin old man turned on his heel, then walked stiffly down the front steps.

Prescott Worthington IV glanced out at the pla-
toon of worried faces. The men and women peered up at
him from chairs arranged all around the long boardroom
table of Worthington International, Inc. Thanks to several
generations of Worthington breeding and boarding
schools, Prescott Worthington could glance at every one of
the board members without ever actually having to look
one of them in the eye.

Eye contact was reserved for equals, and there were
none in the world whom Prescott Worthington deemed
worthy of the gift of a direct Worthington gaze. This was
doubly true for those harbingers of doom and gloom, the
bean counters who comprised the board of Worthington
International, Inc.

"The report from Hawaii is not good, Mr. Worthington,"
a corporate vice president informed him. "This is the tenth
quarter that Worthington Sugar has seen losses exceed

twelve point two million. It's time to cut it loose. Concentrate on slumping overseas steel, which still could be turned around."

Prescott Worthington looked the vice president square in the nose. "My grandfather added that sugar business to Worthington International when that leper colony was still boiling missionaries in pots," he drawled.

A few throats cleared. Such comments made some members of the board uneasy.

Their CEO was prone to off-color remarks that many considered distasteful. A few years ago some black minister had stormed the boardroom for a sit-in, expressing outrage at some comments that had allegedly been made by unspecified individuals at Worthington International, and had been leaked to the press by disgruntled employees. The siege had ended with a cash donation and the addition of a few dark faces in fancy management jobs, all of which went to the minister's relatives. Prescott Worthington had told each one of them, "Now you be a vice president," and he had handed each one of them a broom as part of their "welcome aboard" ceremony. And then he had gone right on saying whatever the hell he wanted to say about anyone who did not possess the same Anglo-Saxon pedigree as Prescott Worthington IV.

The company vice president, who claimed to be a WASP but who, through Worthington's research, had been revealed to possess a full quarter of Armenian blood, argued that the projections for Worthington Sugar into the foreseeable future were not good.

"There is no way that we can pull it out of the nosedive it's in, Mr. Worthington," the man said. "The only financially sensible thing we can do is cut it loose. For the good of Worthington International."

At the head of the boardroom table, Prescott Worthington exhaled audibly. He was sick of others telling him what was good for Worthington International.

"Send the figures to my secretary," Worthington said. "I

will review them personally. We will discuss the future of Worthington Sugar at a future date."

Someone tried to raise the next order of business, the hemorrhaging red ink stain in India that was Worthington Chemical, but Prescott Worthington cut the VP off.

"No. We're done," he informed them.

The board meeting was adjourned. While the others filed out the main conference room door, Worthington exited through his own personal doorway. Alone, he strolled up a private hallway.

So now the jackals thought they would put Worthington Sugar on the block. Worthington Chemical would be close behind. What would be next? Prescott Worthington was bred to be a king of industry but he was wise enough to know that he ruled over a dying empire and he was surrounded by people who wanted the dying to be neat and orderly.

The hall through which he walked was one seen by few outside the Worthington inner circle. Four large portraits adorned mahogany walls, two on either side. The eyes of Prescott Worthington I through III peered accusingly as he passed. Even his own portrait, painted ten years before when he was fifty, seemed to disapprove of his older self.

Worthington remembered sitting for his portrait. He had been directed to wear a suit. Prescott Worthington hated wearing suits. The New Mexico climate was simply brutal for them. On most days, like today, he wore a simple polo shirt, shorts and tennis sneakers.

His ancestors certainly would not have approved his work attire, even though their portraits revealed a century of gradually relaxing sartorial styles. Most appalled would be Worthington's great-grandfather, founder of the great Worthington business empire.

In his portrait, Prescott Worthington I wore a high starched collar. His face was drawn. His eyes were sunk a little too far down in his sockets, giving the impression that he was forever peering up over a ledge. Even in the portrait one could feel the disdain emanating from this great captain of industry from an age long passed.

The original Prescott Worthington often joked that a handshake deal with God himself had been responsible for his early success, but the Almighty was not likely to have shaken hands with great-grandfather Worthington, since, being omnipotent, He would have known where Prescott Worthington's hands had been. Although he had access to the finest soaps and most delicate perfumes of the day, Worthington could never wash away the invisible stains of blood and manure.

Cows had started the family fortune. The first Prescott Worthington had run slaughterhouses in Chicago in the nineteenth century. Thanks to hustle and luck, by the 1880s Worthington Meats fed half of North America.

It was a natural offshoot of his initial business success that the first Prescott Worthington would want to control how the cows were carted from Worthington stockyards in the southwest to Worthington slaughterhouses in the east. To that end, great-grandfather had moved quickly into the railroads. Next was the telegraph, and from there it was steel, lumber and coal.

In that great gilded age that saw the rise of the great families of Rockefeller, Vanderbilt, Lippincott and Forsythe, Prescott Worthington reigned supreme.

It came as a shock, therefore, to the business world when Prescott Worthington I announced that he would be moving the corporation's national headquarters to New Mexico. The elder Worthington had been diagnosed with tuberculosis, contracted, as Prescott Worthington often announced, from "those filthy Irish devils" in his Chicago slaughterhouses.

"My own fault," he said at the going-away party thrown by the elite of Chicago business. "Could've delegated. Didn't have to stay so close to my business interests. But I didn't delegate, you see. Not in my nature. Must have my

hand on the lever. And what did I get? Filthy Paddy bas-
tards coughing their disease at me. *Who knew?*"

The Chicago business aristocracy all agreed that the
Irish were presenting a terrible problem to the nation that
should be dealt with, either by stricter immigration control
or, failing that, another good, solid potato famine.

After saying his goodbyes, Prescott Worthington I had
packed up his business and moved southwest, where it was
hoped the dry New Mexico climate would hasten healing.

No one save the Worthington family physician ever
learned the truth behind his medical problem—that
Prescott Worthington I had not, in fact, contracted tuberculosis from his slaughterhouse employees, but from the staff
of an establishment far from the blood-drenched Chicago
stockyards.

The eldest Worthington would often take his private
train on the Worthington Continental Railroad to tour his
southwest cattle ranches. And on every visit to the region,
he would cross the border into Mexico for a rejuvenating
pit stop at his favorite bordello. It was during one week-
long stay, in the room the ladies dubbed the "Worthington
Suite" for all the time he spent there, that Prescott Worthington contracted the tuberculosis that necessitated his
move south.

The transition was not as difficult as some skeptics had
thought. America was growing smaller, thanks in part to
the telegraphs and railroads Prescott Worthington had
helped build. It was no longer vital that one base oneself in
New York, Boston or Chicago. Prescott Worthington and
his business thrived in the New Mexico climate.

Unfortunately, the move brought him into happy prox-
imity with the same establishment which had given him his
tuberculosis and which was eventually responsible for the
syphilitic dementia that resulted in the great family patriarch running naked through the streets of Albuquerque and
diving underneath the hooves and wheels of a charging

Wells Fargo wagon. The New York papers announced that
the first Prescott Worthington had died peacefully in his
sleep, and the nation mourned. President McKinley even
said a few kind words of condolence from the White House
south portico.

As they were scraping great-grandfather's pox-scarred
body into a box, Prescott's grandfather—Prescott Worthington II—assumed control of Worthington National.

Grandfather had moved the business into banking and a
new thing called radio. Worthington National became Worthington International.

Grandfather saw that there was money to be made in the
manufacture of appliances. Housewives with Worthington
toasters, blenders and ovens soon became the envy of the
neighborhood.

Prescott Worthington II was taking the first tentative
steps toward moving the family communications empire
into something called "television" when he was cut down
in his prime. A heart attack at fifty-five, the Worthington-
owned papers had announced somberly.

"Killed with an ax by the Mexican gardener," Prescott
Worthington III had confided to his young son. "Dusky
SOB found your grandfather in bed with his fourteen-year-
old daughter. Can't blame the Mexican, young Prescott.
No. In their nature to be hot tempered. My father should
have known not to bed one of those people. Lying down
with dogs, you know."

Three decades later, Prescott Worthington III had apparently forgotten his own advice. The Worthington patriarch
immediately preceding Prescott Worthington IV actually
had died of a heart attack while in the passionate embrace
of the upstairs maid.

Prescott Worthington IV's first act as head of Worthington International was seeing to it that the sobbing woman
was stripped of all her worldly possessions and deported
back to Mexico. His second act was to crack open the

books and see what kind of shape his deceased father had left the company in.

The news was not good. The television division which his father had founded had been sold off. All steel production had moved out of the country. The Japanese were negotiating to purchase the electronics division. There were still the cattle ranches, but Worthington Meats was being pounded by the competition.

Bit by bit over his fifteen-year stewardship of Worthington International, Prescott Worthington IV watched the corporation being chipped away. Next would be Worthington Sugar. The Armenian vice president was right. The losses were unsustainable, and Worthington knew it. But for now they were acceptable.

These were indeed dark days for the Worthington empire. The portraits that he passed only deepened his gloom.

Worthington passed through the hall of his ancestors and made his way back to his office. His secretary—whom he always suspected was some Russian mongrel mix—was not at her desk.

Grumbling displeasure, he slapped open his office door. Worthington marched halfway across the room when he suddenly stopped dead.

There were two men in his office. One was old and bored, the other young and even more bored. The younger one looked from Prescott Worthington's pink polo shirt to his white short pants.

"Howdy doody, little boy," Remo said. "Is your daddy home?"

"Who the hell are you?" Worthington demanded. "How did you get in here? Where is Spence?"

Raymond Spence was a Worthington bodyguard. He was supposed to be stationed outside Prescott Worthington's office door at all times to prevent just this sort of thing from happening.

"Big guy? Not too keen on heights?" Remo gestured to the window.

The front entrance to Worthington International ended in a circular drive around which was a semicircle of a dozen flagpoles, from which hung flags of a dozen nations. Raymond Spence—all 210 pounds ex-Navy SEAL of him—was suspended just above the British flag. It looked as if the pole had entered as nature had clearly not intended. The Albuquerque fire department was on hand. A hook-and-ladder was extended. Firemen were scratching their heads and wondering why the manual did not cover flagpole-impaling. When an acetylene torch was lit, Remo closed the blinds on the scene.

"He wasn't friendly to us," Remo said. "Would you like to be our friend?"

Worthington slowly became aware that his mouth was hanging open. With an effort, he closed it.

"Uh . . . sure . . . sure thing," Worthington said. "What can I do for you gentlemen?"

He smiled tightly from the young man to the old man. The older one seemed uninterested in Worthington.

There was a large glass case in the corner of the office which contained model replica engines and cars of the original Worthington Continental Railroad. It looked as if someone had taken a glass cutter to the front of the case. A perfect circle had been scored in the glass. The circle had been removed and set on top of the case.

The Master of Sinanju sat on the floor near the case. An expensive toy replica engine, coal car and cattle car were at his knees. A few little ceramic cows stood in a cluster. Chiun steered the little train up to the cows.

"Chug-chug-chug-chug," said the Master of Sinanju.

"Leave him be. He's busy," Remo told Worthington. "We're looking into that border guard group that got slaughtered around here. We tried the headquarters first, but the town is a zoo right now with rallies and the place is closed. Since you foot the bill, you were Door Number Two."

"Of course," Worthington said. "I have the information you need right here."

"I haven't told you what we wanted."

"Woo-woo!" said the Master of Sinanju.

"Membership rolls, things of that nature, right?" Worthington said to the obviously dangerous and deranged young man. As he spoke, Worthington backed slowly to his desk and slid open the top drawer. Wheeling, he stuck an automatic pistol in Remo's ribs. Or, at least, he tried to.

"Aha!" came out of his mouth first. And then, "Huh?"

Remo's ribs seemed to swing out of the way of the barrel, as if on hinges. The gun missed Remo entirely and kept on going. Then the pistol was in Remo's hands, and there was a hideous screech of metal, and Remo was handing the gun back to Worthington with the barrel twisted in a knot. The knot had two tiny bumps near the middle.

"It's a doggy," Remo explained. He pointed to the bumps on his gun barrel balloon animal. "Those are his ears, see? Gimme one of those real long barrels—like a rifle or something—and I can make a giraffe."

Worthington felt his legs go wobbly. The young man caught him and guided him to his chair.

"What do you people want?" Worthington gasped.

"Look, we're not here for trouble," Remo explained. "If your goon had listened to Chiun and let him play with the trains in the first place, he wouldn't be hanging on a flagpole right now."

"I am not 'playing'," Chiun said. "I am model railroading. Czar Nicholas used to have a set like this, back when Russia was civilized. Of course, the lights of that set were diamonds and it was trimmed in gold. But this is a nice set too. The czar gifted his set to my grandfather." These last words were directed, with level voice and eye, at Worthington.

"You want those, they're yours," Worthington said.

The words were no sooner spoken than the small engine and train, as well as the tiny herd of cows, disappeared in the folds of Chiun's silk kimono.

Worthington was perspiring. The office seemed to be swirling around his head.

"Here," Remo said. He reached a hand to the base of Worthington's spine and touched a cluster of muscles.

Instantly, the world came back into focus. Worthington felt the air flood deep into his lungs. His head cleared.

"We're not here to send you into cardiac arrest," Remo said. "Those guys of yours who were murdered in the desert. You have any idea who might be behind it?"

Worthington shook his head. "Are you with the government?"

"I'm with him," Remo said, jerking a thumb toward Chiun.

"But only for as long as I allow it," Chiun said.

"Well, whoever you're with, I'll tell you what I told them. General Santa Anna is behind it."

Remo's gaze grew hooded. "General Whoozit?"

"Santa Anna," Worthington said. He held up a hand to ward off protests. "I know how it sounds. Certainly the FBI wasn't interested when I told them. But the fact remains that General Santa Anna is a shadow figure behind everything that has been going on politically in the illegal immigration movement for over a year now."

"You actually think a one-legged Mexican general who's been dead for over a hundred years killed your people?"

"Of course not," Worthington said. He waved a manicured hand. "Not that Santa Anna." With a sigh, he leaned back in his chair. "I formed the CBP to call attention to the illegal immigration crisis. We've been successful in our mission, as far as we can take it. Thanks in part to the work of the CBP, the American people understand now that there's a real problem. A crisis, I would say. But we have also attracted the ire of groups with an interest in preserving the status quo. For months now there has been chatter around these groups about someone calling himself General Santa Anna."

"Maybe it's some kind of dippy code name."

Worthington shrugged. "My people at CBP thought he was a myth. They learned the other night that this might not be the case. You know, if you are with the government you should know that I told all this to the FBI this morning. Why am I not surprised that they failed to report it?"

The bitterness in his tone was thick.

"We're not with the FBI," Remo said. "Just consider us a couple of concerned citizens."

"Well, if that's true, which I doubt, you should be concerned," Worthington said. "We all should be. Five hundred thousand annually."

"Excuse me?"

"That's the latest estimate. Five hundred thousand illegals stream into this country every year. But, of course, no one knows the true number. Can you imagine that number? Because most people can't. That's why those first pro-illegal rallies last year were such a shock to middle America. Five hundred thousand is the equivalent of the entire population of Albuquerque entering the country every year. How can that number be sustainable?"

"Can't say I blame them for wanting to get in here," Remo said. "I've been to Mexico. If they told me I had to live there, I'd gnaw off my own foot to escape."

"I can't blame them either. But our government is scarcely able to sustain the system we have in place now. Have you been to a public school lately? I have. Worthington International sponsors dozens of inner city schools. The system is falling apart. It's already overburdened. It cannot absorb into it the children of every foreign country in the hemisphere."

"So we do what? Toss them back over the border?"

"Forgive me if it seems harsh, but yes," Worthington said. "That is precisely what we should do. At least there they'll be back in their own culture. The idea of a U.S. melting pot is dead. What we've got now is an all-new policy of separate but equal. They do what they want, get what they want, but heaven help us if we make any demands of citizenzhip on them. Or do you think that someone like me would be able to waltz into Spanish Harlem and come out alive?"

"That depends," Remo said. "Are you riding your polo pony at the time?"

Worthington allowed his lips to twist into a tight little smile. Despite the smart aleck comments, he could see some of his words were registering with this brute, who was clearly some impossible-to-decipher mélange of gutter breeding.

"Do you really think . . . what is your name?"

"Remo."

"Do you really think, Remo, that it's fair, what we're doing to the illegals that manage to sneak in here? All of these handouts have been designed with a specific purpose in mind: votes. A perpetual underclass that politicians want to keep in squalor and ignorance. Believe me, I've heard it enough. If by some miracle they do manage to crawl up into the middle class, all of a sudden they resent having half of their paychecks going to people they never met, people who don't work a lick for their entire lives."

"Last time I checked, picking grapes in hundred-degree sunlight for ten cents an hour constitutes work." For a moment, Remo was distracted.

Worthington saw that the young man's eye had been drawn to a section of paneling beside his desk. When he glanced back at Worthington, there appeared to be a knowing glint in his deep-set eyes. Of course, that was impossible.

Worthington plowed ahead. The manicured hand waved

once more. "I have nothing against these people, Remo, believe me. Look at it from a strictly legal standpoint. We have immigration rules for a reason. Is it fair that someone who plays by the rules and jumps through every hoop the government sets out for him doesn't become a citizen for some silly technicality, while another who gets into America by hiding inside the empty tank of an eighteen-wheeler immediately has access to schools, social programs, medical care, and everything else this country has to offer?"

Remo grunted that Worthington was probably right.

Worthington flashed an unctuous smile. "Of course I am. It is simple economics."

Remo knew that it was more than economics for Prescott Worthington. Clearly this man was a racist weasel of the highest order. But although he questioned his motives, Remo found himself agreeing with the weasel's basic premise.

Worthington lifted a slat in the blinds. "Well, I see that they've nearly gotten Spence down. I'm a busy man, so if you gentlemen have nothing further. . . ."

Once he realized he had nothing to fear from these two, the frightened man who had nearly passed out a few minutes before had nearly reverted back to his everyday condescending form.

"One more thing," Remo said. "Where exactly were the bodies found?"

Worthington gave them directions as he showed them to the door. He smiled at Chiun.

"Enjoy your trains," he said. "By the way, I have nothing against the Chinese."

"You should," Chiun replied coldly.

"I see," Worthington said, smiling, not seeing at all. The instant he shut the door, the smile vanished. He went straight to his desktop computer and dashed off an inter-office memo to the head of the personnel department to terminate Raymond Spence. What good was a bodyguard

who, at the first sign of trouble, got himself stuck on a flagpole like a decoration on top of a Christmas tree?

Worthington had begun writing a second note to the accountant who handled Worthington International workers'
compensation, ordering him to obstruct any claims Spence
might make for his alleged injury. As he typed, a door near
his desk slid open. The door blended in with the paneling
and to visitors, it should have been completely invisible.

It was the same part of the wall Worthington had seen
Remo take an interest in. But, of course, he could not have
known there was a secret passage hidden in the wall.

A woman stepped into the office.

She was in her early thirties, with a figure that would
have turned heads even on a Malibu beach jaded by quotid-
ian beauty. Her face was a little too wide, but the imperfec-
tion only enhanced her looks. She had pale, flawless skin
that had never seen acne, wrinkle or makeup. Her long
honey-blond hair was drawn into a ponytail that bobbed as
she walked.

"You were a big help," he growled.

"You were the one who wanted to keep some of your
own help on," she replied. Her voice was like church bells
on a winter's midnight. "I can work some of your security
for you, Mr. Worthington, sir, but if you insist on keeping
these brainless linebackers in your employ as well. . . ."

She let her voice trail off and shrugged.

Prescott Worthington watched her shrug. Her chest did
wonderful things when she shrugged.

And besides her chest, the woman had one of the most
perfect derrieres Worthington had ever seen, like a pair of
peaches wrapped in silk. He had once tweaked one of those
saucy little cheeks. The next thing he knew he was coming
to on the floor of his office with a high heel on his throat.
Towering above him, the woman had smiled that warm,
aw-shucks Midwestern smile of hers.

"Well, gosh and golly, Mr. Worthington, sir, I hate to be

a party poop, but if you try that again I'm going to have to chop you up and feed you to your dogs. But dang if I won't feel really, really bad about it."

He had never pinched her bottom again.

"I need someone full-time," Worthington said.

"Mr. Worthington, sir, I can only ever be a temporary consultant," she said. "That is how I run my business, and that was your father's (God rest his soul) arrangement with our mutual friend, my mentor, Benson Dilkes."

Worthington knew well of Dilkes. He was a free-lancer who had arranged security for heads of corporations as well as heads of state. He had also been one of the greatest hired killers in the world twenty years before. This woman was Dilkes's number-one protégée.

"Dilkes would have come on full-time," Worthington challenged.

"Now, now," she said, shaking an admonishing finger at Worthington. "We both know that's a little bitty fib. Benson never took a permanent job anywhere. That's how his business worked, and that's the way mine works too. I'm more a consultant. I like to delegate. I'd get into the trenches more but, gosh darn it, blood is just so dang difficult to get out of silk." The smile she flashed seemed icier than before. "But if you want me to staff your security forces with folks who are actually competent, who will actually protect you, then by all means I'll take the contract with a big fat thank-you."

"Okay, it's yours. And the first order of business is finding out who those two are and making sure they don't get in my way. With all this border stuff going on, I'm in the middle of something important, noble even, and I don't even know what side they're on. I don't want them messing up everything I'm trying to do. Who the hell are they anyway?"

"A couple of things, Mr. Worthington, sir. One. They're not on your side. And two, I know very well who they are.

Thanks to the house-cleaning they did a few years back, I'm one of the last in my line of work who does."

"Good. So you can deal with them."

She shook her head. "That's a bit of a tall order, Mr. Worthington, sir. You see, Benson Dilkes, whose services your family valued so highly, is dead because of them. And that young one—the cute one—Remo? Well, you see it's like this. I killed him once a few years back." Rebecca Dalton flashed pearl-white teeth. "But shucks and shame on me, it didn't seem to take."

Outside, as they walked toward their rented SUV, Remo told Chiun, "You were busy playing but I noticed that Worthington has a hidden panel in his office. Probably a secret room."

Chiun's head snapped in Remo's direction. "Do you think he is hiding more model railroads there?"

"I don't think so."

"Pffff. Who cares then?" Chiun said.

They did not see her as Rebecca Dalton came out on the steps of the Worthington office complex and watched them walk away.

She had seen them before, hated them before, and despite how she should still have hated them, she knew there was something special here that she did not understand.

Rebecca had first heard about it from her mentor and teacher, Benson Dilkes.

Dilkes, who had never shown fear in all the time she had known him, had spent his life terrified of the men from the House of Sinanju. He told her about his fear, calmly and rationally, in the gazebo of his Zimbabwe ranch.

"They're like nothing you've ever seen," Dilkes said. His soft Virginia drawl had emigrated with him to the plains of Africa. "And believe me, Rebecca, my dear, they are nothing you ever want to see."

At the time, Dilkes had been a distinguished man in his late fifties. His hair was still dark, but tinged with strands of gray. Deep laugh lines and a dark tan crimped the skin at the corners of his eyes.

Benson Dilkes had been ruggedly handsome, cut from the John Wayne mold. It was only natural that Rebecca had fallen in love with him. There were few women who were not drawn to the natural virility of Benson Dilkes, but still when it happened, it had come as a surprise to her.

Rebecca had had a bit of an antisocial streak when she was a little girl. She was not afraid to admit that, mostly because she had put it behind her.

She had never really liked playing with the other girls and boys. At the orphanage she used to hear them whisper that she was emotionally scarred. "Beyond all hope," she had once heard the facility's nurse whisper.

They said she had been so damaged by the deaths of her parents and grandmother, but the truth was she did not remember much about that day. They told her it was a terrible accident, that her father had been decapitated, and that Rebecca had been wedged in the ditch for almost a day with a headless daddy and dead mommy and gram-gram before they could get her out. But if Rebecca could not remember, then how could it have damaged her?

Through hard work, she had proved to them that there was nothing wrong with her. The brightest in her class, nothing but A's, college paid in full with academic scholarships. So what if she never had any friends? She could stand up on her own two feet, friends be darned.

She had almost not gone on the trip to Africa at the end of her senior year. A group of volunteers was going to help dig outhouses for savages, or something. Rebecca really didn't read the flier.

The truth is she did not care much about helping others. No one had ever helped her. But the price was cheap, and she had never been outside of Illinois in her life. It really

was a once-in-a-lifetime opportunity. So she had signed
on, flown to Zimbabwe, told her shocked classmates that
she was "so, so sorry" but that she wouldn't be helping "in-
oculate smelly babies or whatever after all," and had gone
off on her own to explore.

She had found that this was not the wisest course of action when, the next day, she was nearly gang-raped at
knifepoint in a public bar.

It was on a dirty, scarred Formica table, next to a picture
window in full view of the street. The first gentleman in
line was about to perform his nasty business on her, when
his eyes suddenly bugged out of his head and he fell on top
of her. At first she thought he'd had a heart attack, but as he
toppled to the floor she noticed the knife handle sticking
out of the base of his skull.

And that was when she saw the very calm, very tan
white man sitting at a private table in the corner of the bar.
Next to his mug of imported American beer, and his ash-
tray in which smoldered his pipe, were two knives with
handles identical to the one sticking out of the back of her
would-be rapist's head, and a Colt .45.

The man crossed his legs and picked up his pipe.

"I am sorry, Mr. Dilkes," the bartender apologized. As
he zipped up his fly he was sweating profusely. "We did
not know the young lady was with you."

Rebecca Dalton had never seen such delicious fear in all
her admittedly short life. All the men in the bar, even those
who had not lined up for their turn with the beautiful
American college student, slowly backed away. Appoint-
ments were suddenly remembered, drinks were abandoned. In less than a minute, the bustling bar was empty,
except for Rebecca Dalton and the man who would become her lover and teacher.

Rebecca took to the art of murder like a fish to water.
She absorbed all that Dilkes could teach her, and when
there was nothing more he could offer, she learned new

things on her own. Eventually she had outgrown him, as he told her repeatedly she would.

"You have the world, Rebecca," Dilkes told her wistfully. "This little country, where they treat you well if you know how to frighten them, is my world now."

She had often wondered why a man so youthful and fit would retire from the business. It was on their final night together that he at last told her.

"Their art is called Sinanju," Dilkes said. From his whitewashed gazebo, they watched the sun burn red fire over the African plains. "That's also the name of their village in North Korea. There's one pupil and one teacher in each generation. They're called Masters of Sinanju, and if you are very, very lucky they'll suffer you to ply your trade, as they did me. But if you cross paths with them, Rebecca, my dear, run for all you are worth and don't look back."

Rebecca had not believed that these men from the East could be as dangerous as Dilkes claimed. Five years ago, when Dilkes came out of retirement and hired her in a scheme to kill both Masters, her suspicions that he was just being dramatic were confirmed.

But then a funny thing happened. Benson Dilkes was killed. There was no obituary, no wake, no funeral. She never saw the body. But the earth opened up and swallowed him whole. Rebecca knew he was dead.

The saddest part of the whole affair was not her mentor's death. As a sociopath used to abandonment, Rebecca Dalton always assumed everyone would leave her and did not much care when they did. No, the thing that most saddened her was the fact that Dilkes had not lived long enough to learn of her success against a vaunted Master of Sinanju.

In the end, they were not as tough as Benson Dilkes had thought. With just a little cunning and an assist from modern technology, Rebecca had killed the younger one.

Or so she had thought for five years. Until just now in the office of that annoying pest Prescott Worthington IV.

Rebecca Dalton stood on the steps of the Worthington office building and watched Remo and Chiun walk away.

"We have a debt to pay," she said softly to herself. "A very large debt."

The late afternoon sun blazed like a lake of fire
suspended above the scorched New Mexico desert as
Remo parked their rented SUV at the shoulder of the
lonely stretch of empty blacktop.

Worthington's directions had led them straight to the
spot where the dead CBP men had been discovered. But it
was obvious immediately that the area was a mess. Footprints of investigative teams had churned dust and if there
had ever been any tracks, they were all gone by now.

Remo and Chiun were examining the ground, looking
for something, anything, when they heard the sound of an
approaching engine. It took several long minutes for a Jeep
to appear on this highway to nowhere.

The vehicle did not pass. Kicking up another cloud of
choking dust, the Jeep pulled to a stop behind Remo's
truck.

The Latin beauty who was driving climbed down to the

hot asphalt. She wore a pair of sensible flat shoes and what looked to be the slacks of a pantsuit, but she had discarded the blazer. Her navy blue blouse was sleeveless and untucked. The top several buttons were open.

She had driven with the windows down. Her long hair was tousled, and she shook her head back, running splayed fingers through the thick black curls. The grooming took seconds and, not bothering to check a mirror to know that she looked perfect, she marched directly up to Remo who was squatting, looking at the ground.

"Conchita Diaz," she said, in a crisp, businesslike voice. She extended her hand.

"Not interested," said Remo without looking up. "I get my insurance from Geico."

The woman's hand wobbled in the air for a few seconds before she let it drop to her side. "That was rude," she sniffed.

"No, that was maybe abrupt. But not rude. Rude would have been me knocking you upside the head for stomping in here and kicking up even more dust on a crime scene."

It was clear from the look on her tawny face that Conchita was not used to having men talk to her that way. She had yet to meet a man who did not fall under the spell of her natural beauty. With her aristocratic cheekbones, raven hair and caramel skin, Conchita was used to hearing men gasp. They tripped over their own feet to open doors, hail cabs, pull out chairs. A man ignoring Conchita Diaz was like a thirsty dog turning up its nose at a bowl of water.

Maybe this one hadn't noticed. He had not really looked at her. She squatted next to him, leaned her face close and smiled.

"Conchita Diaz," she repeated.

This time she got a reaction. Remo turned to her and said, "If you're looking for the mouthwash, it's in aisle five next to feminine hygiene products."

He rose and walked away. Conchita did not know what

to say. Such casual dismissal of her stunning beauty was something she had not experienced since her first blush of womanhood. After a lifetime of men slobbering for her attention, she considered the reaction her natural right.

As Conchita stood, blinking her surprise, she felt a gentle touch on her forearm. When she glanced over, a wizened face was peering knowingly at her.

"Forgive my son's rudeness, beautiful lady," Chiun said. "I have done my best to instill manners in him, but one can only do so much when the raw materials are faulty."

"I'm right here, you know," Remo called over.

Chiun dropped his voice but still loud enough for Remo to hear. "Consider yourself lucky that you do not have to eat with him," he confided. "I live in constant fear that I will get too close and lose a finger."

She had not gotten anywhere with Remo. She turned her attention to Chiun. "Conchita Diaz," Conchita said.

Chiun did not take her offered hand either but he did allow a slight tip of his head.

For the third time in as many minutes, she found her hand hanging in dead air. This time when she withdrew it, her fingers clenched white at the insult.

"Are you with the police?" Conchita asked.

"If we say yes, will you promise to invoke your right to remain silent?" Remo called.

She looked from Remo to Chiun. She had not imagined that these two could possibly be police. "What do you think you're doing here?" she demanded.

"Right now?" Remo asked. "Ignoring you. Little Father, over here."

Remo was crouching down a few yards away from where their SUV was parked.

Chiun padded over. His simple wooden sandals made not a single scuff in the soft dirt. Conchita marched along beside him, kicking up sand as she walked.

In the dirt near the toe of Remo's loafer was a shiny silver object. He dug it up and tapped away the dirt. It came off easily. The object had not been there long.

"What do you make of that?" he said, dropping the item into the Master of Sinanju's hand.

Conchita forced her way between them. "That is a Mexican army button," she said. "But it is an antique. Those have not been used in more than one hundred years."

Remo counted off on his fingers. "Didn't ask for your opinion. Don't know who you are. Don't give a rat's rump what you're doing here. I think that covers everything. Chiun?"

Chiun flipped the button over in his palm. He tapped it with an exploratory fingernail. "This is new," he said.

Conchita frowned. "It cannot be," she insisted.

Remo closed his eyes and counted to ten. "All right already," he said, exhaling. "I can see I'm not going to get a minute's peace until I ask who the hell you are."

She drew herself up to her full height. "I am Conchita Esperanza Diaz. I am a Web consultant for MacroWare Computers, Incorporated. Who are you?"

"Lady, I can pretend I care only so much, and answering your questions is a bridge too far."

But he had given her an opening, and she was not about to back out now.

"That must be an antique," Conchita insisted, leaning to peer at the button. "I have seen similar buttons in museums in Mexico as well as on this side of the border." But as she examined the button more closely, her conviction wavered. It was unscratched and glinted sharply in the sunlight.

"Looks like our guys dropped it here when they dumped the border patrol bodies," Remo said. He turned to Conchita. "Any idea who would be wearing buttons from Mexican uniforms that went out of date a hundred and fifty years ago?"

"Why?" she sniffed. "Because I am Mexican you expect me to know what every other Mexican is up to?"

"No," Remo said reasonably, "but because we are out in the middle of nowhere examining a spot where a dozen murdered bodies were discovered, presumably killed and dumped here by someone sympathetic to illegal aliens, and because you are here in the same spot, when there isn't a Chi-Chi's within fifty miles. And, yeah," he added, "because you are Mexican. Sue me for the hate crime."

Conchita was too shocked to be angry. She found herself answering Remo calmly and rationally.

"No, I do not know," she said.

She was surprised when he took her at her word.

"Too bad. Would've made my job easier."

Shrugging, Remo turned and began combing the area once more. Wordlessly, the aged Master of Sinanju joined him, and Conchita was not certain what to do.

The previous week, she had set off on a quest that seemed impossible and now, five days into it, the chance for success seemed even more bleak than when she had started. But at this, her darkest hour, perhaps she had been guided to salvation.

These two seemed to know what they were looking for, and at the moment, she was unsure what she should do next. Perhaps if fate had arranged this meeting, these two might be able to help her in her search.

Remo and Chiun said nothing as she joined them.

The trio combed a widening area away from the road, until the last traces of human involvement blended to undisturbed desert landscape. After twenty minutes of vain searching, the three of them gave up.

"That's it," Remo said, frustrated, when they had gathered back near the SUV. "There are no footprints or tire tracks through the desert. They must have driven up the road and just dumped the bodies here. I should have asked Worthington if he knew where any of his crews were attacked."

Conchita said, "I know where you want to go."

And she flashed a smile more blinding than the sinking desert sun.

They took Conchita's Jeep, which was more suited to the rough terrain. Consulting her dashboard compass, she brought them within a mile of the Mexican border.

The sky was streaked orange with the last few moments of the dying day. The cold blue of twilight was creeping up their backs as they stepped to the sand. Behind them a dead river bed snaked off to the east.

Far ahead, Remo could see the collapsing remnants of a badly damaged chain link border fence. Every day, all across America, children on playgrounds climbed more challenging obstacles.

They found the spot where Rob Scott's Civilian Border Patrol unit had been slaughtered.

The area was less disturbed here than back near the road. Back there had been the bodies and graffiti, and so it had naturally drawn all the focus of media attention. Here was just a long ride through desert heat and a few patches of blood soaked into arid ground. Even the authorities had not lingered. There was evidence of only a perfunctory search of the area.

In the riverbed, Remo and Chiun found the spot where Rob Scott's life had ended. At the base camp, they found disturbances in the sand consistent with falling bodies. The blood spatters caused by bullets were visible to their Sinanju-trained eyes.

Although the desert seemed devoid now of human activity, Remo sensed the low hum of electronic equipment.

"You feel that, Chiun?"

The Master of Sinanju nodded. He seemed interested in a distant spot in the ground.

"Feel what?" Conchita asked.

Remo's attitude toward Conchita had softened on the

bumpy ride out to the desert. She had been quiet on the long drive and now, as she surveyed the desert, the last glint of dying light revealed glistening tears in her soulful brown eyes.

"There's something electrical out here," Remo said.

So lost in thought was she that she seemed startled she was not alone. Quickly wiping away the tears with the back of her wrist, she shook her mane of raven hair.

"The fence?" she suggested.

"No," he said. "The fence isn't electrified. That might make it actually effective, and we can't have that, now can we? This is closer."

"The CBP volunteers who died, they used electronic equipment to watch the border," she said. "Perhaps it is that." But when they looked around they could see no evidence of the devices the CBP had been using earlier that week. Everything had been packed up and shipped off.

"It is this way," the Master of Sinanju said.

Like a dog on a scent, Chiun struck off before them in search of the source. Remo and Conchita trailed after.

"I suppose," Conchita said, "you will not tell me how you are able to detect electronic signals. Assuming, that is, you actually can do so and are not insane."

"With him, the one does not preclude the other," Chiun called back.

"If you could give me ten years and your undivided attention, maybe I could begin to tell you how," Remo said. "In the meantime, now's as good a time as any to tell me why you're out here."

"I am here because of my idiot cousin Juan Carlos." Conchita spat the name as if it were poison. "Past generations came to this land through Ellis Island, and were proud to announce the fact for decades. That" . . . she waved to the border fence . . . "is where my cousin chose to enter."

The Master of Sinanju was walking a few yards ahead of Remo and Conchita.

"I do not blame him for sneaking in," the old Korean called back. "One does not want to be seen entering this nation for the same reason brothels have back doors."

"I told him I would help him," Conchita said. Anger seeped into her husky voice. "I am a naturalized U.S. citizen. The process can be daunting, but it is not impossible to come here legally. Legal Mexican immigrants are the largest foreign national origin group allowed into this country. Nearly thirty percent. America certainly does not bar Mexicans from entering. Not even worthless imbeciles like Juan Carlos, who I explained this to. But he has always been stupid and lazy. The legal way takes too much time, and he had his own timetable. So he hired a coyote to sneak his family across the border. Fool."

"This woman is the fool," Chiun said in Korean. "Ask her why her cousin did not rent a circus elephant or a giraffe to cross this border. Why a coyote? Perhaps he could have retained the services of a dolphin and swum a magic rainbow to the gold-paved streets of America."

"No, Little Father, I've heard about coyotes before," Remo said in English.

"Professional smugglers who traffic in human beings," Conchita said, and this time she did spit. "The lowest of the low. My Tia Elena called me frantic when she did not hear from my cousin and his wife. They were supposed to phone her when they made it safely across the border."

She thought of her Aunt Elena. The woman meant well, but was frustratingly old-fashioned. Conchita could not stand the way her aunt and the other women in her family so easily accepted the constraints society placed on them. For all the advances the world had made, Mexico was still at its heart a backward patriarchy. And so her aunt, a bright woman, let her idiot son Juan Carlos make a stupid decision that had put his entire family at risk.

Worse than Aunt Elena's long silence was her insistence to Conchita that she would find guidance in her search for her cousin and his family. A devoutly religious woman, Tia Elena had prayed to Jesus and the Virgin Mary to find her missing son. When she finally called Conchita to ask for help, she claimed that she was told in a dream to do so.

"I do not have time to take off work to go looking for Juan Carlos, Tia Elena," Conchita had said when the long distance call came through from Mexico.

"You must," her aunt had insisted. "The Virgin Mary has said that you will help him find rest."

Conchita was still a believer, but she was not as religious as she had been in her youth in Mexico. Sometimes she went to church, but mostly just for holidays. She could not remember the last time she had prayed.

Her aunt had insisted.

"You will do this thing," Tia Elena had said. "But you will not do it alone. You will find help in your search. The Virgin Mary says that an angel will protect you."

"Protect me from what?" Conchita has asked.

But on that particular topic, the Virgin Mary had apparently fallen silent.

Conchita eventually relented. She had agreed to take one day off from work to try to find her missing cousin. It was now five days later, she had eaten up five vacation days more than she had ever wanted to spend on this fool's quest, and she was no closer to finding her missing cousin than she had been on that first day. And if her aunt was right and a guardian angel was going to help her, he was certainly taking his own sweet time flapping his way down to find Conchita.

Tramping through the desert, Conchita pushed a wayward lock of curly ebony hair away from her eyes.

"I am angry at my aunt," she said to Remo. "She should have called me weeks ago to tell me that my idiot cousin had hatched this stupid scheme. I do have some sympathy for my sister-in-law, who is old-fashioned and allows Juan Carlos to dominate her. But, in truth, I am here for the children. If not for the fact that he dragged my little niece and two nephews along with him, I would not even be out here."

"It's a big border, last time I checked," Remo said. "He could have come across anywhere from California to Texas."

"I know he crossed near here. The coyote he hired favors this stretch of the border."

"So why don't you ask him?"

"I tried," she said. "He has disappeared."

Despite the harsh words she had had for her cousin, worry laced her voice.

"When I learned that the CBP was here, I thought I had gotten lucky," she said. "They had been monitoring border crossings here for almost a week, so I had hope that they had some information on Juan Carlos. Then I learned that they had been killed and I thought all hope was lost." She smiled. It was not a smile of manipulation, a smile intended to use sex to win over a man. It was the first sincere smile she had given him. "Then I met you."

Despite himself, Remo returned the smile.

Up ahead, Chiun held a finger to his papery lips. "Shhh," the old man hissed. "Do you hear that?"

Then Remo heard it too. Both Masters of Sinanju stopped dead in their tracks. When Conchita plowed into Remo, it was like walking into a wall.

Remo and Chiun exchanged glances. Conchita caught the strange looks on their faces. There seemed an urgent energy that coursed between the two men, and to Conchita it was almost as if a jolt of electricity had hopped from one to the other. She thought it must be her imagination when she felt the fine hairs on the back of her neck stand at attention.

"What is it?" she asked.

The hushed words were scarcely past her lips before the first shot rang out.

They came up out of nowhere. A dozen dark shapes moving through the dusk.

Conchita did not feel the pressure waves of the bullet that sang toward her exposed chest, nor did she feel the hand that grabbed her by the shoulder a split second before the bullet hit and launched her safely out of harm's way. There was the gunshot, a brief sensation of movement, the zing of the bullet whizzing harmlessly by, and she was sitting on her rear in the dirt. Remo's stern face hovered above her. Streaks of gray dusk smeared the sky behind him.

"Stay put," he commanded. And he seemed to float away.

More bullets fired. Single shots at first. Then, as targets were missed, the firing increased. So many bullets pierced the air that Conchita knew some had to be hitting home. Yet, although they should have been cut to ribbons, Remo and Chiun continued to fly at the firing men.

And then they were among them and the real carnage began.

Remo took out the first charging man with an easy backhanded slap that looked almost gentle. The man's head detached from his shoulders and gently bounced away across the desert floor.

Chiun caught the barrels of two rifles. Metal cried out in pain, and the barrels were perfect V's aimed into the startled faces of the pair of soldiers. The men did not see the simultaneous slaps, and were only vaguely aware for a single flashing instant of something flying at their faces. A pair of bayonets shot into a pair of open mouths, piercing soft tissue and coming to rest deep in two shocked brains. They fell to the ground, twitching like a pair of oversized trout caught on two misshapen hooks.

Sitting amid the scrub, Conchita twirled, panicked, at the center of the maelstrom. For the third time today here were men uninterested in her beauty. Worse, they were killers. And there was shooting, and someone was yelling.

And Conchita realized that the person doing the yelling was herself, but she did not care because the world had gone insane.

"What is happening?" she cried.

A scuffed foot nearby. Another soldier.

He was dressed in the livery of a nineteenth-century Mexican army soldier, but with a few modern alterations. The style of dress allowed for more freedom of movement than the stiff uniforms of old, and the jacket and trousers were stained with camouflage blotches. Strapped over his eyes were night vision goggles.

There was nowhere this soldier could have come from. Like the others, he had seemingly materialized from thin air. When Conchita cried out, he wheeled, gun leveled on her chest. Seated before the gunman, Conchita screamed.

Before the finger could brush the trigger, tearing the scream from Conchita's slender throat, a blur passed between her and the soldier. A horrid crunch, and the blur had scarcely resolved itself into the shape of Remo before the soldier was falling to the ground.

During that flash, in which Conchita was only vaguely aware of movement impossible for her eyes to focus on, it appeared as if the soldier's chest had collapsed. The arms and head were the same size, but the torso was freakishly smaller, as if compressed as easily as a wad of tinfoil.

Remo did not pause to see if she was all right. He moved back into the advancing line, calmly and efficiently dismantling human beings along the way. Chiun worked from the other direction, back toward his pupil.

A loafer heel launched fragments of shattered pelvis up into a soldier's abdomen.

One long fingernail harpooned a broad forehead. A burst of gunfire ripped the top off a cactus as the soldier collapsed to a heap.

All around bodies fell, arms and legs torn away, skulls reduced to quivering masses of jelly.

In all, it took less than two minutes. The last soldier dropped with shattered sternum and a fatal hiss of collapsing lungs. When the last man fell, Remo surveyed the scene. Thirteen bodies lay at broken angles across the desert. Not a sign of life breathed from a single one. Remo frowned.

"Damn," he said. "Chiun, you didn't keep one alive."

The Master of Sinanju was at Remo's elbow. His hands were tucked inside the billowing sleeves of his kimono. "It was not my turn," Chiun replied.

"Yes, it was. This time, it most definitely, one hundred percent was your turn. It was my turn last time. Remember that terrorist cell Smitty sent us after in Australia six months ago? I kept one of mine alive for questioning back then. That was my turn. This one was yours. Yours, not mine."

The old Asian offered a tiny shrug of bony shoulders. "Who can recall? Perhaps if you had not shunted me off to a dusty corner of your life these past few years, perhaps if you had not ignored and abandoned me, perhaps if you actually involved your spiritual father in important decisions that concern the House of Sinanju and, yes, will impact on my place in the Sacred Scrolls as Master and teacher, perhaps then I could keep better track of whose turn it is or isn't."

"Dammit, Chiun, it was your turn and you know it. Why do we even bother taking turns if you're just going to keep skipping yours? I was keeping the girl safe."

"You have done your usual excellent job I see," said the Master of Sinanju.

"What do you mean?" Remo asked. He glanced around. All he could see were the bodies. Conchita was gone. "Now what? Where the hell'd she go?"

All at once, ten yards distant, a head appeared out of the ground like a gopher from a hole.

Conchita smiled at Remo and Chiun. "I have found the source of your electricity," she said.

* * *

The trapdoor in the desert floor was disguised with sand, stone and clumps of scrub brush.

"I tripped over the handle," Conchita said. She was back up on level ground. "See? They looped a piece of rope through here. And look at that."

A hole in the ground yawned wide. Below was not all darkness. Amber light filtered from some hidden source. A simple wooden ladder leaned against a cinderblock wall.

A few yards distant, Remo spied another irregular square in the earth. It would have been difficult to see in daylight. At night, only eyes trained in Sinanju would be sharp enough to spot the trapdoor.

The soldiers had appeared from several different locations. There must have been multiple spots like these peppered throughout this area of desert closer to the border.

"Remember, Little Father, if we find any more, we need to keep one of them alive for questioning."

"If you are correct, then that was my turn," the Master of Sinanju said, tipping his head toward the field of bodies. "That makes this your turn. Do not mess up."

Not giving Remo a chance to argue, the old man was over the edge and scurrying down the ladder. Remo followed Conchita down.

A tunnel opened up at the bottom of the deep well. Yellow extension cords ran from lintel to lintel. Bare bulbs dangled from the low ceiling. Underfoot was packed earth and an occasional dust-dry board.

Remo could sense from the emptiness of the air before him that the tunnel extended well over to the Mexican side of the border.

"The people I spoke to said that the coyote my cousin hired sometimes used a tunnel for border crossings," Conchita said excitedly.

Remo had to restrain her to keep her from bounding down the tunnel ahead of them.

"Let us take point," he suggested.

Conchita seemed ready to struggle from his grip, but rationality overcame passion. She stayed close behind as they made their way up the tunnel.

Here and there, short alcoves cut open on either side. Cinder block walls and ladders ran up to the surface.

The deeper they traveled, the more the sense of emptiness grew. A quarter of a mile in, there were no more ladders. By then, Remo and Chiun had come to a shared conclusion.

"There is no one here," Chiun announced.

"There must be," Conchita insisted.

"Trust us," Remo said. "Everyone who was down here is up there now." He shot a glare at the Master of Sinanju. "If someone hadn't had a hissy fit and skipped his turn, we'd have somebody to question right now."

"And if someone had been more respectful of the man who had taught him everything worthwhile he ever knew, then he would not be squabbling with his teacher over silly details. But then someone has always been selfish."

"Stop it," Conchita said.

"By 'someone' I mean you, Remo," Chiun added.

"Just stop it!" Conchita snapped. She pushed between them and hurried down the tunnel.

"What's her problem?" Remo asked.

Chiun shrugged, uninterested. "She is female, and therefore needs no excuse to start an argument. They snap at you if it is their time to make a baby or if they've burned your dinner. Believe this, for I have been married. Placidity is unknown to their nature."

They followed Conchita down the tunnel.

Although the routes to the surface had stopped a few dozen yards back, other, larger chambers opened off this longer stretch of tunnel. These appeared to have been dug more recently than the main border tunnel. The supports were sturdier and sunk into mortar. Remo noted the Home Depot stickers still fastened to a few of the beams.

They found Conchita standing at an open door. Remo and Chiun slid in beside her.

"Madre de Dios," Remo said, whistling.

The room was filled to the rafters with guns and explosives. Cases of ammunition were stacked floor-to-ceiling.

"Looks like someone's ready for the revolution," Remo said.

Conchita was not listening.

In the corner, behind a pile of wooden crates, two pairs of boots jutted into the light.

Conchita hurried across the room. When she stopped over the bodies, she gasped. Hands shaking, she fished something from the pocket of her slacks.

A photograph was clutched in her hand. Remo saw that the face in the picture was that of one of the dead men.

"Your cousin?" Remo asked softly.

She shook her head. "This is Gustavo Acevedo," she said, voice hollow. "The coyote my fool cousin hired."

"That could be good news," Remo said. "If your family isn't here, that means he maybe got them through safe."

Conchita did not accept his soothing words. She spat into the dead man's face and turned on her heel.

"Do not even think of bringing this one home," the Master of Sinanju warned Remo. "The bills to clean the carpet will land me in the poor farm."

"You're probably the richest man in Asia," Remo commented absently. "Hey, get a load of this."

There was a map of North America unfolded on a table near the door. Although the paper was new, the picture itself must have been copied from a very old map.

"The borders are all screwy," Remo said. Frowning, he folded the map and tucked it in his pocket.

The next room was some sort of communications center. Motion devices and hidden cameras tracked activity in the desert above. On one monitor, Remo saw a distant view of

Conchita's Jeep, illuminated in the ghostly green haze of the night vision camera.

Staring sternly out at them from dozens of framed photographs all around the room was the image of a fat-faced man. His skin was ravaged from a failed battle with teenaged acne. Balding halfway back, his hair grew long at the sides and swept up his temples where it was plastered to his forehead. His uniform was a throwback to a bygone era. A high gilded collar brushed his cheeks, and a pair of huge epaulets gave the false impression of broad shoulders.

Under each picture a legend was inscribed in simple, archaic script: General Santa Anna.

Conchita peered at the face in the nearest photograph. She looked as if she had eaten something foul.

"This is not Santa Anna," she said.

Chiun cast a disdainful eye up and down the picture. "How can she tell?" he asked Remo. "All generals look alike."

"That's not true, Little Father. You're starting to sound like Worthington now. You can't see the difference between this guy and Norman Schwarzkopf?"

"I do not know this Dummkopf friend of yours."

"A general. For our side."

"Fat and blustery, isn't he?" asked Chiun.

"Yeah, kind of."

"See? All generals are the same. They could be Roman or Greek or this pockmarked creature here. Peas in a pod."

"I do not know who this man is," Conchita said, steering them back to the photograph, "but I certainly know one of the most famous figures in the history of Mexico. And given his success at the Alamo, there are few Texas schoolchildren who would not know him as well. Whoever this man is, he is not the real Antonio López de Santa Anna."

The voice that answered Conchita belonged to neither Remo nor Chiun.

"Oh, he's definitely General Santa Anna. He just isn't the one you expect."

The tinkling female voice was scratchy, electronic but one Remo had heard before. He glanced around and saw that a computer monitor had flicked on across the room. A familiar, beautiful Midwestern face smiled out at him.

"And, good gosh, how could it be the same Santa Anna after all these years?" the woman asked. "He'd have to be over two hundred years old by now. Hello, Remo."

A camera was mounted on top of the computer monitor, a dull mechanized eye staring across the subterranean room. She could see them as well as they could see her.

"I saw what you did to those men I sent up to say hello," the woman said. "You guys are something else. And this must be Chiun. You must be very proud of your son, Master of Sinanju."

The old Korean ignored the woman on the monitor. "Who is this harlot?" he demanded of Remo. "Is this what you have been doing with your time? You tell me that you have been off on important business, and instead you have been seeing some new hussy behind my back?"

"I wish," Remo said. He did not take his eyes off the monitor. "Her name is Rebecca Dalton."

A light dawned in the old man's hazel eyes. "This is the one who tried to kill you?" he said. His gaze narrowed as he stared at the face on the computer monitor.

It was during the Sinanju Time of Succession, the last ritual test Remo had been forced to endure before taking his place as Reigning Master. Assassins from around the world had tried to kill Remo with poison, bullet and blade. Only one of the otherwise run-of-the-mill killers the world's governments had sent against him had posed a challenge.

"Back then everyone I met was trying to kill me," Remo said. "She's the only one who succeeded."

"Well, that's mighty generous of you, Remo," Rebecca

Dalton said. On the monitor, she shook her head. Her ponytail bobbed. "But the fact that you're still standing there is proof that I dropped the ball, wouldn't you say?"

"Actually," Remo said, "it's a little more complicated than that."

"Enough," Chiun snapped. He floated between Remo and the computer screen, as if to shield his pupil from harm. "You did not learn from your master, wench. Benson Dilkes knew his place. Sinanju tolerated his existence as long as he did not stray into our path. The moment he did, he was no more." Hands flashed a warning, fingernails like knife blades slicing air. "Heed his lesson and begone."

"So you did kill poor Benson," Rebecca said. "I figured as much, but I had no way of knowing for sure. That was a crazy time. There were so many in our business who vanished thanks to you, it was hard for a gal to keep track."

"To suggest, little girl, that we are in the same line of work," Chiun said aridly, "is to claim that the worm and the lion are the same because both breathe air."

"Gosh, you're just cute as a button," Rebecca said. "I could eat you up. Actually, I can't leave like Benson. Wish I could, but I'm way too busy these days. I have a whole bunch of big-name clients now. The good general is just one of many. I'm busy, busy, busy. I've gotta give you a big thank-you for that, Remo. You eliminated virtually every big name in the business. This is a golden age for assassins."

The camera shifted slightly toward Conchita.

"Well, aren't you a pretty little thing," Rebecca said. "And who might we be?"

"I am Conchita Esperanza Diaz," she said.

"That a MacroWare badge hanging from your pocket?" Rebecca asked. "You should have gone into work today." She pouted her lower lip. "Gosh 'n' golly, am I ever sorry to have to do this. Especially to you, ma'am, since you seem to just be at the wrong place at the wrong darned time."

Remo had heard enough. Rebecca was obviously far away from here. There was nothing to be gained by listening to this cheery jibber-jabber any longer.

"Okay, kitten, you've had your fun," Remo said. He started for the computer, ready to rip it from its extension cord. Rebecca stopped him before he could reach it.

"Just because I failed the last time it doesn't mean a gal should stop trying," she said. There was suddenly a hint of cold steel in her cheery tone.

Remo glanced up. And as they all watched, Rebecca raised a cell phone to the camera.

"I'm sooooo sorry about this," she assured them. And a slender finger pressed the pound key.

It took two seconds for the first sound to reach their ears. A soft, distant foom. The lights blinked, then faded.

Foom-foom-foom!

Explosions, one after another, rocked the tunnel. A violent cloud of dust exploded up the tunnel and vomited through the door behind them. The ground heaved beneath their feet.

On battery backup, the computer continued to glow through the earthquake. For a minute in the dark, Rebecca Dalton seemed to be trying to watch the result of her handiwork, a deeply sympathetic look on her face.

"Again, I'm real, real sorry about this," Rebecca said over the growing thunder. "I hope you're not mad at. . . ."

And then a boulder crashed down, the monitor and camera sparked and smashed to pieces, and a thousand pounds of desert crashed in around Remo, Chiun and Conchita's ears.

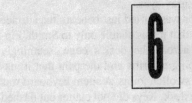

The sedate brick building that sat amid the trees
and sprawling green lawns on the northern shore of Long
Island Sound was a throwback to another era.

Travelers who passed the front gate scarcely took notice
of the old building, which was the sort of structure one
could easily ignore. Common at the time it was constructed
a century before, so there still remained enough examples
of its architectural type to make it unworthy of more than a
glance.

Sometimes a child in a car's backseat would notice the
granite lions that stood silent sentry at the front gates and
wonder what fascinating things must be going on inside for
the building to have such fierce stone guardians.

A simple bronze plaque at the front gate read "Folcroft
Sanitarium."

In the back of the building was an office, as far from
passing cars and childhood illusions as was possible. And

in that lonely post, behind a slab of desk so black it seemed hewn from coal, Dr. Harold W. Smith watched the world pass before his sharp, gray eyes.

A computer monitor was buried just beneath the surface of the desk, canted so that it was visible only to Smith. Fingers played nimbly across the desk's edge, seemingly oblivious to the creeping arthritis and the pain that it visited upon twisted and swollen joints. A silent keyboard was buried at the lip of the desk. Keys did not clatter but flashed light at Smith's confident touch.

Data from states at the nation's southern border scrolled across the screen, reflected in the spotless lenses of Smith's wireless glasses.

There were several more large immigration rallies planned for the day. The biggest was in Los Angeles. Already marchers were on the scene.

Smith had taken down from a shelf his small black-and-white television. The set was perched on the edge of his desk. Although turned on, the volume was off. Smith had tuned in to one of the big cable news outlets and occasionally as he worked he would glance up at the screen.

Live reports cut from Las Cruces and Albuquerque in New Mexico to Phoenix and Los Angeles. Smith watched the massive gatherings of humanity with pinched concern.

For a year now, civil unrest had become a regular occurrence for those sympathetic to the plight of illegal immigrants. But so far the self-inflicted damage to the cause had been welcome news to advocates of stricter border enforcement. Waving foreign flags, carrying upside-down what few American flags they had been issued, even going so far as singing the national anthem in Spanish . . . it was almost as if some heavy hand were behind it all, attempting to use the guileless protesters as a pawn in some greater scheme. But if there were a guiding force, Smith's computers had so far been unable to find it.

Smith's fingers withdrew from his keyboard. Leaning

back in his cracked leather chair, he removed his glasses, pinching the bridge of his nose.

Smith spun his chair to the big picture window at his back. The window was special one-way glass. Smith could see out, but outside the glass was mirrored, so that no one could see what took place in the dusty corner office.

It was spring on the East Coast. The buds on maple and birch had sprouted into early leaves. Weak and yellowish now, seemingly too fragile to survive, they would soon grow hearty and green. From spring bud to summer leaf, Harold W. Smith would scarcely notice the change.

Harold W. Smith did not have time to fritter away on the natural beauty of his surroundings. His job was to make certain that others had the time for such frivolity. His Spartan Folcroft office was the place where he felt most at home. Field, woods or nature trail were as alien an environment to him as the surface of Mars.

When other men his age had started retiring from the workforce more than a decade before, duty kept Smith at his post. Without his work, Smith would have been as oxygen deprived as if he had been deposited on the red planet. His selflessness and dedication to work and country had been with him since his New England upbringing, and were as natural a part of him as any limb. Even more so, for a limb could be amputated and Smith would still find a way to crawl to his desk every day, rain or shine.

Some called Smith's the "greatest generation," but he did not agree with that assessment. The very idea that one generation was greater than another automatically diminished the accomplishments of all others not in some venerated fraternity. Smith understood that in every generation there was potential for greatness, and he did not view the blood spilled at Normandy and Iwo Jima as any more precious than that which soaked the sands of Kabul or Tikrit.

But agree or not, Smith was wrong. Greatness was not measured in lost blood alone. It was sometimes measured in the will of a man to stay in the game long after his prime, compelled to fight the good fight solely because of the knowledge that—although he received no accolades or awards—the work he accomplished on this earth made a real difference. In this, in a lifetime of diligence, humility and self-sacrifice, Harold W. Smith was truly the greatest of many great generations.

A sloping green lawn led to the shore of Long Island Sound. A rotting boat dock bobbed on frothy waves. It was to that dock that Smith had come over forty years before.

He had been in early middle age then. His perspective on age had changed over the years. He now believed that the man who had stepped out on that dock had been young.

The secret agency CURE had been in its infancy. Smith had been its father, had guided it, molded it. An agency which by mandate would break the law in order to save the nation.

No one would have believed the priggish, unimaginative Smith could have undertaken such a task; no one but a U.S. president, long dead.

Not even Smith's secretary of thirty years knew the truth of her employer's work. Only a handful had ever known. In addition to Remo and Chiun, CURE was known to each current president. A Sinanju technique assured that every chief executive forgot about the agency the day he left office. During the earliest days, Smith had been assisted at CURE by an old CIA friend, Conrad MacCleary. For a time there was Ruby Gonzalez, another ex-CIA operative. Both had died while in Smith's employ. There were no state funerals for CURE employees. Each loss had been quietly mourned.

Their faces came to him now, forever young in his mind's eye. And, reflected in the window before him, an old man's face. There were times when he saw his own reflection and Harold Smith did not recognize himself.

Smith did not realize his thoughts had drifted to age and

to lost comrades until a knock at his door shook him from his reverie. He checked his trusty Timex which he knew was soon due for its biennial battery change.

Nine o'clock. Right on time.

Smith spun his chair away from the window. "Come in, Mark," he called, as he settled back behind his desk.

The young man who entered the office was in his late thirties. The laugh lines that had once crimped the corners of his eyes had surrendered prominence to a furrowed brow. Dark circles rimmed his eyes. The baby fat had been cut away, as had been the eyes of innocence. This hardened face was a stark contrast to that which the young man had worn the first time Smith had met him in Folcroft's parking lot on a cold winter's evening six years before.

"Morning, Dr. Smith," Mark Howard said as he shut the door behind him.

During his six years at CURE, Howard's light brown hair had begun to gray. Mark pushed his fingers through his salt-and-pepper hair as he took his seat in the hard wooden chair before his employer's desk.

Except for Mark Howard, Ruby Gonzalez and Conrad MacCleary, there had never been another CURE employee at Folcroft. There was no need. Smith had run the agency single-handed for the bulk of forty years. Even when he had had help—MacCleary, Ruby, Mark—at any given time, there had only ever been two at Folcroft with operational knowledge of CURE. For an agency for which secrecy was crucial, it would have been insanity to introduce unnecessary personnel into CURE. There had never been three at a time with knowledge of CURE at Folcroft and there never would be.

"Have you heard from Remo?" Mark asked.

"Not yet," Smith said. An anxious notch formed above his nose. "He should have checked in last night."

"I was here all night. If he tried, the call would have

been routed to my office." Howard saw the worried look on the CURE director's face. "I'm sure they're fine."

Smith sighed, finally replacing his glasses. "Most likely. And we both know Remo has always been" . . . he searched for the right word . . . "relaxed in his attitude toward what we do. Even before I let him go on that long sabbatical."

"I guess we could have included the two of them more," Mark suggested.

Smith shook his head. "No. When we went off after terrorists and left them out of it, it was the right thing to do. We're engaged in an active war. There are just too many forces out there in the global field, too many witnesses, too many opportunities for exposure. No. The decision to hold them back and use them only in cases of extreme urgency was the right one."

Mark Howard knew it was not in Smith's nature to come to frivolous decisions, nor to second-guess decisions once they were made. It was also clear from his tone that Smith was certain that excluding Remo and Chiun from the bulk of CURE's recent anti-terrorist activities had been the right choice.

"Has he ever spoken about where he's been?" the younger man asked.

"Not a word."

"And all I could find out was that he went to East Africa. And then he fell pretty much off the face of the planet. I talked to him once; he told me he was on 'walkabout.' And then he told me to blow it out my ears and to tell you that everything was fine and not to worry."

Smith sighed. "When Remo tells me not to worry, that's when I worry. Still and all, he's back and maybe someday he'll tell us what he was up to. Meanwhile, let's hope he can keep focused on this job. Have you found out anything worthwhile about Prescott Worthington and Worthington International?"

Howard sensed that Smith was as relieved as he was to set aside the issue of Remo's mysterious jaunts to Africa.

"You know, Dr. Smith, it's in my nature to be suspicious of anyone to the manor born," Howard said. "But so far Worthington seems clean. Remember, though, that there's a ton of material to go through. Worthington International has owned some of the same companies going back a hundred years. I don't even think they know everything that's under their umbrella. You think the guy is dirty?"

Smith shook his head. "At the moment I have no reason to think so," he said. "But Worthington could be a target. Those were his men murdered, after all. It could be that whoever is responsible for the CBP deaths has an ax to grind with Worthington himself. Perhaps a disgruntled former employee, a business rival, someone angry with his position on stronger border enforcement. This may not even be a border issue at all."

"I'll keep looking," Howard promised.

Smith knew that he would, and that his research would be as thorough as if Smith had done it himself. He honestly could not imagine how he had managed the crushing demands as head of CURE for so many years without an assistant.

And it had helped their working relationship that Smith had grown fond of the young man. Smith had developed a paternal bond with Howard, a bond that at times felt stronger than the one Smith shared with his own daughter.

Normally an unemotional man, Smith could not help but feel a twinge of sympathy for Mark Howard. Smith was already married when he came aboard CURE all those years ago. Maude Smith had already given birth to their only child. The Smiths' daughter, Vickie, had gone on to give them three healthy grandchildren. There existed for Smith a life outside of Folcroft's ivy-covered walls, even if he did not spend much time there. Not so for Mark Howard.

Howard would never have the wife, the children, the normal life. He had a house in Rye. Smith had insisted that he buy it to maintain his cover as assistant director of Folcroft, the exclusive mental health and convalescent facility. But the house would remain an empty shell and there would be no Thanksgiving dinners, no presents under a Christmas tree, no swing sets in the backyard, no Little League, no Band-Aids on scraped knees.

Smith sometimes wondered if the young man understood what he had surrendered when he signed on to the most secret agency ever to exist on American soil. He doubted it. How could Howard know? After all, Smith had been fully briefed those forty years ago, yet in hindsight he realized he had understood nothing. Knowing a thing and living it were two entirely different things.

Their morning meeting continued, eventually moving off the subject of the current border crisis. There were always other problems that required CURE's attention.

Since late 2001, a digest on global terrorism had become part of the daily briefing. The latest item to be caught in the CURE computer net was a report out of Mexico City.

"It's calling itself the Elite Incursion Martyrdom Brigade," Howard said. "The CIA has got it on a hot watch. The leader is Jordanian, a guy by the name of Zaid Dudin."

"The CIA doesn't know its purpose?" Smith asked.

"Not yet. But it's the CIA and they'd probably miss it even if this Brigade whatever-it-is took out an ad in the CIA employee newsletter. They say they've got them under surveillance. The computers will flag us if they start to move."

They were discussing some other recent al-Khobar chatter out of London when Smith was suddenly distracted by the television on his desk.

He had long felt that television news was now designed for adults with the attention spans of hyperactive children. Most of the time it was next to impossible to see the main image on the screen, so crowded was it by picture-in-picture commentary, pop-up graphics, and the constant news crawl at the bottom of the screen. But the screen on his small TV had suddenly changed to a single image. All the usual extraneous window dressing was gone.

It was an image from an outdoor rally. Smith recognized the Los Angeles City Hall in the background.

The previous year, few American flags had been waved at the first huge pro-illegal immigration protests. This fact, added to the many Mexican flags on hand, had raised patriotic hackles across the nation. Since that time, organizers had been careful to issue American flags to the crowds.

At the protest on television, Smith saw that part of the rambunctious crowd had descended on a group stretching out a large American flag. Hands grabbed at stripes and star field, tearing at the fabric. Smith watched, aghast, as the flag was thrown to the street and ground underfoot.

"Have they gone mad?" he gasped.

As he spoke, someone doused the flag with liquid from a can. A match was struck. Smith watched the American flag go up in flames. To his horror, others raced forward, tossing smaller American flags into the growing conflagration.

The men who had set the fire danced gleefully around the blaze, arms waving ecstatically, faces hidden behind bandanas decorated with the Mexican flag.

Smith could not believe his eyes. No one, no matter how stupid, could possibly think such an act would help their cause.

"What is it?" Mark asked. He came around behind Smith's desk so that he could see the black-and-white screen.

Excited spectators were screaming delight. They appeared to be shouting the same words over and over.

Reaching over, Smith turned up the volume.

Smith understood only a little Spanish. His languages were French and German, the former learned at Putney Day School in Vermont, the latter as part of his service in the OSS during the Second World War. But he did not need to be fluent in the language to understand the words being shouted by the ecstatic spectators.

"Viva Santa Anna! Viva Santa Anna! Viva Santa Anna!"

The bouncing camera suddenly wheeled away from the bonfire, redirected to a distant stage. Zooming, blurry at first, it hastily found focus.

A man was addressing the crowd. His dark skin was pockmarked, and his black hair was plastered to his temples. The high collar of his old-fashioned blue and gold uniform brushed his ears like the neck brace of a whiplash victim.

When a caption finally flashed on the screen, Smith felt his already parched mouth go drier than desert sand.

"I fear the crisis has just gotten worse," he said.

On the screen, the uniformed speaker waved his arms dramatically and shouted exhortations to the wild crowd. The simple caption read "General Santa Anna."

When the world came crashing down in an ava-
lanche of stone and earth, sending up clouds of choking
dust and plunging all into a blackness so deep that no light
could penetrate, one single thought passed through the
mind of Remo Williams. And that thought was, "Crap on a
crust."

The explosions that had caused the tunnel to collapse
had stopped. Through the settling earth, Remo felt the
rumble of the last blast dissipating, rolling across the
desert like a lost aftershock in search of the earthquake
that had spawned it.

Although he ordinarily needed little light to see, there
was no ambient light whatsoever to draw into his eyes.
This makeshift grave of Rebecca Dalton's required sight of
a different kind.

Honed by training, now as instinctive as breathing itself,
Remo extended his senses.

As falling rock came down around them, Remo and Chiun had directed the larger boulders like massive children's blocks. Flashing hands caught rock, steering it into piles, left and right. Before the earth had settled completely they had formed a cavern big enough for three.

In the dark, Remo felt two heartbeats near his own. One was confident and strong, the other hopped nervously, like a frightened jackrabbit. From the darkness, the owner of the more assured heartbeat spoke.

"Move your big stupid feet," the Master of Sinanju squeaked.

"Chiun, how's Conchita doing?"

The woman was on the other side of the old Korean. Her heartbeat was growing more erratic.

"My God, we are . . ." She gasped and choked on dust.

"Don't panic," Remo said. "We'll do okay. This isn't the first time she's buried me alive."

Conchita found no comfort in his words. Panic rattled through her. Remo could hear her heartbeat spike as the realization of their situation set in.

"Little Father?" Remo said.

"Bah!" the Master of Sinanju snapped.

Remo heard the rustle of Chiun's kimono. There was a sharp intake of air. Conchita's erratic heartbeat suddenly became more confident. He heard Chiun's hand withdraw.

"She will be calm for the time being," the Asian said.

Remo assessed their situation.

"Straight up?" he asked.

"Not if you wish to save this one," Chiun said.

Remo understood what his teacher meant. It would have been the logical plan for the two of them to cut a straight line up to the surface, tunneling vertically, easing rock back into pockets behind them. But Conchita complicated things. Training coupled with deft manipulation of stone would keep the two Masters of Sinanju safe. But Conchita was essentially dead weight. With her in tow the risk of further collapse was too great. One wrong move and she would be crushed between shifting boulders. That likelihood only grew if she had another panic attack along the way.

There was only one way for them to go.

The tunnel had been an unnatural intrusion, but its collapse had not been total. Both men could sense other air pockets where the tunnel had been, interlocking with their own, many large enough for them to fit through.

Remo was closest to the opening of their makeshift cavern. The Master of Sinanju slid back, placing Conchita between them. With Remo in the lead, the three of them began the laborious task of crawling out to safety.

It was tortuously slow going. Conchita could feel certain hands guiding her in the darkness. Pulled from ahead, pushed from behind; at times it seemed to take hours to crawl inches, at others, she had the sense of being propelled through wider caverns at unmeasurable speed.

The air pockets were thick with settling dust. The Master of Sinanju had torn an inner strip off of his kimono and wrapped it around her nose and mouth. Her heavy breathing turned dust to caked-on mud.

"Wouldn't it be safer to wait for someone to dig us out?" Conchita asked Remo at one point.

"Secret tunnel in the middle of nowhere," Remo replied. "They could dig until doomsday and never find us. Assuming anyone would think to dig for us, which they wouldn't."

Throughout the ordeal, Conchita labored on. At times she felt the fear rise like bile in her throat, but through sheer gritty determination, she quelled her instinct to panic.

In this endless dark of artificial night, her faith in her Tia Elena was suddenly total. Her aunt had been right. These men had been sent by God to help her. The Almighty would not allow them to die. Indeed, did she not feel in their assured movements through sheer darkness the guiding hand of a benevolent deity?

In the blackest midnight of her darkest hour, Conchita Diaz prayed, prayed as she had not since childhood.

She did not know how long it took them to reach the surface. All at once the earth seemed to crumble to light and she felt herself being tossed up onto solid ground.

It was dawn over the desert. She had kept her eyes squinted shut for most of the ordeal below ground. The first harsh yellow rays of daylight seared her retinas.

Conchita pulled the cloth from her mouth and sucked in a great lungful of fresh air. She spent the next five minutes doubled over and coughing up black phlegm.

Remo patted her back. "You did all right, kid."

Conchita did not feel all right. Her eyes watered. She hacked and hacked until her throat was raw. Eventually the breath returned to her. She blinked the dirt from her eyes.

She was a little bloodied, her clothing shredded. Somehow the two men she was with had come through their overnight ordeal unscathed. Remo's T-shirt was a little dusty. A few slaps cleaned the dust away. The Master of Sinanju's kimono looked as if it had just come back from the laundry. His hands were tucked in his sleeves, locked onto opposing wrists. It was as though the old man were part gopher, used to spending his nights burrowing through earth.

She saw that Chiun and Remo were not paying attention to her. Their attention had been drawn by something nearby. When she glanced up, she saw dark shapes moving swiftly across the desert. They came out of the sunlight. Conchita had been coughing so hard she had not heard a sound. The Jeeps were upon them before she even realized that they were there. Eight Mexican army soldiers clamored down to the dusty ground. All were armed. None looked happy.

The commanding officer shouted something in Spanish. Remo, who did not speak Spanish, said, "Keep your skirt on, Lupe Velez."

The man's face went purple. A uniform patch over his

pocket identified him as Captain Javier Jiminez. Shouting something new, and not entirely friendly sounding, Jiminez waved his sidearm at the three of them. His seven men stood ready with rifles.

"What'd he say?" Remo asked.

"Do not ask me," said the Master of Sinanju. "I am merely in your life as window dressing, remember? You have made the choice to be illiterate in nearly every language you encounter, including your native tongue."

As they bickered, Captain Jiminez's eyes narrowed. "You are Americans," he accused in English. His gun grew steadier, aimed now at Remo's chest.

"There is no reason to be insulting," Chiun sniffed.

"Naturalized," Conchita said. Her hands were in the air. She watched nervously as the young soldiers leered at her. "I was born in Guadalajara."

Why were Remo and Chiun not raising their hands, Conchita wondered? These were not costumed fools playing games in the night. This was broad daylight, they were surrounded, and these were trained soldiers of the Mexican National Defense force.

"American," Chiun spat, oblivious to the danger. "Why not accuse me of being Thai? Or even a lowly Vietnamese? This slur cannot be allowed to pass. Who is your supervisor?"

The captain ignored the old Asian. "What are you doing here?" he demanded of Remo.

"Hi-de-ho to you too, amigo," Remo said. "And shouldn't I be the one to ask you that, seeing as how you're driving around on American soil?"

Remo heard a hiss at his back and felt a tap on his shoulder. When he looked, the Master of Sinanju was pointing in the direction from which they'd come. Remo noted the fence far at their backs.

"Ah, hell, we're in Mexico."

A soft gasp and Remo now felt an anxious tug at the back of his T-shirt.

"This is my country," Conchita whispered. "At least, it is my nation of origin. Things work differently here than in the U.S. Allow me to handle this."

But Remo wasn't listening. Fishing in his pocket, he flipped Captain Jiminez a nickel.

"As long as we're here, go bring me back eight million pesos and one clean Mexican streetwalker." Remo waved a warning finger. "And don't forget my three cents change."

Conchita was not exactly certain what happened next. She was aware of eight very angry faces. She was even more aware of eight gun barrels pointed in their direction. She thought they might be shot right then and there.

The next thing Conchita knew, one of the uniformed men was lying in agony on the ground cradling his shattered testicles, and Remo was leading the remaining Mexican soldiers in a song, the title of which seemed to be "North of the Border/Up Hoboken Way."

"I demand an apology," the Master of Sinanju said, as the perspiring soldiers sang about lost love on the banks of the Hudson River. "Remo, does Mexico have a king?"

"A president," Remo said.

The Master of Sinanju exhaled angrily and threw his hands up at the uncaring heavens. "Thank you yet again, America," he complained. Folding his arms, he sulked at Remo's side.

Remo was not paying attention. He pulled Captain Jiminez from the chorus. The officer was singing louder than all the rest. Veins bulged in his neck. Both hands were locked protectively over his groin.

"Want to tell me why you were being nasty even by *federale* standards?" Remo asked.

Jiminez's eyes darted from Remo to the soldier who lay moaning on the ground. "Do you not know?"

"If there is something to not be known, rest assured he does not know it," the Master of Sinanju said.

"Enlighten me," Remo said.

"Overnight, the protests in your country have grown in intensity," Jiminez told them. "My people have been instructed to take to the streets of America in force today."

"Your people?" Remo said, brow arched. "It used to be people came here to become my people." He suddenly remembered where he was. "Came there," he said. He waved toward the fence. "Over there. You know what I mean."

"No one knows what you mean," Chiun said.

"Don't help," Remo warned.

"Our presidents have exchanged words over the border issue," Captain Jiminez continued anxiously. "Some of your senators have announced they are coming down to tour the area to see the problem for themselves."

"Politicians are coming and you're getting pissy with us?" Remo said. "If you had half a brain you'd be home locking up your hooch and your daughters."

"There are already big rallies overnight in some of your major cities," Captain Jiminez said. "Los Angeles has been shut down by the marching in the streets. Migrants demanding their rights have swarmed the city of Albuquerque."

Remo was about to point out that, not to be technical or anything, only citizens of the United States had the legal standing to demand guaranteed U.S. constitutional rights. But he was distracted by a piercing sound.

A train whistle shrieked across the desert.

Remo had heard the train rumbling toward them for the past several minutes. He had spied the tracks about a mile distant. They ran up from the south and spanned the border between the two countries. The train was apparently trusted by both nations, for there was not a border checkpoint on either side. Just a section of fence tripped by an unseen electric switch that rolled back invitingly as the locomotive approached. When the section of gate opened, three distant figures scrambled up from out of a patch of thick scrub brush where they had been hiding and made a mad dash across the border into the United States.

"Are we giving away free balloons to the first nine million customers?" Remo groused.

The train had finally come into view, rumbling along on hundred-year-old tracks. When Remo saw it, he frowned.

"Chiun, let me see that train you got from Worthington's office."

The Master of Sinanju fished in his robes and produced the toy locomotive.

Remo held the toy train up to compare it to the distant locomotive. The model of the old-fashioned steam engine matched perfectly the train chugging toward them.

"It's the same train," he said.

"That is Señor Worthington's private line," Captain Jiminez explained. "He has much industrial land in the Chihuahua region."

"What do you say, Little Father?" Remo asked, handing the toy train back to his teacher. "You want to ride the rails back to civilization?"

Chiun hid the train back inside the folds of his kimono. "Unless this contraption traverses oceans, one cannot get to civilization by train," he sniffed in reply, then flounced off, pipe stem legs billowing the skirts of his kimono as he ran.

Remo turned to Conchita. "You want to trust yourself with them, or hitch a ride back with us?"

By now the Mexican army chorus had sung themselves hoarse. They were only too eager to see Remo leave so they could get back to shaking down tourists and abusing their fellow countrymen.

Conchita hesitated. "What about my Jeep? And your truck is still back at the highway."

"Your Jeep's your business. My boss will probably tell Hertz where to pick up my rental."

"It was a Budget rental," Conchita said. "I saw the window sticker."

Remo shrugged. "Hertz, Budget, whatever. I'm a big-picture guy. I don't fuss over details. I'll probably just tell him it was stolen anyway. You coming?"

Conchita seemed torn. The tunnel had been a conversion experience for her. Somehow, despite the fact that by all rights she should have suffocated in a coyote's tunnel, she was breathing clean air. Had her aunt's prayers truly had been answered in these two miraculous men?

"The train's leaving the station," Remo warned. He took one step toward the tracks.

Conchita nodded. "Ye—" she began.

It was all she managed to say before she felt herself being lifted off her feet and flung over Remo's shoulder. He took off at a lope toward the speeding train.

The Master of Sinanju had already reached the tracks. He looked like a casual commuter awaiting the morning train on an invisible platform in the middle of the desert.

The approaching train had the look of a turn-of-the-century steam engine, one of the last before the introduction of diesel and electric engines. There was an engine, two cars and a caboose. At some point it had been converted to diesel. No steam billowed from the engine is it chugged at fifty miles per hour along the straight stretch of track.

An engraved sign on the side of one of the coach cars read, WORTHINGTON CONTINENTAL RAILROAD.

The train showed no signs of slowing. As the locomotive raced past, the Master of Sinanju reached out a hand and latched onto a railing. A swirl of kimono hems and he was suddenly standing on the back platform of the red caboose.

Remo raced to catch the departing train, Conchita balanced lightly on his shoulder.

Conchita did not get the sense that they were running at all. There was not the jarring bounce of feet pounding earth that one normally associated with running, just a gentle gliding across the uneven desert surface.

They should never have been able to catch the speeding

train. But then they were somehow at the caboose, and Conchita had a fresh sensation of floating, but she had actually been hurled like a javelin and then she found herself being plucked from the air by the Master of Sinanju and placed firmly on the train's rear platform. A light skip, and Remo landed beside her.

"You think the dining car is still serving breakfast?" Remo asked.

Smiling at Conchita, he reached lightly for the door handle and, finding it locked, said "Oh, well" and ripped the rear door off the caboose and tossed it over his shoulder.

Two minutes earlier Prescott Worthington IV was busy multi-tasking. Others of his station might have difficulty juggling his morning shave, watching cable news and berating his barber simultaneously, but Prescott Worthington IV was more than up to the challenge.

Worthington only vaguely knew about twin blades, cans of shaving cream and disposable razors. Worthington believed in hot towels, fresh lather and straight razors. Worthington also believed that others of lesser station should be the ones to use all said supplies on smooth Worthington skin. Worthington's father had never taught his son how to shave, but that was not to say that there was no teenage rite of passage in the Worthington manse. Worthington III had given strict instructions to Worthington IV on how to properly berate others while shaving him.

"Be careful, you brute," Worthington snapped as the razor scraped whiskers from his right cheek. "You're shaving a Worthington, not sheering a sheep."

"I apologize, Señor Worthington."

"That razor feels like you've been using it to shred lettuce for tacos or some other ghastly gastronomic nightmare you people indulge in between prison sentences. You haven't been using it to shred lettuce, have you?"

"No, Señor Worthington."

"Well, see that you don't," Worthington sniffed.

His barber, a dark-skinned, white-haired, dignified older gentleman originally from a small village in the Valley of Mexico certainly would never use Mr. Worthington's expensive titanium straight edge razor to slice vegetables. He did, however, and after days where he felt particularly mistreated by his employer, clean off Mr. Worthington's special shaving cream brush in the toilet. He found it quite good for getting up in that hard-to-reach spot under the rim.

"Here! You just got that in my mouth," Worthington complained as the barber applied a smidge more shaving cream.

"I am very sorry, Señor Worthington."

"Be more careful. It's not like there aren't thousands more just like you sneaking into this country every day." Worthington waved to the television, on which was videotape footage of the Los Angeles immigration rally. "Just look at this unruly mob on television. I could buy any one of them to do your job for a fraction of what I generously pay you."

The barber was apologizing again, even while making secret plans to bring the brush home for a really good scrubbing, perhaps in the broken sewer line that sometimes backed up in the basement of his modest one-bedroom bungalow, when the caboose door was unexpectedly torn off in a shriek of twisted metal. The startled barber jumped and nearly slit his employer's throat. As it was, he made only a tiny nick near Prescott Worthington's Adam's apple.

Worthington was as startled by the cut as by the sudden disappearance of his train's back door. He saw the vague shadow of the door against the sky as it flew from sight.

"What the devil!" he said.

There was no way anyone could board his train, let alone get inside. Worthington had made certain of that. The windows were welded shut. The locked doors only opened from the inside. There were no recesses beneath the cars where illegals could stash themselves away. The train was barreling at fifty miles an hour through the desert and would not stop until it reached American soil. It should have been impossible for the three people who were now entering the caboose to even be there.

And then Worthington saw who the two men were and his already tense shoulders tightened visibly. He seemed to make a conscious effort to relax. Sighing audibly, he sank back in his barber's chair.

"It's a pleasure to see you gentlemen again," he said, "but in polite society people knock first."

"I'm only up to soup spoons in my Emily Post," Remo said. "I think the trains chapter is at the back."

Chiun did not deign to speak with Worthington. The wizened Korean offered the seated man his back. Looking out a window, he watched the train speed through the gate into the United States. The fence rolled shut behind them.

Worthington's frantic barber was trying to dab the nick on his neck with a bottle of liquid styptic. The old man's hands shook. Worthington slapped him away. The barber took the cue and hustled from the caboose.

"To what do I owe the pleasure?" Worthington asked. He grabbed a towel so white it would have put an angel's robes to shame and pressed it to his bleeding neck.

"Just a little trouble with the *federales*," Remo said. "Figured we'd hop a ride with a friendly face."

Worthington's face was anything but friendly as he studied Conchita. "And who is your foreign companion?" he asked. "Perhaps I should know since apparently I am sneaking her into my country." His eyes were dead.

"I am an American citizen," Conchita insisted, wondering even as she said it why she felt the need to justify herself to this arrogant gringo.

"I see," Worthington said. He managed to draw out the word "see" into three syllables, all of them condescending.

It looked to Remo as if Conchita might punch Worthington in the mouth. Her fist was balled and she definitely had a spark of fiery indignation in her dark eyes.

Remo stepped between Conchita and Worthington. "This is some choo-choo you got here," he commented. He caught Conchita's fist—which she threw out when Worthington wasn't looking—and placed it back at her side. "What kind of mileage you get?"

"Sadly, this is the last of my family railroad. Worthington Continental once serviced all the major cities on the East Coast, with a line straight from Chicago down to here. Serviced our ranches and slaughterhouses. When the rest of it shut down, my father kept this section open. It's only a couple hundred miles of track. A single line from my business interests in Mexico to my home in Las Cruces, and another line into Albuquerque. This is the last train with the Worthington name. I guess maybe I keep it as a memento of my youth."

Worthington's tone had grown wistful.

"Must be tough being down to your last railroad car," commiserated Remo Williams, who had spent his childhood in an orphanage which was often without hot water, and sometimes at the end of a month had to ration toilet paper. Remo had just noticed Worthington's TV.

On the wide plasma screen another rally was playing out, this one in Albuquerque. The word "live" was superimposed in one corner.

On a platform, a fat-faced man in an out-of-date uniform bellowed in Spanish at the cheering crowd. His pockmarked face was red and glistened with sweat.

"It's him," Remo said. "The guy on those posters in the tunnel. Chiun, get a load of this."

The Master of Sinanju stepped in beside his pupil, along with Conchita. Beside them, Worthington grunted disdain.

"He has been all over the news all morning," Worthington droned. "Their new hero apparently." His lip curled at the sight of the man on the screen.

Conchita's anger with Worthington was forgotten. As she listened to the man on the television, her face paled. Even the Master of Sinanju was interested. The old Asian's back grew rigid and his eyes narrowed as he watched Santa Anna.

"Remo, this is very bad," Conchita said. "He is issuing a call to arms to all immigrants, legal and illegal. He is calling for revolution in all of the southern border states."

Remo looked at the faces of the people in the crowd. He had seen zealotry before. In the eyes of some was a glowing enthusiasm. They studied their new leader, absorbed his every word, with the unquestioning gaze of fanatics.

"Yeah, that could be pretty not good," Remo agreed. He turned to Worthington. "Hey, Daddy Warbucks, you think maybe I can borrow a phone?"

When the blue contact phone at last jangled to life, Smith snatched it up on the first ring.

"Remo, where the devil are you?" Smith demanded.

"Smitty, I spent all night buried under the desert and all morning trying to coax harmony out of a Mexican army unit that's never going to make *American Idol*, so if you could please ease up on the sweet talk, that'd be just swell by me."

Smith placed a hand flat on his desk. "Remo," he said, forcing composure into his lemony voice, "there is a major crisis developing."

The CURE director had watched the rally in Los Angeles turn to riots, thanks to the rabble-rousing of this new Santa Anna. At the moment, police were attempting to quell the civil unrest while fire officials had been called to dozens of blazes set by rioters all around the city. A call had already gone out to the National Guard.

After jump-starting the riots in California, the pockmarked man in the anachronistic uniform had disappeared for a time, only to resurface at another rally in New Mexico. On the television screen, Smith watched General Santa Anna screaming encouragement to revolt at an Albuquerque mob. Santa Anna's black eyes were wild. Frothy white spittle launched from the corners of his mouth as he shouted. The crowd bellowed his name in appreciative chorus, arms upraised as if in worship of some acne-ravaged deity.

"I know what's going on, Smitty," Remo said over the phone. "I'm watching him on TV right now. Who is this guy?"

"We do not know," Smith said. "I have Mark researching him at the moment, but so far he is a blank slate."

Smith heard the Master of Sinanju's squeaky sing-song chime in somewhere in the near background.

"This rebel general has had the temerity to threaten your southern provinces while Sinanju stands beside your throne, Emperor," Chiun called. "Rest assured that this insurrection will be dealt with expeditiously, and this wicked general with the dirty face will be dealt a swift end for this attempt to undermine your absolute sovereignty."

To Smith it sounded as if the old Korean was actually excited by all this. He was not surprised. The Masters of Sinanju had served kings and caliphs for five thousand years. The Korean house of assassins had in its time seen more than its share of palace intrigue, usurpers of crowns and murders. Certainly there had been territorial threats against their many and varied clients, and Chiun would have found an army of Vandals galloping over the horizon far more interesting than the untroubled borders of the United States.

But Smith was not intrigued. This was the twenty-first century, and the United States had not seen a serious border dispute in one hundred and forty years. Secession had only been dealt with once in the history of the country, and Smith had no desire to see a repeat of that bloody time on his watch.

"Santa Anna is still in Albuquerque," Smith said. "Where are you right now?"

"We crossed in from Mexico about twenty miles back, and we've been picking up steam ever since."

Smith had switched off his portable television and set aside all other work. He was now watching nonstop cable coverage on his computer monitor. He glanced at the screen. As Santa Anna spoke, a special language program translated his words into English text. The words scrolled across a black bar at the bottom of the canted monitor.

"He appears to be giving the same speech that he gave in Los Angeles. That took him well over an hour." Smith clenched his free hand in frustration. "Still, assuming he gives the exact speech, that does not give you enough time to drive to Albuquerque before he is finished."

"Anyone ever tell you you give up too easy, Smitty? How fast does this thing go?"

The second question was directed to someone other than Smith. The CURE director heard an unfamiliar voice reply from somewhere nearby.

"One hundred fifteen, maybe one hundred twenty-five."

"You said this track goes straight to Albuquerque?"

"Actually, it goes straight to my Las Cruces home, which is where I was going before you hijacked me," the strange voice replied. The man sounded cultured and bored; a voice born into privilege and unused to real adversity. "However, yes, the line can be switched. The track runs straight as the crow flies into Albuquerque."

"Get us on that track," Remo ordered. He came back onto the phone. "It'll be close, but we can make it, Smitty."

"Of course we can," Chiun called. "Tell him we will deliver him the head. Heads of generals are quite pleasant, both as souvenirs and cautionary objects. He may hang it on the gates of Fortress Folcroft as a warning to any other general that may challenge his absolute rule."

"I'm not schlepping this guy's head halfway across the country, Little Father."

"Of course not, Remo," Chiun said. "Because I may ask you to, and to do so you would have to honor a request by your father and teacher who has given you everything, not to mention glorifying your emperor."

"Still not doing it," Remo said.

"We can overnight the head to you, Emperor," Chiun promised. "What is your FexEd account number?"

"Tell Master Chiun in no uncertain terms that I do not want Santa Anna's head delivered to Folcroft."

"I'll try, Smitty, but just in case, if you get any basketball-size boxes, make sure your secretary's not in the room when you open them. And on the off chance we don't make it to the rally on time, maybe you'd better see if you can get the local cops or Feds to pick this guy up."

"I'll try but the crowd is already too dense and unruly. And after the Los Angeles riots, we don't need any more. I think we could lose a lot of people."

"Which leaves us. Gotcha, Smitty. We'll be blowing through red lights from here to Albuquerque."

"Bring me the head of Santa Anna!" Smith heard the Master of Sinanju shout the instant before the buzz of a dial tone sounded in the CURE director's ear.

Smith returned the blue phone to its cradle.

On his monitor, Santa Anna had paused for applause. The gathered multitude screamed support and frantically waved flags. Most of the flags were from Mexico, but Smith spied several from Central and South America. Smith did not see a single American flag in the mob.

This crowd seemed even more worked up than the one in California earlier that morning. Word of Santa Anna's wild reception in Los Angeles had obviously reached these protestors. For Smith, their crazed excitement was distressing. But at the same time he realized their enthusiasm could work to his advantage.

Smith had set a simple timer program to compare the length of this version of the speech to Santa Anna's earlier

time. Due to prolonged pauses in order to give time for increased cheering this time around, the mysterious general
was already five minutes slower than he had been in L.A.

There was time for Remo to get to Albuquerque before
the speech ended. Time to stop this madness.

The general preached his words of revolt. One zealot
had thrown a brick through the window of a closed florist's
shop. As Santa Anna delivered his stem-winder, the crowd
was showering the stage with liberated flowers.

And as he watched the insanity play out before him from
his Folcroft office, helpless to do anything to stop it, Harold
W. Smith allowed himself a rare prayer for his nation.

"Muchas gracias," Remo said. He tossed Prescott Worthington the cell phone he had borrowed.

Worthington snapped the phone shut and carefully
slipped it in the pocket of his white tennis shorts.

Chiun and Conchita were still watching Santa Anna on
the television. Chiun held both hands out as if trying to
judge scale for a head-size box. Conchita was chewing her
right thumbnail anxiously.

"What's he saying now?" Remo asked.

"He is calling on immigrants to reclaim land lost to the
United States over one hundred years ago," she said. "He
wants them to form an army to take back by force that
which he says is theirs by right."

By the looks of the faces in the crowd, many men were
all too eager to take up the cause.

Remo turned to Worthington. "Talk to your engineer,"
he said. "Tell him to keep the pedal to the metal."

The billionaire flashed a mouthful of orthodontia worth
more than two years of his barber's salary.

"Glad to offer a helping hand to someone who's with me
in the cause," Prescott Worthington IV drawled.

The old Worthington line carried them like a bullet into the heart of Albuquerque. The crowds grew more dense the deeper they sped into town. By the time the train was encased by a sea of protesters, the engineer had cut their speed to five miles per hour, although from the look on Worthington's face, Remo got the distinct impression he would rather have driven over the crowd than slow for it. The train stopped at a private platform inside the gated grounds of an old boarded-up warehouse. A faded sign on the wall of the dilapidated brick building read P. WOR-THINGTON TEXTILES, INC.

Remo and Chiun hopped lightly to the cracked concrete platform. Beyond the fence, the protesters all seemed to be drifting in the same direction.

"Looks like the fun is that way," Remo said.

"I recognized the area where he was speaking on TV,"

Conchita said as she climbed down beside them. "I used to work at the MacroWare plant here in town. I will lead you."

Worthington hustled down behind Conchita. "I'll come too," he said.

Remo glanced at Worthington's white shorts and pink polo jersey. "If this was a rally for spoiled rich albinos objecting to unfair squash court schedules, sure. But with this crowd, probably not the best idea. Plus if they recognize you as the guy who sponsors that volunteer border patrol group, I'll be scraping billionaire off my loafers for the next month."

Worthington glared at Remo. "As an American citizen concerned about the integrity of our nation's borders, I'm interested in whatever it is this fellow is up to."

"Your funeral, Jeeves," Remo said.

The four of them hustled out the gate and into the moving mass of humanity.

Worthington and Conchita had to struggle through the throng. For Remo and Chiun, the mob split like water off the prow of a ship and they moved unmolested through the crowd. Conchita and Worthington tried to stay close and follow in their wake.

"At least this Santa Anna whoever-he-is doesn't look like he'll be much of a threat," Remo said as they ran.

"The threat is not to us but to Smith," Chiun replied.

"Smitty's a little on edge, but he's always like that, Chiun. He's not going to come unglued over some fat guy in a Mexican Halloween costume."

"You are wrong," Chiun said. "Smith is lunatic in many ways, but he understands the importance of maintaining the integrity of his kingdom's borders. If he loses this region, others will follow. The Spanish will attempt to reclaim Florida. The British will sack Boston and turn that province of bean eaters into grazing fields for their stringy beef cattle. Some foul Canadian warlord will wrap a towel around his head and ride out of Toronto to claim New York as his own."

"I don't think we have to worry too much about that stuff, Little Father. Just Santa Anna."

Off to the side, a group of three surly men accosted Conchita and Worthington. Seeing her in the company of Worthington, one screamed that Conchita was a race traitor. Without breaking stride, Remo spun the man like a top and he twirled into one of his companions. Conchita and Worthington were forgotten as a fight broke out among the trio.

"This one who calls himself Santa Anna is enough to worry about," Chiun continued, as if there had been no interruption. "He wants to raise an army, and that is always a dangerous thing. The first Santa Anna was a bumbler, as is true of most generals, but he did manage to make himself leader of Mexico three times."

"Three times?" Remo asked.

"Every time he got the job, they threw him right back out," the Master of Sinanju said with a shrug. "It was Mexico, after all. They get nervous if there has not been a coup by four in the afternoon." His hazel eyes grew wistful. "Did I ever tell you that an ancestor tried to find work for the House there, since the nation is so rich with intrigue?"

"Couldn't afford us, could they?"

"Unfortunately, no. A shame, for unlike the United States with its insane system of government and orderly transfer of power every four years, Mexico has always been just the sort of country Sinanju could learn to love."

"I bet it just killed your ancestor that they were too poor," Remo said.

"It should bother you as well," Chiun replied, "for it is in corruption and betrayal that we find work. Stability does not feed the babies of Sinanju. Order does not keep the poor of our village clothed, or give the elderly kindling for the fire. If Mexico were not so poor, I might well have taken work there rather than in America. A wealthy Mexican emperor would pay handsomely to keep himself in power. But, alas, such a man does not exist."

"Maybe this Santa Anna guy has money," Remo said. "He had all those guns and computers in that tunnel. That must have cost him something. And Rebecca Dalton seems to be working for him and she doesn't come cheap. He certainly seems well financed."

"Perhaps," Chiun said. "Or perhaps he is just the latest in an endless parade of poverty-stricken Mexican dictators. They are less selective than even America. My Master once observed that everyone will become emperor of Mexico at one point in their life. When it is your turn, Remo, do not leave the royal palace even to put coins in the parking meter or some peasant like Santa Anna will have declared himself ruler in your absence and be sitting on your throne upon your return."

The side road they had been hustling along broke into a main avenue. The crowd grew in number and decibel.

There was not a hint of police presence. The mob had taken control of Albuquerque.

The street was packed from one end to the other. In the distance, a temporary platform had been constructed. Booming over loudspeakers that had been set up on rooftops, light posts and parked vans, a lone voice addressed the crowd.

Santa Anna had grown hoarse from shouting. Yet still he screamed words of revolution. The people scarcely heard, so caught up were they in the heat and emotion.

"Santa Anna! Santa Anna! Santa Anna!"

In the multitude were true believers, revolutionaries who were ready to seize an opportunity to finally take vengeance for years of imagined transgressions. Those who had come as innocents in support of a simple cause now found themselves sucked into the quicksand of revolt.

Energy emanated from the revolutionaries, seeming to

jump the distance between them and those who were at the rally only to show support for immigrant rights.

There was danger in the crowd. Both Remo and Chiun felt it flood their senses the moment they stepped into the square and it grew stronger as they approached the stage.

Remo was not certain how he sensed the gunman. In a crowd this size, with so much shouting and general disorder, it should have been an easy thing for the man to slip up beside Remo, stick a gun in his back and pull the trigger.

Maybe the man walked differently, maybe his breathing or the anxiety just before the kill gave him away, maybe Remo felt the pressure waves of a weapon directed at him. After all these years, Remo did not know the how, he only knew that within the crowd was a man, and that man had a gun and he was now one step behind Remo and was squeezing a trigger. Before the man could fire, Remo reached back and snatched the gun. "Hot potato," Remo called.

He sailed the gun over the top of the mob. The weapon bopped off a few heads like a stone skipped across a pond before landing in a sidewalk trash receptacle.

As he tossed the gun with one hand, Remo reached out with the other. Snatching the would-be killer by the collar, he twirled the man around before them.

Worthington and Conchita were shocked to see someone materialize in front of them. It had happened so fast, neither of them had even seen Remo disarm the man.

The killer was short and fat, with a loud shirt and a dark complexion. Panic and disorientation filled his face. Not yet realizing his gun was missing, his trigger finger squeezed repeatedly on empty air. He seemed baffled by the lack of holes erupting in Remo's chest.

"You have no future in this business," Remo said.

Finally realizing that he was somehow without a pistol, the man in the purple and green bowling shirt fumbled in his pocket, pulled out a blade and slashed at Remo's chest.

"Remo, look out!" Conchita cried.

"Actually, you've got no future at all," Remo told the man. He danced around the wildly slashing blade. "Sloppy form," he said. "You're all over the place. Your opponent's chest should be your main focus. With a knife, you want to sink it dead center. But—and here's the trick—don't picture it sinking into the chest, picture it coming out the other side. So actually, the spot behind my back is the target you're shooting for."

The lesson was a good one. It was one of the earliest instructions Chiun had given Remo on the use of a blade, back when Remo still thought that knives were weapons to be feared rather than tools suited only for kitchens and camping. It was a lesson wasted on Remo's attacker.

The man slashed and hacked air, his sweating face contorting with frustration every time he missed his target.

"You're not going to learn anything if you don't open your ears," Remo said.

"Remo, stop these games," Chiun snapped.

Remo nodded. "Sorry," he said. "Force of habit."

With a sharp upward slap, he swatted the knife from his assailant's hand. It buzzed high above their heads, the blade at last coming to a quivering, half-buried stop in the second-story ledge of a nearby apartment building.

Only when he had disarmed him a second time did Remo notice something in the man's other hand. It was a small scrap of paper which the man had crumpled into a wet ball.

He snatched the scrap of paper away from the man. The man tried to grab it back, but Remo held him at bay with an outstretched hand pressed to his forehead. The man swung his arms helplessly.

Remo frowned. "It's us," he said.

It was a photograph of Remo and Chiun. Conchita was partially visible in the background. The picture was a little grainy, the light a little off. Remo recognized the room where it had been taken. It was about two hundred miles behind him, and buried now under a thousand tons of dirt.

"Rebecca Dalton strikes again," he said. He handed to Chiun the photo which had been lifted from images taken from Rebecca's security room computer camera.

"It is a bad likeness of me," Chiun said. "I look angry. Where is the joy in my eyes?"

"Some people just don't photograph well," Remo said.

"Give it to me!" the would-be killer demanded.

Remo had forgotten all about him. His hand was still pressed to the man's forehead. At arm's length, Rebecca's hired goon continued to try to swat at Remo. His fingertips nearly brushed Remo's throat, but his target remained frustratingly out of reach. For some reason, he could not even pull away and skip around the outstretched hand.

"Sorry," Remo said. "Slipped my mind." A stiff finger sank deep into the man's frontal lobe. Remo's finger withdrew from the forehead and the man collapsed in a heap on the ground. "It's slipped yours now, too."

"Is he dead?" Worthington asked, stunned. "My God, I didn't even see your hand move."

"If you did, his head would still be in one piece and I'd have a broken finger."

"That's amazing," Worthington said. He looked down at the dead man on the ground.

No one in the crowd seemed to notice the corpse. All other eyes were on the stage and Santa Anna.

"I said that's amazing," Worthington repeated. Prescott Worthington was as unused to offering compliments as he was to being ignored. This young mongrel in the black undershirt not only ignored the rare Worthington accolade, he suddenly seemed unaware that Worthington even existed. "Here," Worthington said, his blue blood beginning to boil. "Young man, I am talking to you."

"I guessed that,'cause your lips are moving," Remo said absently. "You got them, Chiun?"

Remo's attention had been drawn to a nearby building. He was looking up at the roof where a dark figure crouched.

Chiun was studying the roof in the opposite direction. Another figure hid from view, only his head and shoulders visible against the backdrop of blinding New Mexico sun.

"Yes," the old Asian said.

On the stage, Santa Anna had finished his speech. His scarred face glistened with sweat. The high collar of his uniform was stained dark blue. In a closing flourish, he threw both arms high into the air. The crowd screamed adoration for the fat little man.

And on the roofs all around the square, more figures began popping into view. Slender, black rifle barrels poked one by one over ledges.

Conchita did not see the gunmen, did not see the barrels swing in their direction. She tugged urgently at Remo's sleeve. "Why have we stopped?" she asked. "Remo, he has finished speaking. We must hurry."

"*Un momento, por favor,*" Remo said tightly. "Got a little business first."

He was looking up at a nearby roof. Conchita could not see why. Nor did she understand the hand gesture he made in the direction of the roof.

Before she could ask what he was talking about, the jubilant air was shattered by a succession of rifle shots.

Conchita had a disoriented feeling of being thrown through the air. She landed in a heap behind a pair of mailboxes. Something soft cushioned her landing.

"Get off me!" Prescott Worthington grunted from the sidewalk where Remo had tossed him.

Worthington's words were the last thing Conchita heard before the crowd stampeded, the square erupted in panicked screaming, and hell came down around all their ears.

* * *

Miguel Fernando Pagaza's father had raised his son to be an accountant. Or maybe a bank vice president. Math was very important in the Pagaza household.

Or maybe little Miguel would be a writer or teacher. English, not Spanish, would be crucial for either occupation, and so the study of English had been encouraged as well.

In his wildest dreams, the elder Pagaza had thought his son might become a doctor or a lawyer. Anything was possible in this great country of the United States of America and Miguel was certainly smart enough to become either. Straight A's from first grade, right on through his senior year of high school. The smartest in the entire Pagaza clan. The world was wide open to a boy with brains like little Miguel's, and thanks to a strict but loving upbringing, his son was given all the educational tools he would need to conquer any profession he might choose.

After stressing so much the importance of education, after attending every parents' night at his son's school, after working late every night in the cobbler's shop he owned for ten long years to pay for one of the most expensive East Coast colleges, the one occupation the senior Pagaza never dreamed of for his middle-class American son was that of Latino revolutionary.

"Miguel, are you crazy?" Fernando Pagaza asked his son on the day the boy returned from college. He had gone for three years, gotten excellent grades, and quit before his senior year.

"Of course you think that," Miguel had replied. "You've embraced the whole middle-class, plastic fantastic, Ozzie and Harriet, racist American view of the world. You don't even appreciate where we come from, man."

Fernando Pagaza understood most of the words his son had used, but strung together they made no sense.

"Is this what they taught you in that crazy college of

yours? The crazy college I have worked my fingers to the bone to send you to?"

" 'Crazy, crazy,' " Miguel mocked. "You even use their word. Call it *loco*, dad. Or has the boob tube rotted your brain so much you forgot that part of your heritage too?"

At this, poor Mr. Pagaza had shaken his head, unable to comprehend his son's new intellectual enlightenment.

It was the early 1970s, and the world was changing. When Mr. Pagaza packed his son off to college three years before, Miguel was like any other red-blooded American eighteen-year-old. His concerns back then had been girls, cars and school. Now here he was, back in the Pagaza living room, a college dropout with no job, hair halfway down his back, and speaking of revolution against the hated gringos.

"Do you mean the Andersons next door?" Fernando had asked, still trying to understand, and thinking of the only "gringos" his son had, as far as he knew, ever disliked. "I spoke to him months ago about his dog messing in our yard, and he has it on a leash now."

"I'm not talking about a dog dumping on your precious Scotts lawn," Miguel had said. "I'm talking about a system that dumps all over people like us."

"People like us" were those with Hispanic ancestry. Miguel had gone on to list all the grievances his Caucasian professors had taught him he should have against America, its people and its system of government.

Mr. Pagaza listened to his son rant about stolen land and oppressed people. About inequitable distribution of wealth and a system that made certain that the workers would never control the means of production. Mr. Pagaza heard all of the unoriginal revolutionary thoughts that had been planted by fools in his son's skull, now pouring out of his son's foolish mouth. As Miguel spoke, Fernando Pagaza grew very quiet. And when his son was finally finished, and had folded his arms indignantly over his chest, and Mr.

Pagaza noted his son's smooth, uncalloused hands that had never seen a day of hard work in his life, the older man at last spoke.

"You do not know what it is like in Mexico," Fernando explained quietly to his son. "I guess that neither do your professors, who are so smart that their hands are as unmarked by toil as yours. Miguel, I know what it is like. It has not changed since I grew up there. You have been raised in a house with running water, with toilets that flush. There is food on the table, and your favorite Klondike ice cream bars your mother keeps always in the freezer. We have a television here, and a roof that keeps out the rain. I had none of those things growing up, Miguel. I had hunger and sickness. I had three brothers die because we had no access to medicine that this nation you hate so much hands out to those in need for free. My heart breaks, not for me, Miguel, but for you, because you have known nothing but plenty, so you cannot appreciate the gifts that America gives you every day without your even knowing it."

"Typical bourgeois crap," Miguel had said. "What have you allowed this system to do to you, man? I know you didn't used to believe all that flag-waving John Wayne pabulum. You were cool once. I heard you mention to Mom one time that you were in MOLAP back when you were my age."

MOLAP was short for Mexican and Other Latin American Peoples, a radical Hispanic group that, among other things, wanted the United States to return southwestern land it claimed had been taken illegally from Mexico and the various indigenous tribes of the region.

"When I was your age, Miguel, MOLAP was not the same group that it is today," Fernando explained. "Back then we worried about education and assimilation. We wanted our people to better themselves. We were Americans first back then, and we were proud of that fact. That is no more the case. MOLAP has become a group that does not care about equality or knowledge. For them it is all about power." A terrible thought occurred to Fernando. "Please tell me, Miguel, that you have not joined MOLAP."

To Fernando's great sadness, his son told him that he had. Sadness, not anger, because his son had been given the chance to make a great life in the greatest country in the world, and had squandered it all because of hate. Sadness because he could not allow his unemployed, hate-filled son Miguel to live at home any longer, watching afternoon movies, eating ice cream bars and complaining about a system that did not pay him to do so. Sadness that his son would join a group that would abandon its founding principles and become more and more radical as the years went by. Sadness that he would live long enough to see the son of Fernando Pagaza—proud cobbler, proud Mexican immigrant and proud American—rise through the ranks of MOLAP until he had become president of the New Mexico chapter of that organization.

Fernando Pagaza had died five years ago, an old man in a nursing home with crippled tradesman's fingers and a heavy heart, and so was not present to witness an event that would have made him not just sad for the life his son had wasted, but sad for the loss of Miguel's eternal soul. It happened in the MOLAP offices in Albuquerque on a hot April morning. The MOLAP offices were abuzz with excitement as preparations were made for the speech to be delivered that morning by the mysterious hero of the new revolution, General Santa Anna.

Miguel Pagaza was thirty years older than the radical boy who had dropped out of college. What hair he had left was still long, but streaked with gray.

Miguel embraced the culture he felt his father had rejected. Miguel's father had allowed only English to be spoken at home while Miguel was growing up, and so he had learned Spanish later in life. Although he did not need to speak English with an accent, he did so in order to prove his commitment to his cause. As president of MOLAP, his uniform was a white T-shirt emblazoned with the Mexican flag. His protruding belly stretched the shirt to bursting and abused the flag into concave stripes of elongated green, white and red.

Miguel was scratching at the red stripe and rejoicing at a report he had just received announcing that the police had surrendered the streets to the protesters, when the door to his small office swung open.

"That is wonderful news, Rafael," Miguel Pagaza was saying into his telephone as he glanced up to see who had stepped into the room. "Sí, that too. But someone is here. Yes, I will see you then. Adios, Rafael."

Miguel hung up the phone. "Hola, señorita," he said.

The woman was as white as Wisconsin milk and as American as hot apple pie cooling on a summer windowsill. She flashed her flawless pearl teeth at the MOLAP president.

"A big hello-there to you too, Miguel," Rebecca Dalton said cheerily.

Despite her great physical beauty, Miguel was cool to this woman. It had not always been so. When he first met her two weeks before, he had made a sloppy grab for her chest. When he came to, he was sprawled across his office desk with a lump the size of a billiard ball on his forehead. Having failed to woo the lovely Rebecca Dalton with his machismo charm tactics, these days Miguel only tolerated her, and only then because she was such a close associate of the great Santa Anna.

"Albuquerque, we have a problem," Rebecca said. She pouted her full lower lip. "I've just gotten word that there's going to be an assassination attempt on General Santa Anna's life this morning. As you can imagine, this has put a big ol' buzzing bee in my bonnet."

"I assure you that the general will be perfectly safe," Miguel said. "MOLAP is handling security. Our best mus-

cle from the southwest is on the scene. We even have two
revolutionaries who used to be with Ejercito de los Pobres."
He smiled confidently. "They have both killed before."

Miguel said this in a dark voice, to impress and, yes, to
frighten this frigid gringa puta.

"Wow," Rebecca said, clearly unimpressed. "Killed. Really? That's just super swell. But, see, our problem today is
bigger than anything they've handled before."

"You do not know these men."

"Oh, I know their type," Rebecca said. "I've been in this
business for, gosh, it's going on fifteen years now. I'm sure
your friends are just swell with, say, shooting unarmed
farmers in the back of the head or something. But the fellas
who are coming to kill Santa Anna are going to cause us a
tad more trouble than that."

Opening the office door, Rebecca beckoned Miguel over.

The big outer office was insane with activity. MOLAP
workers raced around carrying press releases and answering telephones. Near the front door was a fat little man
Miguel had never seen before. The man wore a bright purple and green bowling shirt. He had the dead black eyes of
a killer.

"See him?" Rebecca said to Miguel. "That's Pedro." She
waved to the fat little man. "Say hello, Pedro!" she called.
The little man grunted and waved.

"Be with you in a sec, Pedro," Rebecca called. "Pedro
will tell you where to go," she said to Miguel after she had
closed the door once more. "He's like a bloodhound.
That's his specialty. I've used him south of the border a
few times, and he's never failed to locate a target. He's a
positive little darling. You'll love him. Just follow him
wherever he goes. Here, this will help." She handed
Miguel a small black device, the size of a pocket pager.
"He'll lead you to them. Then it's open season."

"What about your friend?" Miguel said, jutting his chin

toward the door. He flipped the black device over in his hand. There was a tiny LED screen on one side.

"Oh, don't fret over Pedro, silly," Rebecca said. "He'll have a gun, and he'll try to shoot them. Gotta let Pedro think he has a fighting chance. But he doesn't. They'll swat him like a fly, poor thing. Oh, but be a dear and don't tell Pedro that, would you? Thanks just loads."

She went on to explain the operation of the device, how it should be attached to his belt, and how it was a failsafe in case he lost sight of Pedro. Fishing in her purse as she spoke, she laid out seven more identical devices on his desk.

"If these killers are so good," Miguel asked, "what makes you think I will be any more safe than your friend?"

"Distance, Miguel," Rebecca explained, snapping her purse shut. "He'll be close, you'll be far away. In distance is safety. My old friend and mentor Benson Dilkes taught me that."

Unsurprisingly, Miguel had never heard of Benson Dilkes, and said so.

"You would have loved him," Rebecca promised, a wistful glint in her eye. "Taught me everything I know."

After Rebecca instructed Miguel how to kill Santa Anna's would-be assassins—a young white man and an old Asian—she brought the MOLAP president and his most trusted men out to her truck. She passed out high-powered rifles while Miguel passed out the devices that would allow them to track Pedro through a pager that would be attached to his belt.

"The crowd'll be big as all get-out," Rebecca said. "Don't want you losing our little homing pigeon. You keep your eyes and ears locked on him, you'll find them."

She instructed him where they should position themselves on the roofs above the crowd and, with a final perky thumbs-up, left them to save the life of the great general.

Of all the aspects of Latino culture Miguel had em-

braced as an adult, the one he liked most was the idea of
women being subservient to men. Rebecca Dalton certainly did not subscribe to this notion. Miguel would have
made another grab at her, would have loved to teach her the
proper place of women, even if it meant knocking a few of
those perfect teeth down her slender throat. But she was a
close associate of Santa Anna, who was about to bring revolution to the southwest and who had recently donated a
substantial amount of money to MOLAP. And so, with
money in his pocket and revolution on his lips, Miguel
Pagaza swallowed his Latino pride and accepted the orders
of General Santa Anna's woman.

Thus, an hour later, Miguel found himself trudging up
the stairs of the Exchange Insurance Company Building,
high-powered rifle wrapped in a blue plastic tarp.

The roof door was open, just as she had said it would be.
As he settled into position, he noted the other MOLAP
men on other roofs, including the two Ejercito de los Pobres killers. No matter what Rebecca Dalton said, these
men were not soft murderers of innocents. They had accepted the rifles as if they were born to carry them, and had
offered instructions to those like Miguel who were not so
proficient with weapons. The two wore death on their hard
faces.

A crowd was already in the square. As the hot sun rose
higher in the sky, Miguel watched more people flood into
the streets. The cheering when Santa Anna stepped out onto
the platform from behind a long curtain was deafening.

Miguel wished he could see the general close up. When
the bodies of the murdered Civilian Border Patrol members had appeared with graffiti hailing Santa Anna, Miguel
still thought the man might be mythical. He had only heard
rumors of him until that morning, and then had only seen
him give his speech in Los Angeles on television.

Miguel was surprised that the general was giving the
same speech he had delivered in California. There was less

energy to his presentation here, as if the grind of travel were wearing him down.

The speech droned on for nearly an hour and a half, and Miguel had consumed three of the four bottles of water he had brought with him, and was beginning to think that Rebecca Dalton was as loco as his father had been, when an electronic beep sounded from his belt.

As Rebecca had explained it, the device operated on something like radar, but here it was a moving target that bounced a signal that alerted the stationary devices.

Miguel looked over the ledge.

When he had first gotten up on the roof, he had searched for the purple and green shirt. He had found Rebecca Dalton's sacrificial lamb on the corner, exactly where she said he would be.

Pedro was moving. He glanced down. A little dot on the LED screen on Miguel's belt tracked him as he went.

The crowd was so dense, it took Miguel several minutes to see where Pedro was headed. He lost him twice and had to consult the little electronic device to find him again. The second time he located him, Miguel was startled to see how close Pedro was to his targets.

They were just as Rebecca had said. One was an Asian who looked as old as the desert wind. The other was a young white, although something about his features hinted at more exotic ancestry. There were two others with the assassins, a young Latino woman and a middle-aged Caucasian in short white pants and a light pink shirt.

The older white marched through the crowd as if the streets were his to command and the people were little more than swarming insects. In fact, he had the same bearing and was about the same age as. . . .

Miguel did a double take.

It was him. He watched as Prescott Worthington IV shoved his way through the mob of protesters. He was heading with the others toward the stage.

Worthington's Civilian Border Patrol had been a thorn in MOLAP's side ever since it was founded. For years MOLAP had controlled the debate, crushing intellectual opposition and appealing to emotion. The last thing Miguel wanted was serious discussion of the issue of border security, and Worthington and his hated CBP, along with other groups, threatened to undo years of MOLAP's hard work.

Down below, Pedro had slipped up behind the younger gringo. Rebecca Dalton was wrong. Pedro was going to be able to take those two out easily.

It was a shame. Miguel had been talking revolution ever since he had dropped out of college over thirty years ago. He had hoped to be the one who would fire the first shot to reclaim the Southwest. And for good measure, even though Rebecca Dalton had stressed that he should take out only the two assassins, he would have liked to put a bullet right between Prescott Worthington's eyes.

Santa Anna's speech ended. The crowd exploded in cheers. Mexican flags waved, people screamed.

Miguel saw the thin young white toss something through the air. He saw Pedro's purple and green shirt hopping up and down, saw Pedro struggling at the end of the young white's outstretched hand.

And then, to his shock, he saw Pedro fall to the ground.

He could not believe it. Miguel quickly lifted the rifle sight to his eye for a magnified view of the scene.

The white was staring straight at him. And then, like a child playing, he made a gun out of his fingers, with his index finger for a barrel and his thumb sticking up like the hammer. He pointed the index finger directly at Miguel and mimed pulling a trigger. And then he smiled.

It was the coldest smile Miguel had ever seen.

A hundred thoughts raced through his mind at once. He thought of his father, and the life Fernando Pagaza had wanted for his son. He thought of all the poor choices he had made in his life that had culminated in this hour, with Miguel up on this roof with a sniper's rifle in his hands.

Miguel was no dummy. That "gee whiz" exterior of Rebecca Dalton's was just a front. He thought of her now and realized that she had known precisely the danger he was facing, but had not truly communicated it to him. But most of all, he thought of the face of death that had spied him before he had taken a single shot, and looked up at him now like a grinning skull from amid a mob of screaming protestors.

This was a man who would kill without thought, without remorse. For Miguel Pagaza, this was no longer shooting fish in a barrel. It was kill or be killed.

"Sorry, amigo," Miguel said. "Better you than me."

And, taking careful aim at the young man's black T-shirt, he squeezed the trigger.

The first shot brought an echoing hail of bullets from all around the square. After first seeing Worthington and Conchita were safe, Remo quickly appraised the situation.

The cheering was not so loud that the crowd did not hear the gunshots. Shouts of jubilation became screams of terror. The mob stampeded. Some were being crushed against walls and trampled underfoot by the surging mass of humanity.

On the stage, Santa Anna was watching the sky, but he was not watching the snipers. The general was looking toward the west, away from the gunfire.

Remo could have torn through the crowd like a thresher through an autumn wheat field, but to do so ran the risk of injuring too many innocents. There was only one way to go.

Behind him, the Master of Sinanju had reached the same conclusion. "Take that side!" Chiun commanded.

In a flurry of kimono skirts, the old man leapt into the air. The toe of one wooden sandal brushed the shoulder of a running man. Pushing lightly off, Chiun jumped to the head of another, the shoulder of a third.

In this crazy, zigzagging manner, the Master of Sinanju raced across the heads of the stampeding mob to the right side of the street.

Remo took his teacher's cue. With a single leap, he took off in the opposite direction.

It was like running across the backs of a herd of stampeding cattle. The snipers continued to fire as he ran. Bullets zinged past his head. Some were hitting innocents in the crowd. He heard the soft thwaps of bullets striking flesh, as well as the cries of shock.

He reached the near building. A final toe on the rounded shoulder of a retreating protester, and he launched himself in the air. One hand caught the awning that hung over the door of a coffee shop. He swung up high, landing softly on the second-story ledge.

Bullets pelted the brick around him. He was out of sight for the shooters on his own side of the street. The snipers across the square were trying to get a bead on him.

The gunmen above were firing at the wall across the street where even now he knew the Master of Sinanju must be scurrying, squirrel-like, up the building's facade.

Relieved that they had successfully drawn the fire away from the crowd, Remo began scaling the wall.

The days where he had to concentrate to climb a sheer face were long behind him. Still, it was not easy to keep focus in broad daylight with a rampaging mob beneath him and bullets kicking up brick and mortar dust as he ascended.

He was grateful to reach the top of the five-story building. He grabbed the ledge, flipped up and over, and found himself face to face with a very shocked Miguel Pagaza.

"You know what I'm sick of?" Remo asked.

Miguel jumped. He had been firing at the little Asian who could somehow scale the side of a building as easily as most people climb stairs. He swung his rifle at Remo.

"I'm sick of the fact that the only people I ever meet

these days seem to be people who are trying to kill me," Remo said, answering his own question.

Miguel squeezed off a single shot. At point blank range, it should have ripped through bone and muscle.

The bullet missed Remo, slamming into a chimney which exploded shards of red brick across the hot roof. And then the gun was somehow in Remo's hands, and then it was snapped in two fat pieces.

Remo dropped the rifle halves down the broken chimney.

"Who . . . ?" Remo began.

"Rebecca Dalton!" blurted Miguel Pagaza, who at that very moment had decided that the thing he valued more than *la Revolucion* was his own life. "She is a hired killer. She works for Santa Anna! I don't know who he is, or where he came from. He's Mexican, they tell me, but I've never been good at telling the difference between accents. He could be from Paraguay or somewhere, I don't know. He's donated a lot of money to MOLAP. That's my group. I'm president here in Albuquerque. Wait, I've got a card here."

Miguel Pagaza, great betrayer of the revolution, patted his pockets for a business card. Finding one, he offered it to Remo with a shaking hand.

Remo slapped the card away. "Where is she now?" he demanded. As if in response, the whop-whop-whop of helicopter rotor blades suddenly rose above the screams of the thinning mob.

Remo saw the chopper rise over the low buildings to the west. It cut in low, moving toward the platform. Santa Anna signaled the helicopter to hurry. The fat general waved his arms frantically over his head.

"Dammit," Remo said when he saw the face of the chopper pilot.

People scattered from the downdraft and the spinning blades. Like a metallic nesting bird, the helicopter piloted by Rebecca Dalton settled to one side of the big platform.

"It is her," Miguel said. He sounded hopeful, as if her arrival meant this frightening killer with the dead man's eyes would leave him safe and go after her.

Remo was about to do just that when he saw Rebecca fiddle with something next to her seat. Almost simultaneously, he heard a tiny click nearby, too soft to be detectable to normal human ears. It came from a little black object attached to Miguel Pagaza's belt.

Instinct honed by training kicked in.

Remo dropped to the roof and sent both feet hard into Miguel's back. Albuquerque's MOLAP president did not have time to experience the shock of being suddenly airborne. One instant he was on the roof, the next he was launched high into empty air over the street five stories below.

A fraction of a second later, the device on his belt reacted to the signal Rebecca had tripped from inside the helicopter and Miguel popped open like a whacked piñata, showering the square in meat, flame and shrapnel.

The precise moment Miguel's tracking device exploded, seven more explosions ripped the air. On roofs all around the square MOLAP gunmen burst apart, splattering red rain across rooftops and down on the remnants of the mob.

For an instant when he flipped back to his feet, Remo worried for Chiun's safety. But he need not have bothered. He spied his teacher scrambling down the side of the building opposite.

On the platform, Santa Anna had struggled aboard the helicopter. With a furious whoosh of rotor blades, the aircraft lifted off the stage.

Remo was up and over the edge of the roof in a flash. Toes did not search for narrow spaces between brick. He relied only on the force of his fingertips to keep him from plummeting to the ground. Even so, his descent was so fast an observer would think he had flung himself over the side.

At the first floor, he gave a shove, flipped in midair and landed sprinting. Friction stung his fingers.

Remo met up with the Master of Sinanju before the stage.

The helicopter had climbed above the rooftops. Rebecca angled the nose down and spun the craft toward the west.

"We can take it down, Chiun," Remo said.

He glanced around for something to hurl at the rotor assembly. Spying a metal folding chair that had been kicked onto its side, he snatched it up and hauled back. The instant before he let the chair fly, he hesitated.

"No," he said.

Rebecca was following a path that took her directly over the main city street. Hundreds of people still crammed the road beneath the belly of her helicopter.

"There are too many innocents," Chiun said. "She knows we could take the craft down easily, but she knows we will not if it means that hundreds will die in the process." He stroked his thread of beard, nodding appreciation.

"Don't you dare," Remo said. "Don't even think about being impressed by her."

"She is clever," the old Korean observed. He tucked his hands inside his kimono sleeves. "More clever than you, Remo. Although, granted, that is hardly a compliment. She had hoped to kill us with bullets at a distance and, failing that, with the booms attached to her hirelings. But she had planned for a third alternative, in case we dealt with her gunmen and explosives. Assassination has become such an ugly thing, particularly as it is practiced by Americans, that there are not many who would be so thorough in this day and age. It is refreshing to encounter such a clever young lady."

The old man padded slowly away.

Rebecca Dalton had clearly understood Remo's dilemma. The helicopter slowed and hovered. When it turned slightly in the air, she offered Remo a cheery smile and wave.

And then the helicopter nosed down once more and flew off. It vanished behind the low buildings.

Remo heard the engine fade into the noise of humanity, and the everyday bustle of a major city.

A low growl rose from deep in his throat. Digging in one heel, he spun at the waist. The folding chair flew from his fingers at supersonic speed. When it struck the first story facade of the Exchange Insurance Company, so great was the force with which it was thrown, the brick surrendered as if it were no more solid than warm marmalade. The chair buried itself halfway into the side of the building, quivering legs jutting out over the sidewalk.

"There," Remo snarled. "If she's so damn clever, can she do that?"

An infuriating sing-song replied, "She does not have to, for this clever girl, who is cleverer than you on your cleverest day, has gotten you to do it for her."

And the old Korean's cackling laughter left Remo searching the immediate area for another chair to fling.

"You let him get away."

Smith's tone held an edge of thin rebuke.

"I didn't let anybody anything," Remo said. "And I could have taken him out, but it would have meant squashing about a million people under his helicopter. Not to mention the other million who would have been chopped to ribbons when the blades broke off and went skipping off down the street. You want me to start crashing helicopters on innocent people in order to get the bad guys, Smitty, just give me the word. Otherwise, back off."

Remo was on a sidewalk pay phone.

The insanity had ended. Police and rescue officials had arrived to restore order. Amazingly, there had been little rioting. When the shooting had begun and the crowd dispersed, the instinct of most of the protesters had been to run to their own homes. The majority had come through the ordeal unscathed.

But some were not so fortunate. Dozens of people had been injured in the stampede. Several more had been hit by sniper fire. But, Remo realized, the carnage could have been much worse. For all the bedlam, there had been only three fatalities.

From the corner sidewalk pay phone, Remo watched paramedics lift a sheet-draped gurney into the back of a waiting ambulance.

"You did not say there were extenuating circumstances," Smith said.

"Well, extenuate this. Remember our old friend Rebecca Dalton? You know, the lady assassin who buried me in an anthrax tunnel out in Iraq during the Sinanju Time of Succession? The woman you promised me you'd track down five years ago and never did? She's the one who airlifted Santa Fatso out of here. So technically if you want to blame someone, blame yourself, Smitty."

"Rebecca Dalton? Are you certain?"

"Sweet as honey as she pours acid down your throat? Yeah, I'm sure."

"I did track her down several years ago, Remo, but all I could find was her past, not her present," the CURE director said.

Remo could hear the sound of Smith's fingers drumming the capacitor keyboard at the edge of his desk.

"Sure," Remo said. "And I bet her folks were a couple of rich leftover hippie wannabes who just thought that anything little Rebecca did was fine, as long as she kept taking her Ritalin."

"Not exactly," Smith said. "Here's her file. It starts at a state orphanage in Illinois."

Remo's brow furrowed. "She's an orphan?"

"Parents died in a car accident when she was six. Her grandmother too. No other living relatives. She was a troubled child. According to her orphanage psychiatric file, she remembered the accident."

"She was in the car?"

"Yes," Smith replied. "I found a newspaper story about it. The car was stuck in a ravine. It seems she was trapped in the back seat for almost twenty-four hours before she was rescued. Her father and grandmother died on impact, but the mother survived almost all that while and the girl had to watch her die. The ordeal left emotional scarring. She was never adopted." He read from the orphanage report, "Moody. Prone to violent outbursts. Unwilling to get along with other children."

"Watching your family die isn't exactly a trip to Candyland, Smitty," Remo said.

"I didn't say it was," Smith said. "This is all from her file. Don't develop any sympathy for her, Remo. Need I remind you that she is a hired killer?"

"Need I remind you that I'm one too?"

Smith cleared his throat. "I have the whole file," he said. "Public education, scholarships, very bright."

"Get to the part where I can find her."

"You can't," Smith said. "After college, she disappeared from all public records. She stopped paying taxes. No bank accounts or credit cards in her name. Aside from a school-sponsored trip to Zimbabwe her senior year, there are no travel records, no passport. My investigation hit a dead end. There was nothing more I could do, so I stopped searching."

"You say she went to Africa?"

"That is correct. It is the only record I have of her leaving the country."

"Benson Dilkes lived in Africa," Remo said.

Smith was intimately aware of Dilkes's reputation as a hired killer. Against his better judgment, he had at one time retained the man's services. Smith had hired Dilkes to kill Remo, but Dilkes had wound up being killed by Remo. Even though Chiun had encouraged the CURE director to send Dilkes after Remo as part of Remo's final rite of passage in Sinanju, the subject was still an uncomfortable one for Smith.

"Er, yes," Smith said. "He had retired to Zimbabwe for a time before you . . ." Pausing, he struggled for the least distasteful words. "Before he died. It is possible that Rebecca Dalton came into contact with him at some point while on her college trip."

"And he took her under his wing and turned her into the Pollyanna maniac she is today. Chalk another one up for Dilkes. The guy just doesn't give up. I put my fist through his head five years ago and that still doesn't stop him from annoying the piss out of me."

"Remo, what exactly has Rebecca Dalton done this time?"

"The usual. That tunnel I told you about? She blew it up on us. I don't flatter myself to think she had that set up for us, though. She must have had it rigged to go up if someone found the tunnel. We just lucked out. Speaking of which, I overnighted you a package of stuff."

"What kind of stuff?"

"Just a button we found out in the desert. It's new, I think, but it's old-fashioned looking. Maybe you can use it to find out where Santa Anna's getting those costumes made. We found a map down in the tunnel too. The southwest border is all screwed up. I put that in too."

"Is that all?"

"Yeah. Why?"

"Remo, you did not let Master Chiun put anything . . . extra into the package you sent?"

Remo understood. "I told you, Smitty, Santa Anna got away. This isn't a surprise party. His head's not going to roll out onto your blotter when you tear open the envelope."

Smith did not seem entirely convinced that Remo was telling the truth. "Is there anything else?" he asked.

"Yes," Remo said. "Apparently Santa Anna has been giving donations to MOLAP. Their president told me so before Rebecca Dalton blew him to smithereens."

"We have been looking into MOLAP as well as several other radical groups. I'll keep looking for a link. If this Santa Anna is tied in with them, we will redouble our efforts. Perhaps we can trace the money back to his location. I will also try to find Rebecca Dalton once more. If she's connected to him, she could lead us to him. I don't hold out much hope of finding her, though. She's managed to evade us pretty well."

"Okay," Remo said as he dumped the phone in the cradle. He wished Smith had not told him about Rebecca Dalton's childhood. Having grown up under the watchful eyes of the nuns at St. Theresa's Orphanage in Newark, New Jersey, Remo was naturally predisposed to sympathize with a fellow orphan, although in this case that sympathy was a bit strained by Rebecca Dalton's repeated attempts to kill him.

The Master of Sinanju was standing halfway down the block near a parked ambulance. Conchita Diaz was sitting on the back bumper while a paramedic applied a small light-tan bandage to her forehead. Except for the scrape to her head, she had come through the commotion unharmed.

Behind the ambulance was a black limousine with a driver in chauffeur livery standing at attention alongside the open rear door. Remo glimpsed Prescott Worthington in animated conversation on the vehicle's phone.

Remo sidled up to Chiun.

"Smith is on the case," he said. "He's checking into MOLAP and trying to find Rebecca Dalton. He was afraid that you'd mailed him Santa Anna's head."

"Did you tell him I would have gotten him his prize if you had not been outsmarted by that female friend of yours?"

"He doesn't want it, Chiun," Remo warned. "He made that clear again."

"He says that now, but he will change his mind once he sees how effective a deterrent it will be to other rebels. Properly displayed, this Santa Anna's head will keep the Vikings from sacking Smith's Maine province for years to come. Decades, if it is pickled properly."

"I'm just telling you. Smith doesn't want a pickled head for Christmas."

But the old man merely patted Remo's forearm and offered a paternal smile. "You are still so young in so many ways," the Master of Sinanju said.

The paramedic had finished with Conchita's bandage. Refusing a ride to the hospital, she got down from the ambulance bumper and took a wobbly step toward Remo and Chiun. Remo grabbed her arm and helped her find her balance.

"You okay?" he asked.

"I am fine," she insisted. "This . . ." She waved vaguely at the bandage. ". . . Is nothing. My only problem is I have not slept in two days. Between all that's happened last night and today, I had not even thought of it."

Conchita appeared exhausted. Remo could see that. But he could also see that the ordeal of the past day had invested her with a strength she had not known she possessed. Some few lucky people responded that way when they faced the crunch. There was now a pride in the way she stood that had nothing to do with something as ephemeral as natural beauty. In adversity, she seemed to have discovered her true self.

The previous day she had just been another arrogant looker, coasting through life on beauty alone. But trial by fire had burned the shallowness away. Despite the dirt and sweat and bruises, Conchita Diaz was more beautiful than ever, because the beauty she now radiated came from a deep well of internal strength.

Remo touched her arm and squeezed gently. "You've done good, lady. And that bandage is real cute."

With a raised eyebrow, the Master of Sinanju noted the exchange.

"You can do better," Chiun warned.

"I'm not so sure about that," Remo said, smiling at Conchita. She smiled back.

"I was not talking to you," Chiun said.

Before Remo could answer, he saw Prescott Worthington coming toward them.

"Hello! You!" Worthington said. "It's Remo you said, isn't it? Listen, Remo, I've got to run, but I've got a proposition for you. I've got someone who's supposed to be handling security for me, but they're not doing the best job. You've managed to breach my security twice, which is two times too much. And anyway, my regular security person has too many other clients, not enough time to devote just to me. I like my people to be exclusive. How would you like to come work for me?"

"Thanks, but no tha—. . . ." Remo felt a sharp swat on the back of his head. "Ow! Dammit, Chiun."

"I do the negotiating," Chiun said imperiously. He turned toward Worthington and nodded. "You may talk to me."

Worthington deflated. It seemed an effort to turn to the old Korean. He forced politeness into his voice. "I meant only him," Worthington said.

"There is no 'him,'" Chiun said. "There is us. He is young and foolish. Sign a contract with him and you would be taking advantage of the mentally incompetent. There are laws in this country against that. In truth, I have only allowed him to think he has an important position in the family business to boost his low self-esteem."

"Great job, Dr. Phil," Remo said, rubbing the back of his head.

With Chiun in the mix, Worthington seemed to cool on the idea of bringing Remo into the Worthington, Inc., fold.

"Hmm . . . yes," the billionaire said. "Let me talk to my people. Crunch some numbers. You sure I can't just hire one of you?"

"Sorry," Remo said. "We're like salt and pepper shakers. We only come in a set."

"Like . . . Lewis and Clark," Chiun said, looking to Remo for approval.

"Martin and Lewis," Remo said.

Worthington nodded. "I see. Very good then." With a sigh, he looked around the square.

Trash littered the street. Benches had been overturned and limbs had been broken off decorative shade trees. Two police officers were examining the folding chair that was sticking out of the wall of the Exchange Insurance Company Building. As one prodded it with his baton, the other scratched his head in amazement.

"It's an event like this that really changes one's perspective, don't you think?" Worthington said. "Perception altering, life changing. All those . . . those various things. Oh, well. Tah."

Worthington trotted off to his limo, all white shorts and tan limbs. Remo decided that all he needed to make his "preppy moron" ensemble complete was a tennis racket under his arm and a sweater knotted over his shoulders. Preferably tied tight enough to cut off the circulation to his head.

"What do you suppose he meant by that?" Remo asked.

"While you were gone, he said he was impressed with the crowd Santa Anna had attracted," Conchita said. "He said he admired their passion. He even thinks he might have been wrong to fund the Civilian Border Patrol."

"Hmm," Remo said. "Somehow deep thought doesn't seem to suit him." He watched Worthington's limo pull away from the curb and take off down the street. Prescott Worthington IV was invisible behind tinted windows.

"I don't trust this guy, Chiun," Remo said.

"I think he is hiding some model trains from us," Chiun said.

"Among other things."

10

The private jet touched down on the sticky Alamo-gordo tarmac and taxied to a slow stop. When the engine whine ceased and the door at last opened, one bleary-eyed figure stepped out onto the steps.

Senator Ned J. Clancy looked around the airport, blinked, and wondered aloud what he was doing there.

"Immigration issue, Senator," a helpful aide told him.

"Oh, yesh. Yesh, yesh," Clancy said, in an accent as thick as a bowl of Boston baked beans. "And here is . . . ?"

"Alamogordo, New Mexico, Senator. Several of your colleagues have come here to take a stand for the rights of the impoverished undocumented worker."

"Right, right," Clancy said. The act of nodding jiggled the rolls of fat at his chins and left him woozy.

With his aide's assistance, Clancy stomped down the steps to a waiting limo and allowed his aide to arrange him in the backseat. The air conditioning was a welcome reprieve from the blast of dry, hot air that had attacked his sensitive skin the moment he stepped off the plane.

At seventy-five, Ned Clancy was a far cry from the fit young man who once played touch football in his early campaign commercials. A lifetime of excess had obliterated the vigor he once possessed and had left behind a hulking, wheezing, staggering shell.

Clancy's bloated face was a network of burst capillaries that, for public appearances, had to be covered with makeup so thick it looked like tan stucco.

He had gained an alarming amount of weight over the years, and had given up weighing himself back when the bathroom scale was no longer visible below his ponderous belly.

So distended had his torso become, his arms looked as if they no longer fit his body properly. Instead, they appeared to be crudely thumbtacked somewhere out beyond his shoulders, and every step risked jarring them loose. He walked with a shuffle that seemed to combine a toddler's first steps with that of someone who had been asked by police to walk a straight line.

As the limo sped from the airport, Clancy fumbled in the pockets of his suit jacket. Secreted around his clothing at all times were little plastic bottles of liquor and little plastic containers of breath mints, the former to help him somehow manage to stagger through another miserable day on planet Earth, the latter to cover the constant stench of booze that poured from his gasping gullet.

He sucked down a mini bottle of Chivas Regal, chased it with half a rattling container of spearmint Tic Tacs, and slumped back in his seat. Crunching candy, Clancy stared morosely out at the hot New Mexico afternoon.

The homes and warehouses he sped past baked in the merciless sunlight. In all of the buildings were people living out drab everyday lives that a millionaire senator, born to power and privilege, could never hope to understand.

At one time, Clancy would have viewed these little people and their peasant problems with contempt but these days he could not work up the energy even for that. The people who inhabited the world outside his tiny bubble might as well have been ghosts. The hospitals and homes, churches and factories the proles built were mere suggestions of human involvement in some other realm that wealth and stature prevented Ned Clancy from ever having to enter. Life was something that would only ever be glimpsed through tinted windows in the backseat of a speeding limousine.

"So this is where the, err-ah, mighty Clancy Clan will be reborn," he belched.

"Excuse me, Senator?" asked his aide. The young man was seated across from Clancy. He had been on the phone with the aide to a prominent senator from the opposite party, a close political ally of Ned Clancy. The aide cupped the phone and stared quizzically at his employer.

"Nothing," Clancy said, waving the question away. "Just thinking out loud."

The aide seemed surprised. He had worked for Ned Clancy for five years, and in his experience the senator rarely thought at all, either aloud or to himself.

As the aide resumed his phone conversation, Clancy's thoughts returned to his family.

The Clancy Clan was a political dynasty that extended back to Ned Clancy's long-dead father. Decades before, a portion of the family bootlegging fortune had been directed into politics, and the sons, grandsons and great-grandsons of Ned's father had all followed the river of cash into elected office. There had been hope at one time that Clancy might run for president. In a senate chamber filled with one hundred blowhards, none blew harder than Senator Ned J. Clancy, and so it seemed a sure thing that he would one day occupy the Oval Office. But personal strife and dissolute living had killed those prospects. Still, even with his presidential ambitions long behind him, Ned Clancy was in his fifth decade in the United States Senate and showed no interest in retirement. Everyone knew that Ned Clancy would tough it out in Washington until the Lord Himself finally announced last call for his state's senior senator.

Clancy's reputation as a survivor had been put to its first test forty years before.

One dark Friday night, back in the late 1960s, the senator's car had been discovered floating upside-down in a flooded, abandoned quarry in a little New England town. Two fourteen-year-old Girl Scouts had been found drowned in the back seat. Their blood alcohol level had tested three times the legal limit. Although he was not found at the scene of the accident, and at first claimed to be out for a midnight jog during the time of the incident, Clancy had been positively identified by a liquor store owner who had sold him vodka, and who had seen the girls standing near his car in the parking lot. It should have been an open and shut case.

On the first day of the trial, Clancy arrived in court in sunglasses and a wheelchair. He claimed victim status, stating that he was only giving the girls a ride home. He insisted that when he stopped at a McDonald's to heed the call of nature, the Girl Scouts had stolen his car. When asked why he failed to report the theft to the police, he sobbed that he did not want the girls to get into trouble.

"If there, err-ah, was a crime here, it was the crime of my concern for the, err-ah, safety and welfare of all the young girls of this Commonwealth."

Against overwhelming evidence that placed the senator squarely at the scene of the crime, the jury voted to acquit.

"I voted for your brother," a misty-eyed elderly juror told Clancy after the trial, echoing the sentiments of the rest of the jury. "This was the very least I could do for his memory. Such a handsome man."

The only legal fallout came days after the acquittal, when the state, in its majesty and wisdom, revoked the liquor license of the store owner who had testified against Clancy.

Although he was legally out of trouble, the political damage was long-lasting. The scandal had forever killed Ned Clancy's viability as a candidate for national public office. To the nation at large, Ned Clancy was a punchline, but back in his home state, he was the beloved patriarch of a revered, if somewhat tarnished, political dynasty.

When the senator had been implicated in a kidnapping scandal over a decade before and run off to Tahiti to avoid jail, his approval rating back home had taken the worst hit of his political career. Only sixty percent of the state's likely voters said they would definitely vote for him while twenty percent said they would probably vote for him.

He returned after a few months in exile and beat the rap again, thanks to high-priced Clancy lawyers who were kept on retainer to deal exclusively with family scandals. The people of the state rewarded his criminal behavior the following election night, when Ned Clancy staggered to his fifth consecutive senate victory.

Detractors opined that Ned Clancy could rape a nun on live TV before an international audience during Christmas Eve Mass, and the good citizens of his state would blame the sister for dressing provocatively and reward the senator with another six-year term.

But despite the reverence his constituents blindly accorded him, despite his longevity in the Senate, despite avoiding serious jail time for several public offenses and several hundred private ones that the world had never found out about, that he would never achieve the greatness that was his right by birth gnawed at him.

Of course, the fact that he would never be President of the United States was not his fault. It was the fault of those two Girl Scouts for not being better swimmers. It was the fault of his father for investing so much energy into Ned's older brothers. It was the fault of the voters outside New England who did not revere him as his constituents did, and who dared to go so far as to mock him. Clancy pointed the finger of blame at everyone but himself. Adversity had a way of challenging a man to be his best, but for Ned Clancy adversity had always been something that happened to other people. Even the challenges of his various court cases might have presented opportunities for personal growth if he had seen them that way, but whenever turmoil erupted around him, Clancy preferred to climb into his bottle and marinate, coming up for air only long enough to play the blame game. And thus did the decades slowly bleed away, until one day he found himself in his seventies, bloated, buzzed, and with precious few grains of sand left to sift through the hourglass of his life.

In this hazy twilight of existence, when all hope of real power seemed lost, opportunity at last tossed a lifeline to Senator Ned J. Clancy. And if he had to trade the damp bars of the Northeast for the dusty saloons of the Southwest to grab it, Ned Clancy would gladly do so.

His closest aides thought Senator Clancy had come to New Mexico to join in a public discussion of the immigration problem. In the backseat of his speeding limo, Senator Ned Clancy smiled boozily.

"The Santa Anna wind is blowing, my friends," he grunted at the passing scenery. "And it just may blow me to 1600 Pennsylvania Avenue. Or wherever it is."

Dr. Harold W. Smith was annoyed with himself.

For most of his time as head of CURE, Smith had risen before dawn and did not return home until well after dark. After Mark Howard had settled in at the agency, the young man had insisted that Smith shorten his hours. At first Smith resisted, but he had eventually agreed to come home earlier two days a week. For several years, every Tuesday and Thursday, Smith left the office at five o'clock sharp.

And with his new schedule, Smith discovered a little miracle. Despite the fact that Harold W. Smith was not hard at work behind his desk, the world did not end.

For the first time since assuming the reins of CURE, Smith had permitted himself to relax. Not much, for tension was as much a part of his wardrobe as his three-piece suit, and Smith felt naked without some worry in his life.

But there had been a few moments since he had begun his new schedule that the constant stress he had lived under for decades felt slightly less suffocating. For Smith, any reduction in stress was like a walk on the beach.

When Mark had recently suggested Smith shorten his schedule a bit more, the older man had offered only token resistance. Now, three days a week, Mondays, Wednesdays and Fridays, Smith did not arrive at the office until 7:30.

There were times that Smith's new schedule stabbed a tiny pang of guilt into the pit of his stomach. But Smith was at his core a logical man, and although the spirit was as willing as it had ever been, the flesh had undeniably grown weak. He was simply no longer up to the daily rigors of constant twelve- or sixteen- or eighteen-hour workdays.

So Smith now slept until after sunrise three days a week, and apparently his body had gotten more used to the new schedule than Smith had himself because this morning, when he had awakened ten minutes earlier, he had been shocked to discover that it was nearly seven o'clock.

His wife had already gotten out of bed and gone downstairs to make breakfast. Smith, trained in the OSS to sleep with one eye open, had not even felt the blankets shift or the box spring bounce.

Exhaustion was partly to blame. Smith had stayed at work until well after one o'clock the previous night. Given the growing crisis in the Southwest, he was needed at Folcroft. He had come home only for a shower and a nap, but his fatigue had apparently been greater than he realized and he slept through the night.

Smith sat on the edge of his bed to lace up his black cordovan dress shoes.

He heard the sound of television voices drifting up the stairs. He could not hear what was being said, but every few seconds he heard his wife shout at the TV disapprovingly. Lately she had taken to doing that and when he had once suggested to her that the people on the television could not hear her, she responded, "Aren't they the lucky ones? Because I would really give them a piece of my mind."

Smith quickly made the bed and, shrugging on his suit jacket and snatching up his briefcase, hustled downstairs.

Maude Smith was a bosomy matron who wore an apron over her housecoat. Smith entered the kitchen as she scraped eggs out of a scratched frying pan onto two chipped plates.

"Good morning, Harold."

"Good morning, Maude," Smith said, quickly sliding into his chair.

The scrambled eggs were runny and the toast was burnt, even though Maude had scraped the worst of the charred black crumbs into the sink.

Her little counter TV, a Christmas gift from the Smiths' daughter, was tuned in to one of the morning network shows and was reporting on the trouble in America's Southwest.

"A difficult news day, dear?" Smith asked.

The chair creaked as Maude sat across from her husband. "It's just terrible, Harold," she said, shaking her blue-tinted perm. "All those poor people. They're saying some senators are going down there to finally straighten out the mess. I hope so."

At that moment, Smith felt warmly proud of his wife and her naïve good faith that somehow politicians might help in this crisis, even though it had been those same politicians who had, over the course of several decades, by strategic inaction and, worse, direct legislative action, caused most of the problems that they were currently blaming on each other.

"I hope so too," he said.

Smith ate quickly. The television droned.

"The latest development comes out of New Mexico, Diane," a male reporter with a face full of Botox, hair full of

lacquer, and an attitude full of himself was saying. "As
several prominent senators arrive in the state, including
Senators Ned Clancy and straight-talking, iconoclastic
Senator Jack Muldoon, Prescott Worthington, chairman of
Worthington International, has announced that he is spon-
soring a town hall meeting where both sides can discuss
this important issue."

At mention of Worthington, Smith's fork paused on the
way to his thin lips. Egg goo dripped between the tines.

"For those of our viewers who don't know," said the female co-host, "Prescott Worthington is the major donor behind the Civilian Border Patrol, a self-appointed border
watchdog group that some have called vigilantes for their
unauthorized surveillance of undocumented workers."

"That's right, Diane," said the reporter. "You may recall
that the Civilian Border Patrol had a run-in earlier this
week, some say with supporters of Santa Anna, the enig-
matic figure who has electrified guest workers and offered
hope to many throughout the border states."

Smith thought that he could no longer be astonished by
anything said by the talking heads of television. But to dis-
miss a dozen murders as a "run-in" had to be a first. And
despite the chaos he had caused in Albuquerque and Los
Angeles, General Santa Anna was receiving neither criti-
cism nor skepticism from anyone on the program. Smith
assumed that, as usual, the other network news divisions
were in brainless lockstep on the biggest story of the day.

He listened to the two television personalities torture their
conversation to include phrases like "undocumented workers" and "guest workers" and "permanent visitors" and ex-
clude the more universal and accurate term "illegal aliens"
for another five minutes while he finished his breakfast.

Smith choked down every morsel, wiped his mouth,
thanked his wife, gave her a tiny peck on the cheek, told
her that, no, he did not think he would be home early to-

night, and hustled out to his thirty-eight-year-old station wagon.

An entire region of the country was threatening to go up in flames. Personal issues such as age and exhaustion would have to be set aside. For Harold W. Smith, there was much work to be done.

Two hundred miles down the East Coast, the President of the United States was receiving his morning security briefing and minute by minute was growing more annoyed.

"How did he get away twice in the same day?" the president demanded.

"We have men at the rallies," the FBI director explained. "But when you've got five hundred thousand people marching and very little cooperation from local law enforcement, our presence is a drop in the bucket."

The president appeared to understand. Sighing, he leaned back in his chair.

They were in the Oval Office. In addition to the president and the director of the FBI, the director of the Central Intelligence Agency was also present.

"How many men did you have in Los Angeles yesterday?" the president asked.

"Two dozen," the FBI director replied. "Some from our field office, the rest sent from Washington. But that's almost twenty-one thousand protesters to each one of my men. And they're saying this morning that crowd estimates may have been under by as much as three hundred thousand. That's thirty-three thousand protesters per agent. Not only are we not in the business of crowd control, even if we were we wouldn't be equipped for a crowd that size. I don't think anyone is, Mr. President, short of the military."

On the sofa across from the president's desk, the CIA director, a former military man, straightened at the suggestion.

"That option is not on the table," the president said. "These are American cities. Even if Posse Comitatus didn't prevent me from sending in the military, I will not have the United States Army marching through Los Angeles."

The FBI director nodded. "I understand that, sir. My point is that we are not up to this. My men couldn't get within two miles of that stage during Santa Anna's speech. And even if they could have grabbed him, they would have been torn to shreds before they got ten yards with him."

With his fingertips, the president massaged his temples. He looked to the CIA director.

"What good news do you have for me?" he said sarcastically.

"None, I'm afraid, Mr. President," the CIA head replied crisply. "This Santa Anna may as well be vapor. My people haven't been able to find him."

The president was not surprised. Once the premier spy agency in the world, the CIA had been in steady decline since the 1970s. These days the only things it seemed able to find were *New York Times* reporters to splash national security secrets on page one.

"Okay, I know we don't have him," the president said, with forced patience. "But you've had all night to work on this. What have you at least been able to find out about him?"

The two agency directors scanned the notes they had spread out on the coffee table before them.

"He's in his fifties. Overweight. Probably dyes his hair," the FBI director said.

The president's eyes were flat. "What can you tell me that I wouldn't have learned by turning on the TV?"

"According to our voice experts, he's definitely Mexican," the CIA director answered. "As you know, there was a question that he might have come from some other Latin American country. Dialect places him more than likely from the Baja area. He doesn't sound like he's very educated."

"Well, that's really got to narrow the trail, doesn't it?" the president said.

The two men began shuffling through their notes. They looked for all the world like guilty fourth-graders who had failed to do their homework because they had stayed up too late watching TV.

As the papers rattled, the president closed his eyes and wondered for the thousandth time since he had taken the oath of office why he had ever wanted this job in the first place.

In sixty years no administration had seen such turmoil. Just a few short months into his first term, the previous administration's economic house of cards had collapsed with a stock market crash. Then came a devastating terrorist attack on Washington and New York that had not only destroyed landmarks, but had decimated the nation's business nerve center. This was followed by a prolonged war against a shadow enemy that could surface and strike anywhere the world over. And then, as if nature herself were plotting against him, came a string of storms that had swamped an entire American coastline and displaced tens of thousands.

He had dealt with each problem as it came along, despite poisonous political sniping not seen since Abraham Lincoln's day. To those around him who sometimes seemed despairing, the president said simply, "Soldier on. We soldier on."

It was a testament to the strength of America—her economy, her military, but most of all to her people—that the nation had not only weathered all storms, both figurative and literal, but had managed to thrive. The president had even allowed himself to think the worst turmoil was over.

And then the immigration situation took center stage and the political vultures wasted no time before circling.

From the Right they attacked him for being soft on illegal immigration. Some wanted him to round up all the illegals and ship them out of the country. But that was as ridiculous as it was impractical. The sheer numbers of illegals already in the country, some living undocumented for decades, made rounding them up a Sisyphean task for law enforcement.

From the Left they called him heartless for not spreading a giant welcome mat over the Rio Grande so that the lawbreakers who were entering the country illegally could do so without getting their feet wet.

For the President of the United States, it was already an impossible situation long before this lunatic who called himself General Santa Anna arrived on the scene.

The name alone was a provocation, conjuring up instant animosity in the hearts of all true Texans. The president already did not like him even before he found out the maniac wanted to reclaim most of the Southwest for Mexico.

And now he was finding out that the CIA and FBI were unable to deal with this new problem.

The two directors were still shifting their papers.

The president stood. "That will be all, gentlemen."

The FBI and CIA heads glanced up.

"I, um, am sure we'll have something for you soon, Mr. President," the FBI director said.

"Sure. You do that," the president said.

He allowed them a few seconds to hastily gather up their papers before ushering them to the door.

"Keep up the research," he said as the men passed through into his secretary's office. "Find out anything you can about this Santa Anna. If you can find out where he gets his hair dye, even that might help."

The FBI director's face reddened, embarrassed. "I'll have teams ready to move on a moment's notice if he surfaces again," he promised.

"No," the president said. "Just do research. Don't do anything operational. Don't confront. You too, Jack," he said to the CIA head. "I don't want your people caught in the crossfire."

"Crossfire, sir?" the CIA director said. "Forgive me, Mr. President, but you can't have crossfire if one side stands down. If you're not using the military, and now you're pulling us out too, we're surrendering the Southwest to this bastard."

"I should point out, Mr. President, that there were local police who actively impeded my men," the FBI director said, nodding agreement with the CIA chief. "There's a lot of sympathy out there for this cause, Mr. President, even among those who have sworn to uphold the law."

"Understood," the president said, and shut the door in the baffled faces of the two directors.

The president went through another door to a private elevator. Up in the family quarters, he took a cherry red telephone from the bottom drawer of his bedside nightstand.

When he had learned from his predecessor what was on the other end of that telephone, this president, like most of those who had come before him, had vowed never to use it. But ugly reality had a habit of subverting the most noble pledges. He had used this phone more times than he cared to remember. Each time he hoped would be the last time.

The wearying weight of his years in office heavy on his shoulders, the president lifted the red receiver.

Smith was stopped at a traffic light, one of nearly three dozen he had to pass through on his short drive to work, when the phone in his briefcase buzzed.

A special direct line at Folcroft connected Smith to the White House. Thanks to CURE's resources, Smith was generally aware of a crisis even before the president, and so was nearly always at his desk already hard at work on the solution when the chief executive called. In case of emergency, he had rigged the special dedicated line to skip to his cell phone. But the newer technology, and the myriad ways it could be hacked, made the CURE director nervous.

Keeping his eye on the red light, Smith popped the hasps on his briefcase and retrieved his phone.

"This line could be monitored," Smith said by way of introduction. "We must keep this short, sir."

"The situation in the Southwest," the familiar nasal twang of the president said.

"My special people are already there."

The light turned green. Smith inched forward. Up ahead the next light, which had been green, promptly turned amber to red. Smith had barely crossed the intersection before the traffic stopped moving again.

"What have you learned about this Santa Anna character?" the president asked.

"Not much, I'm afraid," Smith said. "My people have found a financial connection to MOLAP. In my research last night I found recent large donations to several prominent radical organizations, donations that more than likely come from Santa Anna."

"That's more than the FBI or CIA have come up with," the president said hopefully. "Can you trace it back?"

"I have my people doing just that. But the donations have apparently been given in cash. I only discovered them when I found that the personal bank accounts of many group leaders saw substantial deposits around the same time. That, and there was a sudden pattern of extravagant purchases on the part of various leaders of these groups. Expensive cars, jewelry. One MOLAP leader in Arizona bought a home."

"So Santa Anna has a lot of money behind him."

"It appears so, sir," Smith said.

He had made it through the next light, but as soon as he did so, the following light in line tripped red.

"Blast," Smith swore.

"Excuse me?"

"Nothing, sir," the CURE director replied. "As far as Santa Anna is concerned, my special people will do their best to find him. But in the meantime I must warn you, sir, that this is the greatest threat the United States has faced since the Civil War."

"It can't possibly be that bad, Smith."

"Sir, with respect, it is precisely that bad," Smith replied gravely. "In my lifetime I have seen the British empire shrink from one quarter of the earth's land surface, to basically nothing. The year before the Soviet Union fell, experts said it would never happen."

"You can't actually believe, Smith, that the United States could go just like that?"

"The British and the Russians thought it could never happen to them, sir. The reality is that there was a problem even before this individual who calls himself Santa Anna arrived on the scene. With him acting as a lightning rod, those within our borders unhappy with the United States could find focus for their activity. I fear what a single unifying voice could do to that region of the country."

The traffic light up ahead that had been green for all of ten seconds abruptly turned red.

Smith's hands clenched white on the steering wheel.

One of the reasons Harold Smith had been chosen for his position as CURE director was his incorruptibility. He would never use the power at his command for personal reasons. But at the moment Smith would have enjoyed nothing more than to use all of CURE's awesome resources against whatever gang of city idiots had decided it was a good idea to erect traffic lights every twenty feet through the center of Rye.

Smith's briefcase suddenly emitted a low beep.

The CURE computers were set up to alert him of any developments that might require his attention. Glancing up and seeing a red light and snarled traffic, he cradled the phone between ear and shoulder.

"Excuse me one moment, sir."

Flipping up the lid on his briefcase, he removed his

laptop. It was not the CURE mainframes that had signalled him, but rather a message from Mark Howard. Smith's assistant had forwarded him a news story. As Smith read the brief article, he felt the blood drain from his face.

"My God," Smith croaked.

"What?" asked the president. "Smith, what is it?"

Smith heard honking behind him. The red light he had stopped at was now green. His station wagon did not move. Smith's eyes were glued to the computer screen.

"Mr. President," Smith said, blood pounding in his ears, "the war I was afraid of may just have started."

The first verified incursion of Mexican Army troops into the United States of America since the current borders were established in 1854 took place on a small patch of otherwise insignificant desert inside New Mexico.

A small convoy of Jeeps and trucks broke through the unguarded fence north of Chihuahua, reclaiming for Mexico several square miles of land where the Civilian Border Patrol members had been slain earlier in the week.

In California there were reports, so far sketchy, of a single Mexican Army Jeep driving wildly around the streets of San Diego. The Jeep and the four soldiers in it were nearly caught by police at a Gulp 'n' Go where the Mexican soldiers had stopped to pick up beer, Fritos and lottery tickets.

Most ominous was an unconfirmed story out of rural Texas from a rancher who was awakened by the rumbling of heavy equipment during the night, and who in the light of day found what appeared to be tank treads through his property. Texas law enforcement was looking into this case, but with no outside help from Washington.

Smith had agreed with the president's decision to stand down the FBI and other federal agencies, but such a measure could not last long. The president might get away for a day or two by jabbering about diplomacy and talking to the

Mexican president but that would not last. If the crisis was not resolved quickly, at the rate events were spiraling out of control, an armed confrontation between the United States and Mexico would soon be unavoidable.

The CURE director was back at his desk at Folcroft. Acid burned his belly. Blood pounded behind his temples.

Smith fished a bottle of baby aspirin from his top drawer. He tossed two pills onto his parched tongue and took a deep swig from a bottle of antacid. He set both bottles to one side of his desk. He knew that he would be needing them both again before the morning was out.

The package Remo had overnighted him had arrived a few minutes before.

Despite its old-fashioned appearance, the silver uniform button Remo had found in the desert was clearly new. Smith had sent Mark out to have it analyzed, but he had doubts it would lead anywhere. Most important to Smith was the map Remo had collected from the coyote tunnel.

The map was different than Smith had expected. When Remo had told him that the borders had been redrawn, Smith had assumed that Mexico's territory had been pushed north. But the map spread out on his desk was not an attempt by a renegade Mexican national to reclaim land lost to the U.S. more than one hundred years ago.

Santa Anna's dream, outlined on this new map, was not reclamation but an entirely new nation independent of both Washington and Mexico City.

On the map, all of New Mexico, Nevada and Arizona were part of this new country. Most of Texas and California as well. But Santa Anna's ambitions did not only extend northward. Portions of Mexico were also in his sights. Vast chunks of Chihuahua and Sonora, as well as all of the Baja California peninsula were included in his twisted dream.

Nuevo Mexico.

The bold letters were emblazoned across the new North

American map in print equal in size to "United States," "Mexico" and "Canada." The land was divided into five territories, roughly consistent with current state borders. On the West Coast Los Angeles, not Sacramento, was the capital of the province of California. Houston had been completely obliterated from the province of Texas, replaced with a city called "Nueva Jalapa." The provincial capital of Texas had been moved to San Antonio. And in what was currently the American state of New Mexico, a fat black star denoted Albuquerque as capital of the new country.

Smith was not unused to encountering diseased minds. His public work at Folcroft had exposed him to elderly and brain-injured patients who suffered from all manner of delusions. His secret work as director of CURE often put him in conflict with madmen of an entirely different order. But for Smith, experienced as he was, this was something entirely new. For Harold W. Smith, this dream of Santa Anna's was insanity on a scale beyond all rational comprehension.

Smith was still staring in disbelief at the map of Nuevo Mexico when the blue phone jangled to life. Before it completed one full ring, he snatched it up.

"Smith," he snapped.

"Top o' the mornin' to you, too, Smitty," Remo's voice said. "Before you bite my head off, Chiun and I spent all night shaking people down, but no luck. Everyone was paid in cash, no one knows where it came from, except that it's payola from Santa Anna. A few of the guys gave a pretty good description of Rebecca Dalton, though, so I'm guessing she's been acting as bagperson with the cash."

"The money has become irrelevant," Smith said. "Haven't you heard the latest developments?"

Scarcely pausing for breath, Smith offered a rapid digest of all that had taken place since dawn. When he was finished, the breathlessness with which he delivered his sum-mary had apparently not adequately conveyed to Remo the direness of the situation.

"Big woop-de-doodle do," Remo said.

"Remo, we cannot run the risk of a full-scale war with Mexico," Smith insisted.

"Why not? It's Mexico, Smitty. Wait until noon when all their soldiers take a nap, then sneak in and take their five guns away from them. War over."

"Remo," Smith said somberly, "we cannot take this threat lightly. Santa Anna is undeniably a madman, but it is possible that he could pull off this scheme. He has apparently been spreading money around south of the border as well. After this latest madness broke, the president contacted the president of Mexico. When pressed, he could not say with certainty how much of his army is loyal to him. For all we know, Santa Anna could control most of Mexico's armed forces."

"Smitty," Remo said, "you do know this guy is not the real Santa Anna, right?"

"Of course," Smith snapped. "But we could be dealing with someone here who has a genuine psychiatric delusion. He could truly think he is Santa Anna. On this map you sent me, he has renamed Houston 'Jalapa.' That is the city in Veracruz where Santa Anna was born. And the real Santa Anna would certainly want more than anything to wipe Houston off the map, since Sam Houston delivered him such a bitter defeat."

As he spoke, Smith's computer beeped. Shifting the map to one side, he peered down at the monitor. The mainframes hidden behind a secret panel in Folcroft's basement had flagged a wire story.

"There has been a confrontation in Arizona between Mexican soldiers and sheriff's deputies," the CURE director said somberly. Sharp eyes scanned the scrolling text. "The soldiers were giving cover to a group of five hundred illegals crossing into the country. Eight soldiers and one deputy are being reported dead. Oh, no."

"What now?" Remo asked.

"This report says that the confrontation became violent when the illegals threw in with the soldiers."

"Why does it matter how it started?" Remo said.

"Don't you see? There has never been an incident like this before. Whatever one thinks of illegal immigration, it has, by and large, been peaceful. Those who have been apprehended have almost to a man allowed themselves to be repatriated to Mexico."

"They just live to sneak in another day," Remo said.

"Precisely my point. There has been no fighting the system that has been in place all these years because it has been seen as benign and ineffectual. Why fight when, once returned, you can just sneak back in the next night? The fact that this group would choose to stand and fight means that Santa Anna's message of rebellion is taking root. Not to mention the fact that such a large number would sneak into the U.S. in broad daylight in the first place."

"So what do you want from me, Smitty?" Remo said. "I hit a dead end on the cash. If you can't tell me where their leader is, I'm pretty much spinning my wheels out here. It's not like Chiun and I can patrol the whole border and bop back anyone who puts a big toe into the country."

Smith clenched his fists in frustration. Of course Remo was correct. Finding Santa Anna was still a priority, but in the meantime there were incursions taking place all along the border and illegals already in the country were flexing their considerable political muscle. If those forces joined and territory was taken, the United States would have only two options: military action or capitulation. Both were unthinkable.

For the first time since assuming control of CURE, Smith felt entirely helpless to react.

"Every hour that passes without any kind of response makes us appear more and more weak to the world," Smith said, thinking aloud. "And perceived weakness will only embolden an insane opportunist like Santa Anna."

"Not to mention everybody else who has it in for us," Remo pointed out.

Smith pressed the receiver between cheek and shoulder and reached for the aspirin bottle.

"What is needed now is a symbol," he said. "Something that will show the world that we are only demonstrating forbearance. Something that shows strength to our enemies."

As he was shaking out another baby aspirin, Smith's computer beeped once more. It had been doing so with such frequency that he scarcely glanced at the monitor.

When Smith read the latest report, he dropped the aspirin bottle. It struck the corner of the desk and scattered rattling pink pills across the onyx surface.

His stomach churned fiery hot acid. He did not move. His bottle of Maalox remained untouched.

Remo had heard the pill bottle drop, heard the panicked wheezing struggling past Smith's dry lips.

"What's wrong, Smitty?" he asked worriedly.

Smith's eyes were locked, mesmerized, on the canted computer screen. When he spoke, his voice was that of an automaton, drained of anything remotely approaching human emotion. "I am afraid we have our symbol," Smith croaked. "Unfortunately, the other side has reached it first."

12

It was the largest permanent movie set ever built outside of California.

The exact replica of the San Antonio de Valero Mission in Bakerstownship, Texas, was not the usual Hollywood set. For one thing there were four walls, not the usual one-wall facade. No lumber propped up this structure. Adobe artisans from Mexico had been brought in to help with construction of this painstaking reproduction. Historians had been on hand to offer advice, so attention to period detail had been as precise as humanly possible. The walls were of such solid construction that they could withstand direct nineteenth-century cannon fire without buckling.

Cottonwood trees had been planted in the dry ground around the mission, and unlike the desert trees that had dotted the landscape around the original site, the trees at this facsimile were carefully maintained by a full-time landscaper. The name of the tree in Spanish was *alamo* and it was said that it was from this word that the original mission in San Antonio and this movie set counterpart in Bakerstownship had gotten their famous name.

The replica Alamo had been constructed in 1957 for director John Ford for his classic, *Remember the Alamo*, a Warner Brothers picture starring Jimmy Stewart, Henry Fonda, Glenn Ford and a young Clint Eastwood in one of his early movie roles.

In many ways, the movie set was superior to the actual Alamo. It was difficult for a tourist at the real Alamo to get a sense of history. Although the blood of Texan heroes had been spilled there, and although the actual period costumes and weapons were on display, San Antonio was hardly the lonely frontier outpost it had been in 1836.

The movie set had been built to scale, was deliberately rough in design and had been constructed in the middle of four hundred empty acres of Texas ranch land. Although their bodies had bled their last many miles away, on a cold night, the wind blowing dust up the old trails from Mexico, it was easier to imagine the spirits of Jim Bowie and Davy Crockett finding peace at a lonely movie set out in the middle of nowhere than amid the hustle and bustle of modern-day San Antonio.

Since that first 1957 movie, many other Hollywood productions had utilized the set. It had appeared in over sixty television and movie productions, as well as a handful of music videos. When it was not in use for films, the site was a tourist attraction, open 364 days a year. Greenhorns on vacation from Massachusetts as well as retired Texas school-teachers on day trips could scurry along the walls, trading make-believe shots with an invading Mexican army.

The site had grown over the years and, thanks to the influx of tourist and Hollywood dollars, an entire nineteenth-century town had been constructed behind the mission. The town made the area even more attractive to Hollywood producers, and visitors could walk the wooden sidewalks, snap photos in front of genuine hitching posts and order drinks—root beer only—at the town's one saloon.

On the day that would end with a whole new generation of Americans shouting "Remember the Alamo!" Barry Rutherford and his wife Maggie had just left the Alamo gift shop with their ten-year-old son, Billy.

Maggie was pulling the twenty-six-dollar price tag off the white felt cowboy hat she had just bought. As her husband scowled, she stuck the hat on their son's head.

"I don't think we should be letting the boy wear that thing," Barry complained as Billy ran off, pretending to shoot at imaginary Indians. "You know who wears cowboy hats these days. News flash: It ain't cowboys."

"Oh, don't be such a spoilsport," Maggie said. "Besides, the label says it's authentic Texas."

"Authentic Texas made in Thailand," Barry grunted.

Barry was an RV salesman from Amarillo who was as proud of his Texas heritage as he was nervous about leaving his brother-in-law in charge of his dealership. If it were up to Barry he would never take a vacation, but Maggie always insisted, and so once a year the family loaded up the mobile home for their annual trek around the state.

Barry insisted that there was nothing worthwhile beyond the borders of Texas; at least nothing he was interested in seeing. He allowed that the Grand Canyon might be all right, but it was not worth the risk to drive all the way to Arizona just to be disappointed. Barry had nearly been in Oklahoma once but had made a narrow escape.

He motioned to his son and then scraped the toe of his shoe on the ground.

"This is what they did here, Billy. In a place just like this."

Billy looked down at the line in the dirt, not understanding. His father's voice was soft, as if he were recalling a childhood memory.

"There were one hundred and eighty men," Barry said.

"Out there were six thousand Mexican troops. The commander of the Alamo drew a line in the dirt and asked everyone who would fight for Texas and for freedom to step across the line. They all did and they all knew they were going to die."

"Why'd they do that?" Billy asked. "Who wants to die?"

"Because freedom is worth a life," his father said. "They were heroes. The first real Texans. You're here because of them."

Billy nodded. Although he did not understand it all, he realized that something here in this funny-looking old place meant a great deal to his father, and if Dad thought it was important, then it probably was just the most important thing there ever was.

He dutifully registered that thought for a full five seconds and then ran ahead, waving an index finger over his head as if it were a gun.

"That's how it happened? They all stayed? All one hundred and eighty of them?" Maggie asked her husband.

"Well, one of them hightailed out of here. He was a Frenchman. What else is new?"

Maggie laughed as they walked along the wooden sidewalk. "Should we get some lunch?"

"At these prices?" Barry said. "Are you nuts? We've got bread and bologna back in the RV."

Up ahead, Billy dropped and rolled in the dirt, coming up on one knee and shooting two fingers back at his parents.

"You're dead, Dad!" Billy yelled.

Barry did his best to ignore his son's antics.

"Barry, it is our vacation," Maggie snapped. "You do not have to pinch every penny every minute of every . . ."

The Rutherfords stopped dead.

They had rounded the corner near the saloon. Beyond the blacksmith's shop, the mission baked in the morning sun.

A group of curious tourists was gathered in the street, along with several Alamo employees. The focus of the guests' attention was not the nineteenth-century town, the workers in period costume, or the mission that loomed above all.

Something blockish and drab green was rattling up the dusty main street. Buildings shook as it passed.

"Excuse me," Maggie complained to a nearby tour guide. "I do not think that tanks are period specific."

The tour guide seemed baffled by the appearance of modern battle machinery in the otherwise authentic period town. He hustled over to the slowly moving tank.

"Texas history probably isn't exciting enough for this modern generation, what with MTV and all," Barry said, rolling his eyes in disgust. "Let's just throw in some tanks to make the Alamo more fun. Heck, I know. Why not add some Nazis in go-go boots? Can we go now?"

The tank was an M32 Chenca refit. Rolling treads gouged deep tracks and threw clouds of choking dust into the air.

"Here! Stop that! Hey, you!"

The tour guide was trotting alongside the slowly moving tank. The tank continued to roll forward.

The tour guide shrugged helplessly, waited for the deadly treads to roll past, then fell in behind the tank. Barry lost sight of the man for a moment, and when next he saw him the tour guide was climbing up to the turret.

"Stop!" the guide yelled and pounded a flat palm repeatedly on the top hatch.

As if in response, the diesel engine spluttered and coughed. For a moment it sounded as if it would stall, but then the tank halted, its engine idling.

As the hatch creaked open, the tour guide smiled and offered a thumbs-up to the crowd of tourists.

"I knew it," Barry complained to his wife. "It's all part of the got-danged show." Before he saw what crazy thing they had coming out of that hatch—probably someone in a cartoon owl costume warning kids to stay in school—he turned to find his son. "Billy! C'mon, we're going."

The sharp report of a single shot cracked the air.

Barry Rutherford had been shooting guns since he was old enough to go hunting with his father. On the target range and in the field he had heard many a live shot. And he had been to his share of rodeos in his day and had heard plenty of blanks. To Barry Rutherford, the gunshot that echoed across the replica Western village sounded dangerously real.

He looked back to the tank.

There was a man with a rifle peeking out of the turret. The tour guide who had stopped the tank was falling from turret, to tread, to the ground.

Barry had attended the 9:00 a.m. Wild West Show with his wife and son that very morning. There had been plenty of blanks fired then, and lots of men falling to the ground. One even broke through a railing and fell from the second story of the saloon. After, he had gotten up, dusted himself off and waved to the applauding crowd.

But this time was different. For one thing, if this were part of a staged act, where was the rest of the tour guide's head?

The guide's skull looked like a cracked egg. Fragments of brain, bone and blood scattered, red and glistening wet, on the dusty road. The crowd gasped, horrified.

A woman beside Barry screamed. As if her cry were a cue, sudden movement erupted at the distant fringes of the town. Armed soldiers were swarming into the reproduction village. Most wore modern uniforms, but mixed in with these were outfits similar to the Mexican Army uniforms on display in the mission.

The tank hatch slammed shut and the engine rumbled to life once more. The big diesel motor coughed and the tank jerked forward. Treads caught a wooden sidewalk. Wood splintered as the behemoth rolled inexorably forward.

Maggie Rutherford stood, stunned. As the troops advanced, Barry grabbed his wife's arm and pulled her into the street. "Billy!" he yelled. His son came running.

A thrill of fear coursed through the crowd.

The soldiers were advancing from the direction of the parking lot. There was only one way to go.

"This way!" Barry cried.

With Barry in the lead, the crowd ran in the direction away from the soldiers.

Gunfire erupted behind them. People screamed. Some fell, crimson stains blossoming on vacation clothes. Frightened tourists and workers fled buildings, stumbling, falling. Men grabbed children into their arms.

Behind, the tank rumbled forward, spluttered a few more times before creaking to a stop. In Spanish, a muffled shout complained about running out of gas.

Around the edge of the town raced the crowd, now nearly forty strong. The mission building loomed ahead.

From behind, more gunshots. Men and women fell. Some staggered to their feet, others were hauled up. Limping from injuries, they stumbled forward.

The crowd flooded the front gates of the Alamo. Barry made certain his wife and son were safely inside. At the door, he waved the rest through.

"Inside!" Barry commanded. "Move, move!"

The soldiers had rounded the corner and were racing toward the mission.

A car suddenly appeared from the edge of the village.

The big green Pontiac with Texas license plates bounced a big rut in the road and was momentarily airborne. Two soldiers in antiquated costume whirled and opened fire on the car, shattering the windshield. When the car hit ground, it wiped out both men. Crumpled bodies flew high in the air.

The car screeched to a sideways stop in front of the closing doors, sending up a cloud of dust.

The driver, a man in late middle age, jumped out and popped the trunk. "Here!" he shouted at Barry.

A hunting rifle, three shotguns and a few cases of shells

were scavenged from the trunk. As bullets pinged off the Pontiac, the two men raced inside the mission.

"Close the doors!" Barry shouted.

Inside, the heavy doors were shut and barred. Candy and soda machines were dragged in to fortify the main entrance. Employees were dispatched to seal up doors and windows around the mission.

"Where's the safest place in here?" Barry demanded of a numb-looking young woman in nineteenth-century costume.

"Uh . . . I don't know. The souvenir shop maybe."

"Get the children and elderly in there," Barry snapped. "Maggie, help her."

Barry's wife dutifully began rounding up crying children and confused elderly and herding them toward the rear gift shop. Woodenly, the young female employee joined her.

Pounding sounded outside the door. Muffled shouts of angry Spanish. Muted gunshots thumped the thick door. Inside the mission, the three guns were hastily loaded and passed out. Fire axes were taken down from walls. Display cases were shattered and period weapons were removed. Without ammunition, they would be of use only as clubs.

A sudden explosion rocked the ground beneath their feet. Dust burst from hidden crevices all around the front wall.

"What the hell was that?" someone asked, in a voice pleading understanding.

Barry and several of the men scampered up ladders to the catwalk that ran the length of the mission wall.

When he gazed out across the rural Texas landscape, Barry Rutherford felt as if he had been propelled back in time one hundred and seventy-one years.

Acrid smoke twisted like an angry black serpent into the clear Texas sky.

The tank had managed to crawl a little farther along before spluttering to a final stop. It was just visible near the corner of the blacksmith's shop. A single mortar shot had struck the road near the Pontiac, flipping the car up against the doors as an accidental barricade.

And swarming toward the mission were dozens, scores, hundreds of Mexican Army soldiers. They came from every direction. From the village, and from the parking area. Others picked their way past cottonwood and sagebrush. In the distant desert, clouds from moving convoys rose into the clear blue sky.

The tank turret spun. It was still out of range. Soldiers raced off to siphon gas from cars in the lot.

The defenders on the makeshift battlements of the Alamo had gone white with fear. A few shots rang out from the ground, zinging around their ears. An aluminum extension ladder had been liberated from the groundskeeper's shed. Soldiers carried it over their heads to the front wall.

And through it all, one man remained a sea of calm.

"Save your shots," ordered Barry Rutherford who did not expect that by sunset his name would be inscribed alongside those of other great Texas heroes. "We gotta make every bullet count."

13

Cell phones alerted authorities to the attack. By noon the tiny rural community of Bakerstownship was clogged with state and local police, as well as national media who had reluctantly taken a day off from covering American military atrocities, generally involving shooting back at people who were trying to kill them.

The first news helicopters that had attempted to fly over the mission and adjacent western town had been shot at by Mexican-uniformed soldiers on the ground. Airspace above the Alamo movie set was now restricted, closed to all but police aircraft. Law enforcement helicopters secured the cordon, flying out of range of sniper fire.

By the time the authorities had arrived on the scene, the renegade soldiers, six hundred strong, had dug into their positions around the mission site. Trenches were shoveled out and barricades constructed to hold off any who might try to storm the area. The village itself had become a base of operations for the suddenly-appearing army.

The governor had yet to mobilize the National Guard. Word was that Washington had called for restraint and was consulting with the Mexican government but the U.S. Army was said to be massing.

Before they had been chased from the scene, the first news helicopters had caught images of outnumbered Alamo defenders repelling waves of invaders. It seemed the attackers had not thought of what to do if those trapped at the site followed the lead of their nineteenth-century counterparts. The attackers had only one ladder, which was repeatedly knocked over by those on the walls of the mission. Dozens of soldiers had been killed or injured by the fall. Bodies littered the ground around the mission.

An attempt was made to stack wagons and wooden barrels against the wall to use as a makeshift platform to mount the battlements. Burning arrows fired from within the Alamo walls had thwarted this plan. The result was a dozen serious fire-related injuries and three more Mexican dead. The massive mission doors had yet to be breached. Video taken before the airspace had been secured by police showed a 1977 Pontiac that had somehow flipped on its side and become wedged against the main entrance. The attackers could not get close enough to pry the car loose. Several who had tried to do so early in the siege now lay dead, crushed beneath a three-hundred-pound glass display case that had been heaved out a window of the mission.

Flags of several states, liberated from displays within the mission, were flying on the roof.

To anyone watching, it was a valiant effort but one that faced inevitable ultimate doom. There was no way a band of sixty virtually unarmed tourists and roadside attraction employees could continue to hold off an army of six hundred.

This gloomy thought passed through the mind of Walter Morrison, the Texas Ranger who had been assigned to monitor the siege. He was a man of action, and as he paced beside his Range Rover, Morrison felt a swelling urge to hit, kick or shoot someone.

An armchair psychiatrist might suggest that Morrison was out to prove something. At five feet, five inches, he was the smallest Ranger in all of Texas. Added to that was the fact that he was as bald as a baby's behind. Morrison had lost all of his hair by the time he was thirty. The wig he had been wearing for the past twenty years was not exactly top of the line when new, and in the intervening years had grown worse with constant wear. The frazzled toupee now looked as if it had been crocheted from red horse hair.

Adjusting his wig, Morrison paced back and forth at his command post outside the cordon he and local authorities had set up around the old movie set. He had two hundred heavily armed men at his command, but had been ordered to stay put. Rumor had it that a special team from Homeland Security would be arriving soon.

Morrison had no idea what such a team thought it could do against an army. Besides, there was no need to be patient. It was not like this new Santa Anna, whoever he might be, was here and, as far as Morrison was concerned, getting the renegade general alive seemed the only justification for holding back.

Walter Morrison knew one thing. If Santa Anna had been here, orders or no orders, the Texas Ranger would have marched in to the fire zone himself and given the Mexican general a thumping he would never forget.

Flipping his red mullet, Walter Morrison, Texas Ranger, spun on the heel of his cowboy boots and paced back to his car.

Half a mile down the road, another Ranger waved Remo, Chiun and Conchita Diaz through the first police barricade.

Remo told Conchita, "You know, you don't have to keep sticking with us."

"I must," Conchita said firmly.

Since yesterday's rally in Albuquerque, she had tagged along with Remo and Chiun in their vain attempt to follow Santa Anna's money trail.

In all their time together, Conchita had not told Remo about her aunt's dream. She knew that Remo would think it ridiculous. In truth, Conchita felt foolish for believing it herself. Yet the abilities these men had displayed were otherworldly, and if she was to have any chance at all of finding her missing cousin and his family, she knew that she would have to remain close to these two men.

"You would not understand, Remo," she told him.

"Probably not," Remo said. "But it's your funeral."

At another police cordon, Remo flashed his Department of Homeland Security identification. Over the years, Smith had always kept him supplied with various governmental IDs, but in recent years Remo had found greatest success with the DHS badge. Since the cabinet department was relatively new, many still seemed unsure what the badge was supposed to look like, or what authority it granted the bearer.

Remo told Chiun, "Now leave this one to me."

"Why, pray tell?"

"Secrecy," Remo said. "Smith wants us to try to get in and out of here without getting noticed or winding up on the TV news. That'd be the kiss of death for CURE."

"So the emperor wants us to fight an entire army without calling attention to ourselves."

"Exactly."

"Exactly lunacy," Chiun said. "Is someone going to tell the other side not to notice us?"

"Details, details," Remo said.

A somber Texas Ranger pointed out the man in charge, an angry-faced little man with a ridiculous wig that looked like it had been mugged off a mop. The man's badge identified him as Walter Morrison, Texas Ranger.

Chiun saw him and said, "What is that creature wearing on his head?"

"A bad wig having a bad artificial hair day. Now lighten up; these are the Texas Rangers and they're pretty good."

"Pfffft."

"Ranger, we've got to talk," Remo said.

"Who the hell are you?" Morrison demanded.

Remo showed his "Remo Bloomberg" Homeland Security ID.

Morrison's beady eyes strayed from Remo to the ancient figure standing beside him. The old man looked as if a stiff wind would blow him from here clear to Amarillo.

"You've got to be kidding me," Morrison growled. "This is what I've been waiting for? My big salvation from Washington is you, Fu Manchu here, and a woman? No. No way. That's it. Get out of here, you three. Before I have you arrested. I'm taking charge here." He turned toward a group of Rangers standing near some sawhorses.

Before he could bark an order, Remo leaned toward him, and said softly. "Are you a real Ranger or just a blowhard?"

"What does that mean?" Morrison snapped.

"I grew up hearing about you guys. How you were the best. Now I want to know, do you believe in your slogan or not?"

"What slogan?"

"One riot, one Ranger."

"That's what we live by."

"All right. We got one riot here and I need one Ranger. I need you."

Morrison hesitated for a few seconds. "Okay," he finally said. "But they'll probably send me to the nuthouse for this one. . . ."

"You'll have to wait your turn," Chiun said.

". . . But what do you want?"

"Two things. One, give us fifteen minutes and then you follow us. There'll be prisoners coming out. You herd them toward your men and get them the hell out of here. That's the easy part."

"And the hard part?" Morrison asked.

"When it's done, it was strictly a Texas Ranger operation. You never saw us; you don't know who we are. As far as the world is concerned, we were never here. And keep the damned press away."

"I should have my head examined," the Ranger said. "But go. I'll give you fifteen minutes and then I'll follow."

Remo nodded, then told Conchita, "You'll have to stay here."

"No, Remo," she said firmly. "This is my country as much as it is yours. I have an obligation and a right to defend it."

Remo held up his hand, warding off further protest. "Look, you don't have to prove anything to anyone. You're an American. Fine. We're a nation of immigrants, blah-blah. I get the drill. But there's an entire army in there, and Chiun and I are going to have it tough enough without having to watch out for you. Right, Chiun?"

"Do whatever you wish," Chiun said indifferently. "I will not be watching out for anyone other than me."

Conchita was tensed for an argument, but then the fight drained out of her. Nodding, she turned from them, thought better and, spinning back, threw her arms around Remo's neck and kissed his cheek.

Beside them, Chiun hissed disgust at the public display. Once Remo had disengaged, she spun away, bravely offering him her back. Remo winked broadly at Chiun. Chiun looked around as if searching for a place to throw up.

Side by side, the two Masters of Sinanju left the final barricade and headed onto the grounds of the Alamo.

As they approached the site of the siege, Chiun grew increasingly suspicious. Observing the sun's position in the sky for guidance, he finally shook his age-speckled head.

"Either Smith is more deranged than usual, or this mission is not in the right place," the old Korean insisted.

"Smitty says it's a replica of the real Alamo. They built it for some movie or something."

Chiun's face immediately soured. "I have seen some of your movies on this subject." He clucked his tongue unhappily. "What passes for entertainment in this country. You could at least get some of your facts right."

"Since when are you an expert on the Alamo?"

"Since you whites get everything wrong, which is forever," Chiun replied.

They were moving now through scrub brush. Far ahead, from the mission, they could hear an occasional rifle shot.

"So what facts are wrong about the Alamo?" Remo asked.

Chiun's eyes became suspicious vellum slits, yet a hint of a smile brushed the corners of his own papery lips.

"Everything. Now no more questions," the old Korean commanded. "Lest the state take you away from me on a little bus, and I am forced to end my days on this earth listening to the neighbors complain about how poorly you bag their groceries."

"Eggs on top, watermelon on bottom," Remo said, still grinning. And then a light blinked on over Remo's head. "We were at the Alamo, weren't we?" he said, snapping his fingers. "The House of Sinanju was here."

"We were in the correct place, not this make-believe amusement park."

"Let's see. Who would have been Master in the 1800s? Ik was succeeded by H'si T'ang. It was Ik, right? So what was good old Master Ik doing at the Alamo?"

Chiun ignored the smug expression on his pupil's face. "I have told you that Sinanju sought employment from Santa Anna, but found Mexico too poor to afford our services," the old Korean said. "So Ik, on his return, encountered Samuel Houston, and for a small fee, the Master revealed to Houston some of Santa Anna's war plans he had learned while in Mexico. Houston was grateful for the information, and offered to hire the Master on the spot. But this region was still a part of Mexico, and much money had already been spent on an army to fight Santa Anna. The rebels could little more afford the Master than could Santa Anna. Still, a little money was paid, and so as not to have wasted entirely a trip to this new continent, the Master did travel to the real Alamo. And Ik was there when Santa Anna's force of six thousand men swarmed this doomed mission in the middle of nowhere. And the Master aided the rebel defenders, but, in truth, he did no more than was required of him, for the gold he had been paid was a paltry sum. And on the thirteenth day when Ik had determined that payment for his services had run out, he allowed history to take its natural course."

Chiun padded along up the dusty desert road, allowing the tale of Master Ik to sink in. Sometimes with white skulls that could take days. This time was less.

"Little Father, that is a horrible story," Remo said. "By the sounds of it Ik did a half-assed job helping, let the Alamo guys do all the heavy lifting, and then, when the cash ran out, he let Santa Anna overrun the place."

"Samuel Houston did not think it so horrible," Chiun replied. "In the time that Santa Anna was forced to waste at the Alamo, thanks to Master Ik, Houston was able to raise an army to battle the Mexican general. He rewarded Ik more generously when next they met. So much so, that Ik felt obligated to do a little something extra for the additional gold."

"Like what? Eat a sandwich? Take a nap?"

Chiun stroked his thread of beard. "Something about helping Houston rout Santa Anna at the battle of San Jacinto. But in truth, Remo, it did not take much, for the forces were, after all, Mexican. And Ik was already irritated at Santa Anna for making him waste a trip all the way from

Sinanju, so he was more motivated to pitch in than he was at the Alamo. When he delivered the defeated general to him, Houston, like your madman Smith, refused the Mexican's head."

"So you're saying that Master Ik helped win Texas its independence."

"I doubt Ik would have aided Houston if he knew the mess you whites were going to make of his hard work. Why Texas chose to throw in with the United States rather than become a separate nation is beyond me."

A thought occurred to Remo. "Wait a second. You're saying now that Ik was here first. I thought H'si T'ang took credit for discovering America. Not to mention you too. And while we're at it, I seem to recall about five other masters staking their claim in there too."

Chiun shrugged, a move that scarcely lifted his bony shoulders. "Look around you. Can you blame us for wanting to forget a place like this?" Before Remo could object, a slender finger brushed papery lips. "Silence."

Remo had heard them as well.

The six soldiers had dug a foxhole in the sagebrush beside the road. As they approached, Remo and Chiun could hear the labored breathing of the hidden men as well as six nervous heartbeats. The soldiers did not hear Remo and Chiun approach. To move things along, Remo stamped his feet and hooted to get their attention.

This got a reaction. From the bushes, several urgent voices whispered hoarsely in Spanish.

Remo glanced at the Master of Sinanju. "Were they this bad back in Ik's day?"

"If you think they are bad, try Belgian soldiers," the old Korean said. "They make the French look like Huns."

Remo heaved some rocks into the bushes. "Don't make me come in there," he warned.

In the foxhole, a decision had already been made. As one, the men charged up out of the underbrush.

They had expected to encounter armed U.S. troops. When they saw the two unarmed men on the path before them, their war screams turned to whoops of triumph.

"Yeah, yeah," Remo said. "Rah-rah for the team. So where's Santa Anna? We only surrender to him."

One uncooperative soldier responded with hostility, shoving his bayonet at Remo's belly. Remo responded with more hostility, sticking the bayonet through the soldier's head. His hands were so fast, none save Chiun had seen him move. The remaining five soldiers watched, jaws dropping wide, as their comrade collapsed to the dust.

"Santa Anna?" Remo repeated.

As one, the soldiers threw down their weapons, threw up their hands and shook their heads desperately. A torrent of unintelligible Spanish exploded from their lips.

"They say they do not know where the general is," the Master of Sinanju said. "He is not part of this force."

"Damn," Remo said. "I hoped he'd be here. Why isn't anything ever neat for me?"

Frowning at the line of terrified Mexican soldiers, Remo planted his hands on his hips and sighed.

"Okay, here's the deal," Remo announced to the men. "America." He pointed to the ground. "A-me-ri-ca," he repeated, smiling and nodding.

He pointed south. "Mexico," he said, now frowning sternly. "Mex-i-co."

"Yoooou," he said, drawing out the word as he pointed to the five men, each one in turn. "Go." He waved both hands sharply south. "Mexico. Or . . ." He raised an instructive finger. ". . . Stabby-stabby in head." To demonstrate, he drew the bayonet in and out of their dead comrade's skull.

By the time Remo stomped his foot, pointed south and shouted "Vamanos!" the men were already stumbling over their own feet in their haste to depart. A moment later, Remo saw Ranger Morrison herding the men back toward the Ranger camp. They scrambled through brush, plowed into cacti and ran, yelping and screaming, all the way to the border.

Chiun was shaking his head in silent disapproval.

"Hey, don't knock it," Remo said to his teacher. "You learned a hundred languages, I learned the one you taught me: fear. Now let's find some more of these mopes."

Together, the two Masters of Sinanju struck off up the dirt desert path.

14

In a rundown old ranch complex just a handful of
miles across the border into Mexico, Rebecca Dalton listened to the latest news out of the United States and doodled with a red pen on a pad of yellow legal paper.

Usually when Rebecca doodled, it was mostly hearts
with arrows through them, unicorns with pretty bows in
their manes, and cute little fuzzy teddy bears. She always
doodled with a red pen, because red was warm and inviting.

Today, Rebecca wished she had a black pen. Today, Rebecca Dalton was not in a very unicorn mood.

Rebecca finished drawing a very severe frowny face,
which she underlined three times. After adding two excla-
mation marks, she glanced at the television.

"We aren't permitted inside the airspace directly over
the tourist site, but these are live images from the desert
just a few acres outside the western village, Katie."

The veil of night was drawing closed over Texas.

The bouncing helicopter video showed soldiers running across the desert toward Mexico. Rebecca counted over forty men. Last time there had been thirty. They were fleeing in bunches, gathering up more men as they ran. They all seemed to be herded by one small Texas Ranger. Over the course of the afternoon, the TV had told her that over four hundred men had fled the tourist site in Bakerstownship.

"Something must have scared them into retreat, Katie," the newsman at the scene said. "We're told, however, that a large assault force is still outside the Alamo mission."

Rebecca tried to concentrate on the TV, but two things were distracting her. The first was outside. The thin wooden walls of the ranch were not enough to keep out the sound of marching feet and men shouting in unison. The second distraction was in the room with Rebecca. Behind her it seemed as if a buzz saw was cutting through wet wood.

She suddenly found herself grinding her molars in anger, which was so unlike her that it surprised and annoyed her. Then she realized that being surprised or annoyed was unlike her as well. She liked to concentrate on the happy aspects of life. There was far too much negativity in the world.

The buzz saw gulped, swallowed and began sawing again, more loudly than before.

Rebecca closed her eyes. "One, two, three. . . ."

As she counted, she breathed in and out through her nose. She rarely needed the relaxation technique. Why would she? After all, she was such a bubbly personality. Only a silly billy needed to force themselves calm . . .

The buzz saw noise again.

With a feral scream, Rebecca Dalton leaped to her feet, grabbed a glass end table and heaved it with all her might against the wall. Her note pad and pen went sailing, and the table shattered into a thousand pieces.

She paused, took a deep breath, exhaled.

"Eight, nine, ten," Rebecca said perkily. She smoothed invisible lines in her spotless, cream-colored slacks.

Behind her, the buzz saw continued to buzz, oblivious to Rebecca Dalton's outburst. She did an about-face to the noise, planted her hands on her hips, and put on her best exasperated June Cleaver face.

"Jumpin' gee willickers, but you can sure get on a gal's nerves," she said, sighing.

The snoring lump which was emitting the buzz saw squall grunted and scratched itself.

In repose, Santa Anna was not the same impressive figure he had been the previous day.

The hero of millions and herald of the new nation of Nuevo Mexico was passed out on a sofa. The tequila bottle he had been suckling from had rolled a dribbling caramel-colored arc across the dry floor, coming to a rest against a sofa leg.

Santa Anna had peeled off his uniform trousers and thrown them over a bowl of untouched fresh fruit on the dining room table. Stubby, furry legs assaulted a sofa cushion. He still wore his uniform jacket, but all the buttons were undone. A wife-beater undershirt barely contained his ponderous belly. The nauseating gap between undershirt and too-tight BVDs displayed a thick thatch of fur as well as an elongated slit that was the only visible hint of a long-vanished belly button.

In his sleep, Santa Anna stuck his finger in the belly button slit and scratched around a bit. When, still snoring, he stopped long enough to sniff the finger, Rebecca threw up her hands. "Well, that's the end for me, mister."

She marched into the bedroom. A moment later she reappeared with a bed sheet and tossed the sheet over the bloated, unconscious man. Santa Anna grunted a sleepy complaint and rolled onto his side.

"There," she said, once the general was covered. "I know I should appreciate the beauty in all God's creatures, but even art gets covered when it's a work in progress, and you, sir, are most definitely still a work in progress."

THE NEW DESTROYER: GUARDIAN ANGEL   187

She was thinking about how easy it would be to kill Santa Anna—slit his throat as he slept and the snoring would stop—when a sudden chirping sounded across the room.

Rebecca had set her cell phone to ring the tune to *I Dream of Jeannie*, by far the most adorable ring tone she could find.

When she checked her purse to see who was calling, she blew a lock of blond hair from over her eye and frowned.

P. WORTHINGTON. The name was followed by a home number.

"I have too many clients," Rebecca sighed.

She dropped the ringing phone back in her purse. She would talk to him later. First she wanted to think.

Rebecca sat back down in front of the TV.

More footage of soldiers fleeing. Santa Anna had not been as great an inspiration as everyone had hoped. These men were so ginned up, they should have fought to the death for their general, but instead they were running like scared bunnies. Of course, Rebecca knew the reason.

"Remo, you are just a peach," she said.

It was Remo and the old Master of Sinanju. It had to be. The American military had not gone in. According to news reports, the Texas authorities had not entered the site. She had seen only one Ranger, a curious little man, and all he seemed to be doing was herding the Mexican soldiers into the waiting arms of other Rangers. There was no logical reason why the soldiers should have suddenly fled, clearly propelled by blind terror.

But, as her old mentor Benson Dilkes always said, if something didn't make logical sense in this business, look to the assassins from the East.

In the small Mexican ranch, Rebecca Dalton snapped off the television. She had seen enough fleeing soldiers, and had had enough of the men from Sinanju.

"You fellas are tough bugs to squash, I'll give you that," she said.

With the TV off, the sounds of marching and shouting outside grew louder. In the distance she could hear gunfire.

She walked over to the window.

Hastily assembled barracks had been built around a central compound. Soldiers in livery inspired by nineteenth-century Mexican army uniforms marched to the shouted commands of drill sergeants. In the unseen distance, the crackle of rifle fire echoed from the shooting range.

Santa Anna's ranch was the centerpiece of the military base. Painted white rocks lined the packed dirt path that led to the front porch. Peeking out from beside the ranch, Rebecca could just spy the distant helipad and the drooping rotor blades of her private helicopter.

She could start up that helicopter and fly to safety. Benson Dilkes had done so once, before he had gotten it into his fool head to take on the Masters of Sinanju. She had made a considerable name for herself in the past five years. There was plenty of work for a person of her skills anywhere in the Third World.

But Rebecca was obsessive about her work. She liked to finish what she started and the thought of unfinished business would nag at her.

The snoring behind her abruptly stopped.

On the couch, General Santa Anna blearily opened his eyes. Searching with one hand, he found his tequila bottle. Draining the last few drops into his gullet, he dropped the bottle back to the floor, kicked off the sheet Rebecca had draped over him, and promptly fell back to sleep.

Rebecca drew the blinds.

"There's more than one way to skin a cat," she said.

Rebecca retrieved her cell phone from her purse. She had to wait five minutes to negotiate through the automated system, but once she had pressed enough 1's and 3's, a human voice at last came on the line.

"MacroWare Systems, Incorporated. My name is Stephanie. How may I direct your call?"

"Why, hello there, Stephanie, aren't you sweet," Rebecca said, her voice as sunny as a Kansas state fair in August. "I'm looking for the number of an employee of yours. A pretty little thing. Her name is Conchita Diaz."

15

Dusk was setting in by the time Remo and Chiun
had cleaned out the nests of Mexican soldiers hidden in the
acres surrounding the Alamo tourist site. The two men had
worked separately, chasing the Mexicans back toward
Ranger Morrison, and now they finally met up again at the
western town next to the reconstructed Alamo mission.

But the town now was deserted.

Frantic radio calls from the main attack force out in the
brush had sent word of unstoppable wraiths bringing death
and destruction. Although the reports were questioned as
incredible, as a precaution the soldiers who had taken up
position in the town had been pulled out for a final major
assault on the mission. Once the Alamo fell, the attackers
reasoned, they would have a stronger position from which
to defend against whatever terrible assault force America
had unleashed.

That assault force was currently strolling up the main

street of the Wild West village and wondering where everyone had wandered off to.

"It's like a ghost town," Remo said. He noted not a single heartbeat in any of the buildings they passed.

"That is preferable to the alternative," the Master of Sinanju said, padding along beside his pupil. "Places like this one are usually teeming with men in half-pants, exposing pasty legs without a shred of pride or dignity. Not to mention flabby women pushing unfortunate children around in wheeled infant seats, because heaven forbid an American female burn a calorie lifting the product of one lamentable, drunken Saturday evening."

Remo glanced around the empty town. "You put it that way, it is kind of nice," he admitted.

The raised wooden sidewalk to their right had been shattered under heavy tank treads. Porches had been torn from buildings and had collapsed into kindling. When he saw the broken display window in one particular gift shop, the Master of Sinanju gasped. Stopping, he tugged Remo's sleeve.

Remo looked over. A pile of Davy Crockett hats was stacked up on a rack.

"Get me one," Chiun commanded.

"Don't you already have one of those from that trip we took to Disneyland years ago?"

"Yes, but that one is a collector's item. It was gifted me by the fat Russian leader with the one eyebrow in an act of rare Russian generosity. It is on display back in the Master's House in Sinanju alongside Czar Nicholas's toy train, the last boon a Russian granted a Master of Sinanju."

"I never saw it there, or the train. You sure it's not just wadded up at the bottom of one of your steamer trunks?"

"When next we are in Sinanju I will show you the Russian display. It is in one of the east rooms. Not visited much, because Russian generosity has been on decline since the time of Ivan the Good. But I will have to go in there anyway because that is where we keep the trains, and I must properly display the train set given me by the great American philanthropist Presley Wellburton."

"Prescott Worthington," Remo corrected.

"Blame his parents," Chiun said. "Get me a hat."

Grumbling all the way, Remo climbed over the pile of wood, rusted nails and broken glass, retrieving a Davy Crockett hat.

"Not that one, the other one," Chiun called.

"They're all the same."

"The other one," Chiun commanded.

Remo pawed through sixteen hats until he found the right other one. After, they marched up the road, Chiun proudly flipping the furry tail of his hat with every step.

"I'm probably going to need a tetanus shot," Remo said.

"Perhaps these men will be generous enough to shoot you," Chiun said, flipping his tail to point at the stalled tank in the road ahead.

An attempt had been made to siphon gasoline from cars in the parking lot outside the mission, but the only things the soldiers had been able to find to transport the gas were mugs from the saloon. So most of the gas was lost in the parking lot or en route, and nearly all of what made it back had been poured onto the outside of the tank and on the ground around it.

Although the tank had not moved from where it had last stalled, a crew still manned the machine. When the gringo with the dead eyes and the old Asian the soldiers had been hearing about all afternoon appeared on the main road of the reproduction Wild West town, the men were ready.

The hatch slammed shut and the turret swung ominously in Remo and Chiun's direction.

The explosion from the muzzle and the subsequent mortar blast shook the small reproduction village. When the dust and smoke cleared, the tank crew peered out a tiny slit.

There was a smoldering crater in the road where the two men had been, but no sign of twisted bodies. The soldiers assumed they had blasted the intruders to smithereens. They assumed this right up until a pair of deepset dark eyes suddenly sprang up on the other side of the peephole.

"Yo quiero Taco Bell," Remo called.

Panic erupted inside the cramped tank. The men scampered back from the peephole.

Outside, Remo hopped down from the tank.

"I don't think they're coming out, Little Father," he said. He knocked on the side of the tank. "That right?"

"No," several frightened voices called.

"Damn. I hate disassembling these things." He started to climb up to the turret, but the Master of Sinanju restrained him.

"Why must you do everything the hard way?" Chiun said.

The old Korean stooped down next to the tank. Rubbing thumb and index finger together, his fingertips became a friction blur. There was the briefest puff of smoke followed by a bright burst of flame as the gasoline that had been dumped all over the ground around the tank ignited.

The flames shot up the gas-soaked treads and zipped around the body of the tank. By the time the flame and heat ignited the explosives inside, Remo and Chiun were already on the other side of the blacksmith's shop. As metal rained down around them, Chiun happily flipped the tail of his hat.

"I don't know why you'd want another one of those mangy things," Remo said. He had to step over a smoking leg that had splattered to the ground in his path.

"Because that other one is for the ages," Chiun said. "I want one for me."

Suddenly, they heard a burst of gunfire from the mission.

The Battle for the Alamo II, as it had been dubbed by one of the more sensationalistic news networks, was entering its twelfth hour. Power had been cut to the mission.

Torches blazed from high atop the walls. Remo imagined it looked very much as its namesake had when Master Ik had visited 170 years ago.

More than a hundred Mexican soldiers still remained. Many had taken up posts around the big structure. Each time a head appeared on the walls, shots rang out.

The supply of bullets within the fort had been exhausted an hour before. Since then, the attackers had managed to pry the upturned Pontiac from the entrance. As Remo and Chiun approached, fifty screaming Mexican soldiers attacked the doors with a battering ram fashioned from scrap lumber.

With a final, mighty rush, the doors buckled and swung wide. The first wave of soldiers swarmed into the mission. When they saw the doors finally open, the men who had been shooting at the makeshift battlements raced from their positions. In all, a hundred soldiers swarmed into the Alamo.

Remo and Chiun raced in behind them, blended with them, became one with the swarming soldiers. As they ran, their hands shot out, left then right.

Bodies fell. Ten, twenty.

Inside, the swarm broke apart, racing off in every direction. Remo heard the screaming of terrified children. A group of defenders was holding back the army of soldiers attempting to enter the gift shop.

"Chiun, the kids," Remo called.

The Master of Sinanju nodded sharply and raced off to the gift shop. Attacking soldiers launched from his path as if propelled on rockets.

Soldiers swarmed the ladders to the catwalk. The defenders above were already fighting hand to hand against the invaders.

Remo snatched one ladder and lifted it high into the air. Three Mexican soldiers clung desperately to the rungs.

Remo flicked his wrist. The soldiers were still clinging to the ladder when it rocketed up and out a window.

Two soldiers charged him with bayonets. Remo skipped between the men and redirected their blades. The soldiers plowed into one another, each bayonet buried in another's abdomen.

Screams had erupted from the gift shop. From the corner of his eye, Remo saw bodies flying out the open door.

When help arrived, the tourists who had been defending the gift shop seized the opportunity. Wielding knives and using antique guns as clubs, they raced into the swarm of invading soldiers. The Mexican troops seemed taken aback by the ferocity of the defense. Some were already turning, racing back out the door.

The tide on the floor was turning, but on the walls the battle still raged.

With a hop, Remo was scurrying up a ladder. On the way up he harvested bodies like autumn fruit, heaving them onto soldiers on the ground. Remo tore off along the catwalk. "Remember Ik!" he shouted as he ran.

Soldiers tumbled left and right from his path. One soldier charged him, screaming.

"Ik," Remo said, heaving the man out the nearest window. "Ick," he added, when the man splattered on the metal carcass of the overturned Pontiac.

One officer appeared to be directing the troops on the walls. He was screaming angry orders in Spanish down at his soldiers who had thrown down their guns and were running for the mission doors. As Remo raced by the officer, he pulled away the man's gun, flipped him out a window, and fastened the tails of his coat to the adobe with the soldier's bayonet.

"Don't go anywhere," Remo warned.

Leaving the terrified soldier dangling in open air, pinned to the front wall of the Alamo, he ran on.

The battle was nearly over. Some tourists had snatched up abandoned weapons and were giving chase through the Texas countryside. Remo came upon four soldiers still grappling with a lone figure. As Remo approached, one soldier tumbled off the wall and another fell back onto the catwalk, a mortal wound in his chest.

With a clap, Remo fused the skulls of the final two soldiers and tipped the bodies over the side. He knelt before the bloodied man who had led the tourists to victory.

Deep slashes gouged the big man's chest. Fresh blood gurgled from a wound in his neck. His eyes were already glassy. A thick syrup of nearly black blood pushed past lips that were already turning white. Feebly, the stricken man looked up at Remo.

"Did we win?" Barry Rutherford drawled.

Remo nodded to the dying man. "Don't mess with Texas," he said gently.

The big RV salesman tried to smile, but the effort seemed too great and so he did what came easiest and died.

Ranger Morrison and his men had come to secure the mission and Morrison split off from his men and ran toward Remo who was with Chiun alongside the young man's body.

Chiun saw him coming and said to Remo, "He has to get his own hat. He can't have mine."

"I don't know how you did it," Morrison told Remo. "But one fine job."

"You too, Ranger. Now remember our deal. We were never here." He nodded toward the fallen Barry Rutherford. "When you write this up, here's your hero. He's the one who did it all. Add him to the rolls of your honored dead."

"Yes, sir," Morrison said and tossed Remo a precise military salute. "An honor serving with you, sir."

Remo clapped him on the shoulder. "One riot, one ranger. It still works."

16

Before vanishing with Chiun, Remo leaned out the window, pulled out the bayonet and snagged the hanging soldier by the scruff of the neck. He waggled the man out over open space.

"You speakie the English?" he asked. In the blaze of flickering torchlights he was a hell-sent demon.

"Si," the soldier cried. "That is, yes. Yes, I do speak English. Please do not drop me, señor."

"Where can I find Santa Anna?"

"I do not know."

Remo released the soldier. The man fell six inches before Remo snagged him again.

"Oopsie," Remo said. "My butterfingers. You were saying where Santa Anna is?"

"I do not know," the soldier cried.

Remo could see the man was telling the truth. "That uniform," he asked, noting the soldier's nineteenth-century costume. "Where did you get it?"

"They were passing them out."

"Who?" Remo demanded.

"Representatives of General Juan Pichardo."

"Who the hell is he?"

"He is general of all Mexico's armed forces. His men came to us on behalf of the great General Santa Anna."

"Is the whole Mexican Army in this?"

"I do not know," the soldier said. "I believe most are still loyal to Mexico, to the president. But those like me who were born near the border are sympathetic to General Santa Anna."

Remo knew he would learn nothing more from the man.

"You want me to drop you now?" he asked.

"Do not drop me!"

Remo cupped a hand beside his ear. "I didn't quite catch that. Do not what?"

"Drop me!"

"You're the boss," Remo said, releasing the man.

The soldier hit the ground with a fat splat.

Remo looked up to see Conchita Diaz as she rushed in with the crowd.

She called his name, then raced to him and threw her arms around his neck.

Chiun exhaled and turned away. "If you two think that I am raising the baby like so many other grandparents these days, you are as demented as you are debauched."

Conchita did not even hear the old Korean. "I got a phone call," she announced, breathless. "A tip on my cousin's whereabouts."

"Good for you," Remo said. "Let me know how it all turns out."

Conchita's face fell. She pulled away from Remo. "But . . . you are coming with me."

"Pass," Remo said.

"But you must help. We did not meet by chance. You were guided to me for a reason."

"Listen, you're an all right kid," Remo said. "But maybe you haven't noticed that los Estados Unidos is about to go down el crapperillo. I've kind of got my hands full already. You're welcome to tag along." He nodded to the Master of Sinanju. "Chiun?"

The two men turned and headed for the doors.

Conchita Diaz watched them go, helpless to stop them. All around her the madness swirled. Wounded were tended to, husbands were reunited with wives and children, the dead were grieved. And in the midst of it all Conchita Diaz stood, a lost soul, utterly alone, unable to comprehend why the angel she had come to believe in would abandon her in her hour of greatest need.

"The administration's track record on immigration has been, quite frankly, appalling."

Senator Jack Muldoon smiled. It was a smile chiseled in stone. Tight and calculated, it involved only the muscles of his mouth and did not extend to his eyes. The eyes were black and dead. A shark's eyes.

Muldoon's words elicited whooping assent from the largely immigrant audience.

Although he and the president were of the same party, Jack Muldoon was rarely on the same page as the chief executive. In fact, more often than not he broke with his party's leadership in the Senate.

Whenever the senator badmouthed or backstabbed a member of his own party, the press branded him a straight-talking, brave iconoclast, standing up for all that was fine and decent in the world. Whenever he sided with his party's leadership, the exact same press called him a spineless lapdog, incapable of independent thought. Like a lab rat nudged to the food dispenser by the judicious application of electric shocks, Senator Muldoon slowly learned which lever to pull to release pellets of press corps praise. More and more he betrayed principle for favorable write-ups in the *New York Times* and fawning interviews on *Good Morning America*. The term "iconoclastic senator" became a brand that only he could lay claim to.

"I, eer-ah, agree with my good friend Jack," said Senator Ned Clancy. He had to scream to be heard over the cheering. "If there is blame, let it not fall on the immigrants who are, after all, only coming here for the opportunity to make a better life for their families."

Muldoon's frozen grin pulled tighter, as if drawn back to his ears by invisible wires. "Some in my own party say we should blame the current administration in Washington for not enacting stricter illegal immigration laws, or for not enforcing the laws we already have on the books."

The crowd hushed, shocked that Senator Muldoon would be impolite enough to bring up something as gauche as the law at such an event. From the back came a few boos.

Muldoon continued, "I will always give you straight talk, and I say to hell with them, to hell with the administration and to hell with Washington!"

The cheering was so great that, had the rally been indoors, the applause line might literally have brought the house down. Men and women, their faces painted with the flag of Mexico, jumped to their feet and cheered. The earth rumbled beneath thousands of stomping feet.

The outdoor theater had been assembled on the service grounds of the old Worthington Continental Railroad. Three lonely cattle cars rusting on a side track, unused since the 1940s, were all that remained here of the once great Worthington line. Prescott Worthington's private train was sometimes serviced at the site, but even that was not here.

Worthington hated loaning out his train, even for business. But business sometimes demanded small sacrifices in exchange for great rewards. Like, for instance, having to endure the company of two of the biggest jackasses in the United States Senate.

A grandstand had been set up to one side of the old rail yard. Hastily assembled wooden bleachers were stacked in rows back to the cattle cars. The benches were filled. People stood in every available spot between.

From the stage, Prescott Worthington looked out at the sea of brown faces. With colossal effort he resisted the urge to put both hands over his wallet and run.

Worthington had changed from his customary shorts and polo shirt and he felt itchy in his Savile Row suit. This was only partly due to the heat and the fact that he was unused to such formal attire. The thing that most made him itch was the mass of foreign rabble stretched out before him.

Worthington did not feel safe in such a crowd. He would have liked to have a bodyguard present, yet he had no choice but to face all of these Mexicans alone. The woman who was supposed to guarantee his personal safety and to make sure his plan worked had commandeered his train and now she was not even answering her cell phone.

Senators Clancy and Muldoon were at center stage, beneath a Jumbotron screen. On the screen waved computer-generated images of the U.S. and Mexican flags.

Worthington sat to one side of the senators. As sponsor of the event, he had introduced the politicians. Microphones on stands stood before all three men.

Clancy had remained seated, spilling over both sides of his chair, a sagging water balloon of a man in an ill-fitting jacket. Muldoon had occasionally gotten out of his seat and walked the stage as he answered audience questions.

The tumult from Muldoon's last statement was beginning to die down.

"Yes, marvelous," Worthington droned into his own microphone, a tight smile stretching his tan face. "And can I just add that I am as intrigued as all of you are by General Santa Anna."

The audience clapped hesitantly.

They were unsure how to take this new Prescott Worthington IV. Here was a man who had until the previous day funded the work of the Civilian Border Patrol. Yet he had mounted the stage this evening claiming to have had an epiphany. Prescott Worthington IV was now friend to the illegal immigrant, a friend to Santa Anna and the cause.

Their new friend was looking out at the crowd and calculating how many landscapers, seamstresses and fifty-cents-an-hour field laborers were packed into the old Worthington Continental Railroad yard, and if the Port-a-Johns could handle that much refried beans and jalapeño sauce.

"And in light of my newfound appreciation for the terrible plight of immigrants to this land, I have a special surprise for all of you," Worthington announced.

A nod offstage, and the computer images of the waving Mexican and American flags dropped to the bottom of the Jumbotron. A man appeared on the screen.

The broad pockmarked face of General Santa Anna smiled benignly at the massive crowd.

The audience erupted in cheers. The image on screen was obviously live, because the general nodded patiently, soaking in the applause for several long minutes, before finally raising his hand for silence. The crowd dutifully hushed.

"Hola, mis amigos," Santa Anna said. "I will be speaking to you in English this evening, because I want my words to be understood throughout the United States."

It looked to Worthington as if the satellite image was a little out of focus, but on closer inspection it was the general himself who was a little blurry around the edges.

"For those who do not know, I am General Agustín

López de Santa Anna. Although you have all heard of my famous ancestor, until recently most of you have never heard of me. That is because like many of you, my own personal story is one with a most humble beginning.

"I am from you, and so have witnessed your struggles firsthand. Corruption, oppression and lack of opportunity have sent many of you fleeing across the border. But what is that border but an arbitrary line drawn across a continent in another age? Does it really have relevance in this modern time? Was this border there when the United States and Mexico did not even exist and our ancestors, the Aztecs, ruled from Tenochtitlán?

"Borders change with the times, and the time has come—finally come, my friends—for change. We are no longer voiceless nomads. We are no longer running from the incompetence of one government and hiding in fear from another. My friends, mis amigos, this is the dawning of a new, great day. We are today Nuevo Mexico."

On the screen appeared an image of the redrawn North American map, the boundaries of the United States and Mexico pushed back to accommodate the new nation between them.

In the old railroad yard, Santa Anna's words were slow to sink in. Until now, he had been seen as a political figure who would offer change by working within the existing system. He was a firebrand, a revolutionary, yes. But nothing so radical as this had entered the minds of his followers.

When the applause began it was hesitant, almost confused. It quickly grew louder. Men and women jumped to their feet. They screamed; they whistled and cheered. A sound like human thunder rose above Albuquerque. It shook the ground, until all could hear and feel the jubilation of the followers of the great General López de Santa Anna.

The applause lasted for a full six minutes. Santa Anna at last had to signal the crowd to silence.

"Yes, we are about to embark on a bold adventure," the

general said. "I have heard news that some have already acted, thinking they are doing so on my behalf, on behalf of our cause. I applaud their enthusiasm, but I must caution them to restrain themselves, just as I must caution the government of the United States not to underestimate the force we command. See the faces around you. We are strong, we will have our dream, and none can stop us."

More applause. It took minutes to die down.

"In this desire for a brighter future for us all, I have had no greater friends than two of the men who sit before you tonight," Santa Anna announced once silence had returned. "Senators Ned Clancy and Jack Muldoon have worked tirelessly on your behalf in Washington. However, they have met with nothing but resistance." The huge screen image of General Santa Anna looked down at the two politicians on stage. "Not here, my friends. The talents of these two great visionaries have been wasted in the United States. Tonight, I welcome them into our dream of Nuevo Mexico. The skills of these two great leaders will be put to use helping to structure the government of our new nation. There will be understandable objections from the United States. These two men will help explain our position to our neighbor to the north. They will convince the United States that this is in the best interest of all our peoples. And they will never forget, as I will never forget, that this is not our revolution—theirs or mine—but yours. Gracias, fellow Nuevo Mexicanos, and good night."

The image of Santa Anna blinked off the screen to thunderous applause.

The two waving flags, which had remained at the base of the screen throughout the speech, expanded once more. But this time, rather than two distinct flags, they blended into a single flag. There were fewer red and white stripes on the Nuevo Mexico flag, a single red stripe for the seven main districts. The blue star field was gone, replaced by the vertical green, white and red stripes of the Mexican flag.

18

Mark Howard had been at his desk for nearly eigh-
teen hours straight and could feel the fatigue deep in his
weary bones.

Mark never drank coffee but down in the Folcroft cafete-
ria he kept a case of special double-caffeinated cola that
promised the consumer a "super energy boost." Three
empty cans sat in his otherwise barren trash can, and the
promised boost had yet to materialize.

The only break from work had come a half hour earlier,
when Smith had summoned his assistant to his office
where they watched Santa Anna's speech together.

"It's madness," Smith had said. "Two senators calling
for the dismantling of the United States of America. And
what is Worthington up to?" The old CURE director had
just shaken his head in disbelief.

Mark quickly retreated to his office and redoubled his

efforts. He was currently searching through Mexican birth records, with little success.

Santa Anna had finally announced his first name at the Worthington town hall meeting in Albuquerque. That little bit of information might be enough to track him down in the United States. But Mexico's records were not as detailed as the U.S. Plenty of people fell through their government's cracks and Agustín López de Santa Anna was not in any Mexican public record that he could trace.

Mark leaned back in his chair. His office was small, and when he first came to CURE six years ago, he would bump his head on the wall whenever he leaned back.

He crossed his arms and stared at his monitor.

Mark sometimes had an ability to see things that were not apparent to others. If others saw the world only as a giant jigsaw puzzle with pieces scattered haphazardly, Mark had moments of clarity where all the pieces fell into place. But if someone were to think that Mark possessed some sort of magical powers they were mistaken. He wished he could rub his temples like Kreskin and divine what card someone was holding up. But most of the time was like now. The fact was, Mark Howard was in the same boat as everyone else.

The cursor blinked hypnotically in the corner of his monitor.

At rest, the screen and keyboard could be secreted in the bowels of the desk. They rose and descended at the press of a hidden stud near his knee. The desk itself had belonged to Dr. Smith for years. It was sturdy oak, a little worn at the edges from age, but of solid construction.

Mark drummed his fingers on the edge of the desk.

There were no family photographs on walls or desk. Dr. Smith made it feel like a violation of work ethics to bring anything in from home. Still, Mark tweaked the unwritten rule in one small way. On the corner of his desk was a tiny picture of Superman, drawn in crayon. Mark's nephew had given up coloring comic superheroes a few years earlier. In the wink of an eye he was already in junior high school. But Mark kept the picture on his desk as a reminder of innocence and of why his work at CURE was necessary.

As he stared at the picture, the blues and reds seemed to blur into one shapeless, colorless blob. It took a conscious effort to force his eyes back into focus.

For the past two days Mark had been hitting nothing but dead ends, and the wear was starting to show.

The button Remo had sent along was worthless. There were a thousand sweatshops in Mexico that could be stitching Santa Anna's uniforms. A thousand more in other Central and South American countries.

Prescott Worthington had added a new twist to the events unfolding in the Southwest. First he had supported the civilian border patrol and now, suddenly, he had tossed his hand in with Santa Anna.

It was too big a change; too quick and Mark Howard's antenna were vibrating.

What if . . . ?

What if . . . ?

He hunched forward and went back to work at his computer keyboard.

An hour later, all the numbers started to come together. And then a fresh window popped open on Mark's computer. He had disabled the sound years ago. When he started at Folcroft, he quickly found that CURE's system activated the electronic beep so often that, had he not cut the noise, Mark would have put his chair through the screen by now.

It was a CIA report. Mark quickly scanned it. He was on his feet before he had finished.

Standing, Mark tapped a few commands.

The data had not reached Dr. Smith's computer. This particular area had been Mark's responsibility for the past several years. There was too much raw data for Dr. Smith to waste time sorting through it all.

"Never rains but it pours," Mark said grimly.

Climbing out from behind his desk, he hustled from his office.

Smith answered his ringing phone.

"You see it on TV, Smitty?" Remo asked.

"Yes," Smith replied. He had swept the aspirin and antacid into his desk drawer. They would do no good now for his headache or burning stomach.

"So you think he's going to pull it off? Nuevo Mexico? Do you believe it?"

"At this point, anything is possible," Smith said. "Senators Clancy and Muldoon have brought his twisted dream far closer to reality. They lend an air of credibility to the entire affair. The whole thing is wildly up in the air. There are reports that illegals in the U.S. are all starting to head toward the border areas. That could signal outright insurrection. And then we're getting more reports that different groups are mobilizing in Mexico to storm the U.S. border. And I don't know what that will mean. It's getting hairy. Our troops will be on the border. Mexican troops will be on the border. Illegals coming from all over. It may be the biggest riot in the history of mankind."

"Just what the hell is Washington doing?" Remo asked.

"The president's going on TV in a few minutes."

"Well, it's about time he did something."

"I've just looked at his remarks," Smith said. "He's in a tough spot. We certainly don't want to see an all-out border war with Mexico. So he's going to plead for calm; tell everyone in the border states to stay home and sit this one out. And he's going to commend the Texas Rangers for 'their work' at the Alamo. That was a good job, Remo. You bought us at least one extra day of peace."

"Look. Find me where the hell this Santa Anna is. We can stop this in a hurry."

"We're looking," Smith said.

His voice was somber, almost dejected, and Remo said, "You're not exactly Little Mary Sunshine, you know that, Smitty?"

"I am only being realistic."

"Well, it may get worse before it gets better," Remo said. "I found out from one of the guys at the Alamo that there's some muckety-muck who's thrown in with Santa Anna on the Mexican side. Captain Jean-Luc Picard or something."

"General Juan Pichardo?"

"That's it," Remo said. "He important?"

"Yes," Smith said. "He runs the Army and if their president has lost control of Pichardo, then he has lost control of the military. Mexico now has a rogue force opposed to its own government within its borders. Santa Anna may well have power to destabilize the entire North American continent. One moment, Remo."

Smith looked up as Mark Howard burst into his office. He dropped a few sheets of paper on Smith's desk.

"Remo?" he asked, nodding toward the phone.

Smith nodded and as he looked at the papers, handed the telephone to his assistant.

"Hey, Remo, Mark," the young man said. "It's Worthington."

"What do you mean?"

"I was finally able to crack the money trail. He's the one who's been financing Santa Anna, the whole thing."

"You sure of that?"

"Dead sure," Howard said.

Smith took the phone back. His eyes never left the papers that Howard had spread on the desk before him.

"But even Worthington may not be our biggest problem right now," Smith told Remo. And his acid tone threatened to melt the receiver.

19

Zaid Dudin of the Elite Incursion Martyrdom
Brigade let the stars of heaven guide him into the belly of
the beast.

Dudin was Jordanian, born into a family of wealth and
privilege. He had been educated in England, where the
fires of hatred for the West had been kindled. After college,
his father had wanted him to become a diplomat. Instead,
Dudin had joined the al-Khobar terrorist organization.

Dudin had joined the battle on the front lines. Twice de-
tained by American troops in Iraq but, he often gloated, the
fools had released him both times. Any rational Mideast
country would have executed him or at the very least im-
prisoned him for life. Torture was a given either way. Not
America. The United States waved its compassion like a
white flag of surrender.

The twice-released terrorist crossed the border into the

United States on a warm April evening, with six other
Brigade members and a host of Mexican immigrants.

It was amazingly easy.

For weeks he and his men had been hiding out in a
crummy motel in Mexico City, planning how best to enter
the United States undetected. The border strife was a gift
from Allah that Dudin could not refuse. It was all over
Mexican TV. People were walking into the U.S. by the
thousands. And from America's big western cities, illegal
immigrants were heading toward the Mexican border. By
the thousands. By the tens of thousands. Soon it would be
total chaos and thus a simple matter for Dudin and the rest
of the heavily armed Elite Incursion Martyrdom Brigade
to drive to the Mexican side of the border and join one of
the great migrations north.

Even the Mexicans were being accommodating. A group
of soldiers loyal to this Santa Anna person, who Zaid
Dudin had seen on television, had taken over a patch of
American desert north of Chihuahua in New Mexico.

There was an exodus into the United States. Dudin and
his men settled in the midst of the trudging throng of illegals. At the line of Mexican troops, the terrorists paused to
take stock.

In the moonlight they could see about a dozen American
Border Patrol agents and the silhouettes of five Jeeps. That
fool American president has said the U.S. Army was on its
way but the word was that they would be kept miles away
from the actual borders, in order to prevent armed confrontation. The weak-willed West, Dudin thought with the
great contempt of one whose religion countenanced be-
heading women and murdering schoolchildren.

Meanwhile, the small undermanned American line had
given up attempting to detain intruders. There were simply
too many to stop and any attempt to grab one or two risked
an explosive situation as had occurred in Nevada.

Dudin led his men past the Mexican soldiers and chose the widest gap between the small pockets of American agents. In that spot was the shadow of an SUV but no agents were near it. Dudin was certain that the truck was undriveable or else someone would have surely stolen it by now. It did not matter. He would secure a vehicle soon enough.

Dudin knew that there were signs posted on roads near the border warning American drivers not to stop. But for that the Jordanian had a simple enough plan. One of his men would lie down in the road while the rest hid in a culvert or ditch. American fool compassion would compel someone to stop and help, no matter what the signs warned. Dudin and his men would then kill that person and take his vehicle.

And with the Americans focusing all of their attention on their southwestern border, Dudin and his men would easily succeed in their great mission.

In the moonlight, Dudin smiled.

"Look at them," he whispered to his men. "They blindly surrender to the will of Allah."

The loud voice that answered from the night was not that of Allah, unless somehow the cruel universe had been wrong and their great deity—horror of horrors—was actually a very bored-sounding American.

"That's them," said the voice that was definitely not Allah. "I might not speak it but I know Arab gobbledygook when I hear it."

"You had to hear them?" a squeaky sing-song replied. "The only thing that can blot out the odor of Mexicans is the even worse odor of Arabs. Of course if a Frenchman were here we would all have to have our noses amputated."

Zaid Dudin had a brief moment of confusion. No one could possibly have spotted them in this desert crowd, much less have determined that they were not Mexicans. But then he felt a tap on his shoulder.

"If you don't let us stamp your hand, you'll have to pay to sneak in and blow us up again," the same American voice said, this time a breath away from Zaid Dudin's ear.

Dudin's blood turned to ice. He grabbed for one of his three guns.

But another hand had gotten there first. And then the gun had vanished and Dudin was being spun around. He came face to face with the deadest eyes he had ever seen.

A desperate glance, and he saw that his men had been similarly disarmed. In the moonlight, Dudin could see a pile of guns and ammunition boxes in the desert sand.

The other members of the Elite Incursion Martyrdom Brigade were staring at the man in their midst with a mixture of shock, amazement and terror.

"It is him," one man muttered through lips frozen in fear. They had heard stories of the thin, dark-eyed American who had been tearing a bloody swath through the al-Khobar terrorist organization all over the world. Until this moment they had thought it laughable legend.

The legend raised his hand. He was not laughing. "No autographs," Remo said.

"That is only because he does not know how to sign his name," said the second voice.

Another figure appeared before them, this one a wizened Asian with fingernails like knife blades. The stories of the old man were as frightening as those of the American. It was said he could move like a shadow and kill in a whisper.

Neither man was whispering now.

"Let us get this done and be gone from here," the Master of Sinanju said. "I am tired of Smith sending us to the four corners of the earth to clean out nests of this vermin. We are assassins, not exterminators. These murderers of innocents are not worthy of the Master's talents."

"In a sec, Little Father," Remo said. He turned to the terrorists. "Let's go for a little ride, shall we?"

Remo herded the men to his waiting SUV. They got in

one side and promptly tried to climb out the other side.
Remo sealed the door with a slap. He drove them to the
edge of a dried out riverbed, the same one where Rob Scott
and the rest of the Civilian Border Patrol had met their end.

"Okay," Remo said, once he had dumped the terrorists
out of the truck. "Show of hands. Which one of you camel-
jockeys is the leader?"

Remo's reputation was enough to inspire the Elite Incursion Martyrdom Brigade to truth. Five shaking fingers
pointed at Zaid Dudin.

"So my boss got some dippy-doodle report from CIA
that some terrorist cell they've been tracking in Mexico
City is suddenly on the move," Remo said. "Don't ask me
how he knows this stuff, he just does. So he got your location through them, and they followed you as far as the border, and they swear you're supposed to be some sort of elite
squad but, honestly, I wouldn't trust the CIA to figure out
which end of the cat the food goes in, so tell me what you're
doing here and I promise to kill you slightly less painfully."

Zaid Dudin took a bracing breath and puffed out his
chest defiantly. "I will not tell you."

Remo reached over and lifted the terrorist by his ear.
Dudin gasped. Remo gave a little shake. Dudin shrieked.
Most people did when one of their ears was torn from the
side of their head. Remo tossed the ear away.

"Does Allah reward symmetry?" Remo asked. He
reached for Dudin's other ear.

The terrorist screamed and slapped his hand over his
still-attached ear. "We are here for Mustafa," he cried.
"Our mission is to free him."

Remo did not need to ask who Mustafa was. In 2001, the
al-Khobar terrorist was supposed to fly a hijacked plane
into the White House. He had been tried and cheated death,
instead receiving a life sentence.

"That's it?" Remo asked, dark irritation creeping into
his tone.

"Yes, I swear on my eyes," Dudin said. He thought better of his words and pressed his hands protectively over his eyes. "That is a figure of speech," he added worriedly.

"You mean you're not smuggling a nuclear bomb?"

"No."

"Anthrax?"

"No."

"Bird flu? Rickets? Head lice?"

"I am sorry, no," Dudin said. "We can go back and get something if you would like us to."

He peeked hopefully between his fingers.

The first thing Dudin saw was the pile of arms and legs that used to be his crack Elite Incursion Martyrdom Brigade. The appendages were stacked up next to the little Asian. There were torso and head piles nearby. Somehow the old man had disassembled five strong, brave young men without a sound. The second thing Dudin saw was the hand racing toward his forehead. It seemed to come in very slow, but then Dudin realized that this was an optical illusion. It was actually traveling very fast. Faster, in fact, than anything Dudin had ever seen. And then hand met forehead and Zaid Dudin's brain turned to paste, and he didn't see anything ever again.

As Dudin's body collapsed from his outstretched hand, Remo grumbled, "We got sent here for nothing, Little Father. Trust the CIA to get us to waste our time fiddling while Rome burns."

They were heading back to their truck when a pair of headlights came bouncing across the desert in their direction. It came from the Mexican line.

"Halt!" a voice called in accented English. A dark figure stood upright in the passenger side of the Jeep.

Remo and Chiun exchanged a glance. They stood side by side and waited for the Jeep to draw up beside them.

"What do you think you are . . . ?" The man standing in the Jeep suddenly gasped.

Captain Javier Jiminez had noticed some strange activity in this patch of New Mexico desert that had been claimed for Nuevo Mexico. Some dark shapes that were standing in place, rather than trudging through the night. He had not in his wildest nightmares ever thought the small party he had driven out to intimidate consisted of the same frightening men he had encountered back near the old border two days before, the men who had disarmed him and sent one of his soldiers to the hospital. And now they were out in the night surrounded by what appeared to be mangled corpses.

"Forgive me for interrupting, señores," Jiminez said anxiously. "I can see you are very busy men." He smacked his driver on the head. "Get me out of here," he mumbled.

Before the Jeep could start to roll, there came a horrible pop and hiss of air from the back. The Jeep sank. When Jiminez glanced over, he saw the Master of Sinanju removing a dagger-like fingernail from the left rear tire.

"You know what's funny?" Remo said. "You and your guys just happened to be here when we climbed out of that hole the other day. All right, that's fine. Coincidences happen all the time. But now here you are again, and look at you. That's one snazzy new uniform."

Captain Jiminez glanced down at his new costume.

It was a uniform identical to the ones worn by the men who had attacked Remo and Chiun from the coyote tunnel, identical to the ones worn by some of the soldiers at the Alamo, identical to the uniform worn by General Santa Anna himself.

Captain Jiminez attempted a smile.

"It is, as you say, an amazing coincidence, no?"

"It is, as I say, time to let Chiun here do to your eyes what he does to Jeep tires if you don't start doing a little splaining."

To punctuate the threat, the Master of Sinanju sank five sharp fingernails into the front tire. The tire exploded and the Jeep tipped hard to one side. Jiminez had to grab his driver's shoulder for support.

"Promise not to kill me?" Jiminez begged.

Chiun had crossed to the other side of the Jeep. A single thrust took the air from the right front tire. Panicked, Jiminez tumbled against the dashboard.

"On two conditions," Remo said.

20

Smith answered the phone on the first ring.

"Report."

"The Elite Martyrdom Whozits weren't smuggling in anything that could level Pittsburgh, Smitty," Remo said. "They were just trying to bust out Mustafa."

Smith's office was dark. The faint glow from his buried computer monitor cast weird shadows over his pinched, gray features. "The terrorist? He is being held in a top security federal facility."

"I assume they knew that."

"I trust you removed them?"

"There's probably still a puddle, if that's what you mean," Remo said.

"That is not true, Emperor," the Master of Sinanju called from the background. "The heads are still intact if you desire them for your castle walls."

"No heads, Chiun," Remo said.

Smith removed his glasses and sighed. "All right. One crisis averted."

The CURE director sounded defeated and Remo said, "Turn that frown upside-down. I've got more good news. There's a secret base not too far from here where they've been shipping the uniforms from. That's where Santa Anna's been flying in and out of."

"Are you sure?" Smith asked.

"Yeah. And tell Mark he was right; it's some of the old Worthington property. That bastard's been behind this all the while. Anyway, Chiun and I are heading there now."

"Very well," Smith said. "Keep me posted."

"Will do. Oh, and more good news. The mass exodus may be ending soon."

"What do you mean?" Smith asked.

Hundreds of miles from Rye, Remo lowered the cell phone he had liberated from Captain Javier Jiminez and looked toward the border between the United States and Mexico.

The Mexican convoy of trucks and Jeeps that had invaded the New Mexico desert was on the move once more, this time back toward Mexico. Mexican soldiers on foot brandished guns, herding the wave of illegals back whence they had come. Confused illegals darted from the soldiers. Some made a dash into the United States, most hightailed it back home.

With the Mexican Army now on their side, the Border Patrol had jumped into action. U.S. agents were tackling and cuffing border hoppers who tried to run the line.

And the flood of American illegals toward the border had slowed to a trickle. At Remo's suggestion, the Mexican soldiers had begun loudly broadcasting rumors that anyone living in the United States who was picked up by the authorities would forfeit welfare, free medical care, child support, free college tuition, preference in hiring and then be sent to the people's paradise of Cuba. The rumors spread like wildfire and the thousands heading for the border and trouble did almost a military about-face and started back the way they had come.

And through it all, Captain Javier Jiminez drove up and down the line, the rubber of his Jeep's ruptured tires flapping on the desert floor. Jiminez was standing in his seat, arms waving wildly, shouting orders to his men.

Chiun stood at Remo's side, arms folded over his narrow chest as he scrutinized the scene.

"What do I mean? I mean America has now got the Mexican General Patton on our side," Remo said into the phone. "Take care, Smitty."

Remo did not know how to disconnect Jiminez's cell phone, so he snapped it in half and tossed it over his shoulder.

"Let's go harvest us a head or two, Little Father."

21

General Agustín López de Santa Anna stood on the wooden porch of the little ranch on his secret army base and puked his guts into the dry desert dust.

Something was wrong. No one was telling him what it was, but he was not a fool and he could smell disaster brewing.

On the television, the routing of Mexican forces at the Alamo was still being replayed on all stations. He must have seen the same footage of soldiers running in full retreat through the Texas desert a hundred times since the previous afternoon.

And now one network was reporting some baffling news out of nearby New Mexico. Sometime before dawn, Mexican troops had inexplicably begun to help the U.S. with border enforcement and the crowds that had been storming toward the U.S.–Mexican border had turned and were going home.

On the porch, Santa Anna threw up until there was nothing left in his stomach. The dry heaves kicked his guts like a mule.

In the distance was the sound of weapons fire. He was so used to the noises of his army exercising day and night that he scarcely heard the racket.

Some instinct that ran deep in his blood was screaming to him that the tide had turned against him.

It was a strange thing, this soldier's intuitive sense that the war was lost—because Santa Anna was no general. He had never even served in his country's military, but the natural insight of the lifetime soldier may have come to him as a gift in blood from his most famous ancestor.

In truth, Agustín could not remember a time when his insignificant little life was not overshadowed by the towering figure of General Antonio López de Santa Anna, and Agustín often thought how strange a thing it was to have descended from one so famous, yet to be of such humble origins oneself.

A two-room house in an Ensenada slum had been his birthplace and his mother had died in childbirth. His father had tried for a time to raise his son alone, but a gambling problem had eventually put him on the wrong end of a gun. They found him in a ditch in Tijuana when Agustín was only seven years old.

The little boy had gone to live with his grandmother, a woman who was fiercely proud of their family's history. It was she who first told young Santa Anna of the great man who would fire the boy's imagination.

"He was President of Mexico?" Augustin had asked, brown eyes wide with wonder.

They were in the back of the family souvenir stand in Tijuana. There were a few small rooms for personal use, plus one larger room filled with inventory. The front of the small building was a kiosk at the lonely end of an alley down which few customers were ever brave enough to venture.

"They made him give it up three times," his grand-mother had said, eyes lit with sparkling pride. "But he fought to reclaim it. Fought with all his strength. He regained the presidency twice. He was truly a great man."

"Tell me again of how he lost his leg," little Augustin would often ask.

And his grandmother would tell him of the great battle. Pride compelled her to embellish the tale a little more each time. Sometimes their ancestor had killed forty men with nothing but a knife and a broken sword, sometimes he killed fifty with his bare hands. Never was the leg amputated. Most times the French held him down and cut it off while Santa Anna defiantly spat blood in the butchers' faces.

Agustín grew up dreaming of a life of excitement, derring-do and privilege. By the time he was a teenager, he had spent so much time with his head in the clouds that his grandmother began to regret the tales she had told him. "Do not dream so much of the past, Agustín," she told him one day at the end of her life.

His grandmother was bedridden by this time, her lungs riddled with a disease Agustín did not understand. She spoke in a whisper and coughed between every other word.

"I love this land, but it is dead," she told him. "If you dream of anything, dream of the future. You must seek a life elsewhere. The border with the United States is near. Many sneak across it every year. Go, Agustín. Go and make a life for yourself there."

"That land does not belong to the United States," the teenaged Agustín had insisted angrily. "It was taken from us. Stolen by the Americans. I will not sneak onto our own property like a criminal."

"Oh, Agustín," his grandmother had whispered. "I have failed you."

That night her coughing fits grew worse. By morning, they had stopped forever. At sixteen, Agustín López de Santa Anna was alone.

He managed the souvenir shop for decades, just scraping enough tourist dollars to get by. At night he would make the rounds of the local cantinas. And when he drank enough he would brag until everyone knew his lineage. And the bar patrons would mock Agustín López de Santa Anna, the great-great-great-great-grandson of General Santa Anna, now reduced to selling cheap plastic knick-knacks to fat Americans.

It took many years but his dreams eventually died. "This is how it ends, always ends for us Santa Annas," he slurred one night from his cot in the back of his shop. It was the same cot on which his grandmother had offered her last words of hope. "Even you, the greatest of us all, died in poverty. It was your fate, so it will be mine as well."

But at his darkest hour, fate delivered him a savior.

Agustín had heard rumors that someone was trying to buy the block on which his souvenir shop was located, some rich industrialist who had come to Mexico to exploit the people while stuffing his own coffers. Agustín hated the man without ever having met him. He hated him right up until the wealthy man stepped up to his souvenir stand and offered Agustín the chance to turn his family's fortunes around.

"I hear you have an interesting pedigree," the stranger had said. He was dressed strangely for someone so rich. Like a college student on vacation. The man's limousine was parked at the mouth of the alley.

"Señor?" Agustín had asked.

The beautiful female with the broad face who accompanied the stranger flashed a bright smile. "Isn't he just the cutest little thing you ever met?" she said to the stranger.

"Your lineage," the man explained to Agustín. "I hear you have a very famous forebear. I have an interesting proposition for you that will take you away from all of this . . . splendor. Of course, if you prefer. . . ."

The stranger patted a hand on one of the items on

Agustín display counter. It was an ugly ceramic elephant with a tiger hanging off its rear end, an item particularly popular with stupid American teenagers.

Agustín had abandoned his shop without even boarding it up. He left the papier-mâché avocados and plastic, made-in-China burros out for anyone to steal, and departed with the wealthy stranger and his woman.

The rich man's plan was as bold as it was simple. It was a scheme worthy of the legendary General Antonio López de Santa Anna, and of his descendant.

Nuevo Mexico. It sounded insane, but why couldn't it work? His own ancestor had fought for much of the same land centuries ago, why could Agustín not reclaim it now? Borders shifted. Two hundred years ago the world's borders were very different. In two hundred years' time who would recognize the world map of today?

And the power. Agustín would be a figurehead, something for the people to rally around. But he would also be head of the new nation's army, second only in power to the president of Nuevo Mexico himself.

The president would be a difficult sell. Prescott Worthington IV was not someone known for his kindness toward immigrants. But there was even a plan for that and the first step in that plan, the murder of a few Civilian Border Patrol volunteers was a small price to pay for greater glory.

It was a bold act that would inspire illegals to reflexively join Santa Anna. Fear would convince them not to passively await retribution from the United States. Of course, if history was any indication, the U.S. would most likely do nothing. But sowing seeds of worry would be a simple matter among the uneducated people who were already anxious from sneaking illegally into America. And when the army was assembled, Santa Anna would back his gringo benefactor as president of the new nation.

Santa Anna had been hired to play a part, and he accepted his role with relish. He would have the glory of his name restored and Prescott Worthington IV would have his own nation.

And all seemed to go perfectly. The American senators were brought aboard with promises of power. Each would have absolute power in their districts, Muldoon in Arizona, Clancy in California. To pique Clancy's interest, Santa Anna had tempted the senator with all the vices he was known to favor. Muldoon had been easier. All the general had to promise him was face time on television. The most dangerous spot on earth was the space between Senator Jack Muldoon and a TV camera.

All it had taken to bring General Juan Pichardo into the scheme was a massive bribe. The head of Mexico's armed forces now worked for Santa Anna's employer, although he probably thought he was working for the general himself, since Worthington's role in the uprising was still being kept secret.

It had all been planned meticulously and everything was going exactly according to schedule. So why then, why was General Agustín López de Santa Anna leaning on a railing of his porch and dry heaving into the Mexican dust?

He tried to straighten up. His stomach was twisted in knots.

He stumbled back through the door. Before slamming it shut, he ripped down the poster that had been tacked to the facade. Tearing his own stern visage to strips, he lurched back across the floor and fell into the sofa.

Cable news was still airing reports out of New Mexico. A local TV station had gotten to the desert and was broadcasting live. In the early morning sunlight, a wild-eyed captain in one of Santa Anna's own uniforms was seen herding illegals back across the border.

It was coming apart. Somehow, without firing a single shot, the Americans were staging a counterattack.

Santa Anna was still watching the television when the front door burst open and the woman he had first met in front of his own souvenir stand, the woman he had grown to despise for the way she controlled him, hustled into the living quarters.

"Rise and shine, sleepyhead," Rebecca Dalton said. "It's time to leave."

"I thought we weren't leaving until . . ."

"Now," Rebecca interrupted.

The sound of gunfire through the open front door was louder than the usual training sessions of his troops. Rebecca Dalton's head snapped around to the sound.

Santa Anna began to gather up his scattered uniform.

"Please be a sweetie and hurry," Rebecca said.

"Where are we going?" he asked.

"Places to go, things to do," she said airily. She cast a sharp glance at the door. Was the gunfire growing closer?

She was attempting to sound like her normal self, but the usual sugary sweetness was forced. There was now a thin razor edge to her voice and a hardness to her broad, pretty face.

Rebecca paused long enough to dash off a quick note, which she left on the dining room table, before hustling Santa Anna out the door to a waiting car. When he saw they were driving to the helipad at the rear of the ramshackle base, his brow lowered in confusion.

Santa Anna pointed across the desert. "Not the train?" he asked.

"No," Rebecca cut in crisply. "Too slow. And we're only going a few miles."

That would mean the other hacienda at the far of end of this large swath of Worthington property. Santa Anna glanced at the helicopter. A young soldier sat in the pilot's seat. And the rotor blades were already furiously slicing air. Santa Anna knew that Rebecca Dalton ordinarily liked to fly the helicopter. The fact that she had someone already waiting to take them out meant that she did not want to waste time waiting to power up the chopper on her own.

The realization sent waves of fear through his churning gut. And yes, the firing of rifles was getting louder and closer.

Santa Anna had never before met a woman like Rebecca Dalton. Despite her sunny demeanor, she was utterly ruthless and had thus far in their association been incapable of fear. Yet for the first time he could hear fear in her voice.

And Agustín López de Santa Anna knew what the gunfire meant, knew the source of Rebecca Dalton's fear. It was death. And it was coming for them all.

Remo heard the distant sound of the fleeing helicopter and knew even before they reached the ranch that they were too late.

The soldiers who had been firing at them since they first tore through the chain-link fence at the northern border of the secret base had mostly scattered.

One young recruit charged the Master of Sinanju. The old Korean's hands slashed down the man's chest, fingernails tearing right-angle gills through flesh and bone. Bloody viscera slipped through the openings, and the man dropped to the dirt.

The little wooden ranch sat in the middle of the camp. Remo and Chiun leaped up the steps and with a slap, Remo took the door off the hinges.

Inside, the television played loudly to an empty room. Remo saw Captain Javier Jiminez, who had apparently become something of a celebrity thanks to the network morning news, driving in slow circles on bare wheels, herding people in all directions.

There was a white business card leaning against a fruit basket in the middle of the table. Written in script that was loaded with junior high school loops, it read:

"We'll meet again. If you're lucky."

The note was signed "RD." There was a red lipstick kiss in the corner.

"Get a load of this," Remo shouted over the blaring TV. "She even put a little heart over the 'i.' She deserves to be killed twice for that alone."

The Master of Sinanju was over by the television.

"We should leave here," he said.

"Yeah. We will." He picked up the small business card.

"And ignore that nonsense," Chiun said. "She is smarter than you and left it here just to keep us in this place."

"She's not smarter than me, Chiun," Remo grumbled.

His heart wasn't into arguing. He was feeling a twinge of guilt for abandoning Conchita. She had trusted that he would help her locate her missing family members, and he had let her down. But she had to see that there were bigger things at stake here.

"Oh, no?" Chiun said, completing his search. "We should leave."

"She's gone now. And probably Santa Anna with her. What's the hurry?"

Remo folded his arms defiantly across his chest.

They were still folded when, an instant later, the walls of the ranch exploded inward in a spray of orange flame and deadly wood shards, and hell and destruction descended in fire around the two Masters of Sinanju.

Captain Sergio Amor screamed at his troops to continue the bombardment. Tanks and cannon exploded with a thunderous succession of roaring blasts.

In under a minute, the pounding fusillade reduced to a pile of burning rubble the small ranch that had been temporary home to General Santa Anna.

Captain Amor hated to take orders from the gringo woman who was some sort of special advisor to the general. Still, he was pleased that he had succeeded. When the two invaders entered the base, they had encountered only token resistance. Some firepower had been held back until the pair were inside the general's home. Once they were inside the building, the woman's orders to Captain Amor had been to reduce it to ash.

Mission accomplished. The building was flaming rubble. Nothing could be left alive inside.

"Cease firing!" Amor shouted.

It took a moment for the order to be relayed around the lines. When the firing finally stopped, Amor was left with a loud ringing in his ears. That, and the sound of two men arguing very nearby.

"She did not outsmart me."

"She would have succeeded had I not been with you."

"Bulldookey."

Captain Amor wheeled to find the two men he least expected to see alive ever again calmly walking toward him.

Captain Amor looked from the men, to the burning house, and back to the men once more.

"How?" Amor asked, astounded.

"How? That's not Mexican. That's Indian," Remo said. As he passed, he stuffed Captain Amor's head into the barrel of the nearest cannon. To the rest of the shocked troops, he called, "I'm in a pissy mood right now, and there's plenty of empty barrels to go around, so if you're interested, line up in an orderly fashion."

To a man, the soldiers turned and ran.

Remo turned to the Master of Sinanju. "Well, that's it, Little Father. Another dead end."

The old man was looking toward the edge of the camp, and the eastern chain-link fence that opened onto desert.

"Perhaps not," Chiun said.

A whiskered chin pointed off toward the east.

Remo saw what appeared to be some sort of industrial complex in the distance. There were large, low buildings and tall smokestacks. A road fed the site from the south. And from the north was a lonely rail line.

An old-fashioned train sat on tracks that ended at the complex. And with his keen eyes, Remo read the name on the side of the train: WORTHINGTON CONTINENTAL RAILROAD.

A few miles away from Remo and Chiun, as the helicopter landed in an open field near another rundown ranch house, Santa Anna asked Rebecca Dalton the question that had been burning in his mind.

"We have lost, haven't we? What will happen to us now?"

She gave him a slight predatory smile. "You, my dear general, will return to selling paintings of Elvis Presley on black velvet. With luck, no one will ever hear of you again."

"And you?"

"I have a contract to protect Mr. Worthington. There will soon be men from the East who will come to kill him. I will try to do my job and keep him alive. And then, sweetie, I'm going to vanish. There are some people I just don't want to mess with."

22

Conchita Diaz followed the directions given her by
the voice on the phone.

The cheery woman who had called Conchita out of the
blue had not given her name. She had only wanted to say
that she was from a Christian group that aided undocumented workers, and that Conchita's cousin was well, but
unable to get in touch with his family at the moment.

Conchita had pressed her, and the woman had—perhaps
a little too eagerly—revealed that her brother, his wife and
their children were working on a remote ranch right at the
Mexican–U.S. border. It was only a few miles from where
Conchita had first met Remo.

Working on a ranch certainly did not sound like Juan
Carlos Diaz, who had successfully avoided hard work
every day of his life. But the woman had been insistent,
and had even revealed the location of the ranch where her
cousin and his family were working.

"I really shouldn't tell you, you know," the woman had said. She was so cheerful, so friendly, as if she and Conchita had been lifelong friends. "Our group just makes sure migrant workers make their trip safely. But you're just so gosh-darned nice, how can I refuse?"

Maybe this mysterious woman was the angel about whom Conchita's aunt had spoken. One thing Conchita knew for sure; she could not have been more wrong the first time.

How could she ever think that Remo had been sent to help her? Yes, he had saved her a few times but that was in the course of whatever work he was doing for the government. He was not here to help Conchita; he had his own agenda.

Remo was definitely no angel sent to watch over her.

The dirt road on which Conchita drove was heavily rutted. Here and there was evidence of ranch land. Twisted barbed wire hung slack from fence posts that were bent and half buried in windblown sand. Troughs hewn from rock spotted the otherwise barren plains. The fences had not been tended to in decades, and the troughs were baked dry in the unforgiving desert sun. Far off, she saw a railroad engine on a narrow single track.

Conchita stopped between two tall pillars. A sign that had once hung over the road now lay in the dust next to the bleached bones of a long-dead Texas longhorn. She tried to make out the name of the ranch, but the letters on the sign had been blasted nearly clean from years of erosion. This ranch clearly had not been worked for many years but this had to be the right place. Conchita had followed precisely the directions given her by the kind, cheerful woman on the telephone. Maybe only this part of the ranch was no longer tended. Maybe there was cattle and activity closer to the main house. It was not too far up ahead according to the directions.

Conchita climbed back into her rented truck and headed up the bumpy road.

Over hills of black rock rose an old wooden water tower. She followed the road around the hills.

The tower dominated a wide patch of level desert. Near the tower, a sprawling old bunkhouse seemed ready to collapse into ruin. Dozens of ancient barns clustered near dilapidated cattle pens. At some point fire had claimed some of the larger structures. Blackened beams jutted saw-toothed from charred rubble. The fire had been sparked by lightning. No one had been there to put it out.

Railroad tracks so clogged with scrub brush that they looked as if they had not seen a train in a hundred years passed between the barns and disappeared over the horizon.

Conchita drove to the ranchhouse and parked her truck near the long front porch.

There was evidence of recent visitors. Fresh tire tracks marred the dust in the long driveway.

The bowed steps creaked underfoot. Inside was some old furniture, abandoned during a long-ago move. Some bureaus and a shattered mirror. An old box spring leaned against the wall.

There was no sign of human activity in the house.

Conchita went back down the steps and followed the new tire tracks to the rear of the ranch.

There were no vehicles out back. A gleaming silver shovel leaning against an old hitching post caught her eye. Sunlight glinted off the spade. The shovel was new.

Conchita stepped into the massive shadow cast by the old wooden water tower.

There were several big bumps in the dirt that she had to step over. She had taken only a few steps when something new caught her eye and she did a double take.

It had been hidden behind one of the tower legs. A low table draped with a red-and-white checkered tablecloth. The tablecloth was spotlessly new. Arranged on the table were two dozen fat crystal glasses.

Blinking in surprise, Conchita walked over to the table.

So distracted was she, her toe caught a root and she fell to the ground. Cursing her own clumsiness, she got back to her feet and slapped the dust from her clothes.

The glasses were Waterford crystal. They appeared to be dishwasher clean.

A spigot dripped water into the dust. A sign hanging from it read: AGUA/WATER.

Conchita had heard that some generous, sympathetic people were setting up water stations in the desert to aid parched illegals. This tower had obviously been here for many decades. Here at the border, if one were to approach from the direction of Mexico, the tower would be visible from miles away. Briefly, she wondered how many of her former countrymen had availed themselves of the kindness of whoever it was that owned this property.

The day was exceedingly hot. Even in the shade of the water tower, it must have been nearly one hundred degrees.

Conchita picked up one of the crystal glasses and begun to pour herself a drink from the spigot. She was raising it to her lips when a cheery voice behind her called out a command.

"Don't drink the water."

Conchita jumped, and a few drops of liquid splashed on her hand. Immediately there was an itch.

She spun around to see a pretty blond woman crossing from the back of the ranch. The woman wore a pair of khaki shorts and a clean white T-shirt.

Conchita recognized the woman. She had appeared on the computer monitor in the coyote tunnel, the woman who had tried to bury Conchita out in the desert.

"You are just the cutest little thing, aren't you?" Rebecca Dalton said. "I wish I could stay so thin. I bet you don't even work out, do you? I'd put that down if I were you."

And then the woman's voice hit Conchita. The voice on the phone, the voice of the woman in the tunnel. It was the same woman. She cursed herself for not recognizing it when Rebecca Dalton had phoned her, but these past few days had been so insane, and Conchita had been so eager to find her cousin, she had not made the connection.

"Where is my cousin?" Conchita demanded. Her skin had started to burn. There was an odor of singed flesh.

"He's right here, unfortunately," Rebecca said, shaking her head and wearing an expression that was an approximation of the sadness she had seen on the faces of other people. "And I wasn't fooling. You should put that glass down pronto. And be careful, won't you?"

Conchita did not put the glass down carefully. In an act of defiance, she turned it over and poured the contents out onto the table. The tablecloth immediately blackened and hissed, exposing the crackling, peeling veneer of the mahogany table underneath.

Her hand felt as if it was on fire. Dropping the glass, she clasped her wrist in pain.

Rebecca hustled over. She quickly spat on the wounds where flesh sizzled. She dabbed at the blackened areas with the hem of her T-shirt.

"Some kind of acid," Rebecca said. "Don't ask me what. It's produced by one of his chemical plants in India. Take the hide right off of you. Or from inside you, if you drink it. He does like his little games."

Conchita's skin was blistering. The saliva seemed to have slowed the burning. She spat on her own wounds and rubbed them on her pants. Black blisters tore open.

"That's it," Rebecca said, encouragingly. "It stings like the dickens, I imagine. Imagine what it'd be like taking a bath in that stuff." She pointed above their heads at the great wooden tank. "What I had up there, see, is explosive charges. Don't bother looking. They're inside the tank. I had hoped your friends would come here with you, and when they got close enough . . . boom! Bottom comes out, and we get a big ol' splashdown. This whole area would be flooded with acid lickety-split. Anything caught below would have been fried extra crispy. Even they probably wouldn't have been able to get out without escaping some injury. And even if they were only wounded, that would have been enough. So much easier to finish off injured prey. I had high hopes it'd work." She pouted her lower lip. "But, now, I'll never know."

"You are mad," Conchita said.

"Nope, not me," Rebecca said. "I don't get mad. Causes forehead wrinkles and this gal's too young for Botox."

"Where is my cousin?" Conchita demanded.

The sad expression again. "I told you, he's here. You tripped over him on the way over."

Conchita frowned, confused. She had tripped on the way to the tower but that was on a root.

It struck all at once. She wheeled around.

Something dark jutted from the dirt.

Conchita ran over and grabbed the shovel. Rebecca Dalton did not try to stop her.

Conchita did not have to dig far. What she had thought was a root turned out to be a forearm. She dropped to her knees and cleared around the arm with her hands, up to shoulder and face.

Juan Carlos stared sightlessly at the blue New Mexico sky. His throat and most of his jaw had been eaten away.

Conchita was numbly aware of Rebecca standing over her. She ignored the woman.

She understood now what the mounds behind the ranch represented. There were more than two dozen of them, stretching from sunlight near the rear porch to the shade of the great water tower. Crawling on hands and knees, Conchita went to the nearest mound. It was smaller than the shallow grave of Juan Carlos. She dug furiously with her hands. Black flesh where the acid had dripped peeled away, exposing red sores.

Conchita found her niece.

Her stomach rebelled at the sight and smell. Conchita

threw up. Yet no tears came. Just a burning fury that ignited in her churning belly and exploded from her screaming lungs. Hands like claws, she spun on Rebecca Dalton.

But before she could even get to her feet, she felt a jolt to the side of her head and she fell across the shallow grave.

"Now just be careful who you go blaming there, honey," Rebecca Dalton warned. She towered over Conchita, the pistol she had used as a club now held lightly in her slender fingers. "I work as an assassin, a security consultant, a bodyguard, but killing children is not part of my job."

Rebecca caught sight of the little girl's desiccated face, and for the briefest moment her voice caught. And the expression that crossed her face was not one of false sadness, but for a flickering instant one of genuine pain and grief and guilt and loss.

The moment passed. The gun grew steady once more.

"They call it 'shoot, shovel and shut up,'" Rebecca said, inclining her head toward the field of bodies. "Ranchers usually do it for nuisance animals. Bears, wolves, stuff like that. Things that'd kill their livestock, but things the government won't let you kill legally."

Conchita wiped the trickle of blood from the side of her head. Anger dulled the pain in her hand. "Who owns this land?" she demanded.

"A hundred years ago, this was a nerve center for Worthington Meats. He owns miles and miles of this land. Most of the cattle that fed the East Coast was processed through here. Poor little cows, with those big brown eyes. I'm a vegetarian, mostly. Although I do sneak a burger once in a while. Shh. Don't tell anyone."

"Prescott Worthington did this?" Conchita asked.

"Mmm-hmm," Rebecca said, nodding. "His land, he says he has the right to do whatever to whoever crosses it. I wonder when they stopped using the land for cattle? I think they're out of meats now. I never really asked. Tell you what. You can ask him when you see him."

"Why would I see him?"

"Because I signed on to save his worthless hide. The only way I think I can do that is deliver you to him and let him make his own deal. Sorry, sweetie, but that's the way it is."

Rebecca motioned sharply with the gun. Conchita climbed obediently to her feet.

They were halfway back to the rear of the ranch when Conchita heard the growing sound of an engine.

Behind her, Rebecca's lips thinned.

Rebecca watched the helicopter rise from behind the distant barns. From her angle she could not see the pilot. She could only see Santa Anna waving goodbye to her. Kicking up dust, the helicopter raced south toward Mexico.

Rebecca Dalton released a little aggravated sigh, like the prom queen who could not find just the right shade of teal gown to complement her tiara.

"Well, gosh darn it, it looks like we're going to have to take your car. And we'd better get a move on. I don't think we've got but a couple of minutes' head start."

23

On the second-floor veranda of his Las Cruces es-
tate, Prescott Worthington IV stood amid the potted trees
and looked out across the land he hoped someday to chris-
ten Nuevo Mexico.

What he saw was hot and bright and bleak. But it was all
his, to do with as he pleased. Or it soon would be. They
might think that they had stopped him but Worthingtons
did not surrender that easily—especially to the mongrels
who seemed to be hectoring him right now.

Worthington stepped inside and closed the French doors
behind him. The air conditioning kissed the sweat on his
bare arms and legs and chilled his spine.

A pair of malevolent dark eyes followed him as he
crossed over to the desk of his study.

Conchita Diaz's wrists were lashed together. She had
been hung from a mounted wall light. Worthington was

reminded of great-grandfather's beef cattle hung for slaughter.

"You needn't look so hot tempered," he said to her. "I know that's what you people are like. Fiery Latin blood and all that. I could do with a little less of it, quite frankly. But you're safe, my dear. Maybe I can put you to work in the kitchen. Service is where you people shine."

"*Hijo de puta*," Conchita swore.

"I see we can clean you up and give you a fancy job, but you're not so far from scrubbing the grease trap at the corner taco shop as you like to think."

Whistling, he fished his cell phone from the pocket of his white shorts.

It was a miserable little piece of brittle plastic, made in China by pajama-wearing rice-burners. Worthington would have preferred to use a phone produced by a Worthington company, but Worthington Electronics had tried and failed to get into the cell phone market early on. The best phone they could produce weighed five pounds and required the user to lug a backpack and antenna wherever he went.

"Damn panda herders," Worthington grumbled.

There was no number stored in memory. That was strange.

The phone was the same one that creature Remo had borrowed back on Worthington's train. Worthington had been careful not to use it since. Probably some anti-tracing technology. After all, Remo was a government agent of some sort.

Worthington pressed redial.

At first he thought it had not worked. There were nearly two dozen beeps, all the same tone. But just when he was about to give up, it began ringing.

Prescott Worthington leaned back in his chair.

As he read Mark Howard's reports on the various Worthington business enterprises, Harold W. Smith's brow furrowed.

Only now, days after the murderous attack on the Civilian Border Patrol, Smith realized that by chasing Santa Anna they had been looking in the wrong place.

Just Worthington's sugar company alone had lost over one hundred million dollars in two and a half years. In a worldwide corporation worth many billions, this was still an amount that should have made accountants sit up and take notice and now, thanks to Mark and the CURE computers, the money trail was beginning to fill in. For over two years, funds—nearly a billion dollars as could be determined thus far—had been siphoned off from several dead ends in the Worthington business empire. The cash had been directed to activist immigration groups, to General Juan Pichardo of the Mexican Army, as well as political leaders on both sides of the border.

The evidence was clear. Prescott Worthington IV was trying to buy himself a country.

Smith was sifting through damning data when the blue contact phone rang.

"Report, Remo," he said, almost abstractedly, not wanting to look away from the printed Worthington files.

But the voice that answered was not that of CURE's enforcement arm.

"Remo," drawled the delighted man's voice. "What kind of a name is that anyway? It sounds Italian."

Smith's face soured. "I am sorry," he said crisply. "You have a wrong number."

Smith was lowering the receiver when the caller snapped, "This is Prescott Worthington IV and you will not hang up on me."

Gripping the receiver tightly, Smith quickly raised the phone back to his ear. "What do you want, Worthington?"

"I see by your tone that you've figured out it was all me," Worthington said. "Good. We don't have to waste time on pleasantries. What I want is for you to pull your two men out of my country. My new country."

The gall of the man. Smith's arthritic knuckles clenched tight on the receiver. "You have no country, Worthington. Mexico and the United States will never surrender land to you."

"Of course they will," Worthington said. "Neither of them will want to risk the bloodshed they'd get from trying to prevent their countries being torn apart. And this is the direction it was going down here already. I just helped nudge it along. We do it my way, and both countries submit quietly to the inevitable. Nice and neat, we have the birth of a nation and everyone is happy. Maybe we'll commission a Broadway musical."

"We will stop you," Smith said firmly.

"I admit, your mongrel friend and his Chinaman helper are impressive. I tried to hire your Remo myself, in fact. I'm told they had something to do with clearing out the Alamo. Two men against six hundred troops is truly amazing."

"Did Rebecca Dalton tell you that?"

"So you know about her," Worthington said.

"I know that she is a homicidal maniac in your employ," Smith said.

"Yes," Worthington said. "I think she also might be part German. Very pale, but with a very wide face. Could be part squarehead. Heaven hope she's not Irish. But who knows? Still, she gets results. She has given me something that will keep me safe. She tells me your younger friend has a Boy Scout's sensibility. Tell him to keep away from me, to steer clear from Nuevo Mexico, or his wetback girlfriend gets greased." Worthington snorted. "Is that the delightful term? 'Greased'? Heard it on HBO. Grease the greaser. Clever, really. And apt."

Smith glanced at his watch. Something approaching a thin smile flickered across his lemony face.

"For someone who hates Mexicans, you keep odd company," the CURE director said.

In his New Mexico mansion, Worthington smiled

proudly. "You mean Santa Anna," he said, warming to his subject. "Now that was a genuine find. An actual descendent of the real general. Can you believe I found him wasting his time in Tijuana as just another wetback kitsch vendor? His ancestry makes him a terrific face for this enterprise. His lineage will keep Mexico away, and simultaneously attract Mexicans to my cause. And I can finally get it all back. Everything that the Worthington empire has seen peeled away by so-called 'globalization.'"

"So it's all about money?"

"And power. I'll live like a king in a land devoted to industry. For the right price, all will be welcome. There will be no regulations on anything. Pollution, goddamned OSHA rules, minimum wage, health insurance . . . anything. With Santa Anna to back me, these beaners will do whatever I say."

So absorbed was he in this conversation, so proud to finally be revealing to someone the brilliance of his own scheme, Worthington failed to notice a gentle rumbling in the distance. The pens on his desk began to rattle.

"I would not be too sure of that," Smith said.

"Forgive me, but you're just some government bureaucrat. How many servants have you had? Pool boys? Gardeners? How many Mexican factories do you own? None, I assume. I've dealt with these people . . ." He drawled the words with undisguised contempt. ". . . Long enough to know how to manipulate them. Toss them a sack of refried beans and a chicken once a month and they'll beg to come work for me." Worthington sat up, patted his desk. "Now, I would invite you down but, unlike the United States, I plan to be selective about who I allow into my country."

Behind his desk at Folcroft, Smith did not bother to tell Worthington that he had fought against others with the same notions of racial purity sixty years ago in France and

Germany. Nor did he suggest that if a man's worth could be judged solely by time spent on American soil, then Worthington was the newcomer since Smith's own ancestors had preceded Worthington's tardy relations to the New World by more than a century. But Smith said nothing; instead he strained to hear a sound on the other end of the line.

The distant shriek of a whistle sounded far off.

Worthington had heard it as well. "What was that?" the billionaire asked.

"I believe your train is leaving the station, Mr. Worthington," Harold Smith said. And as he slammed down the phone, the CURE director allowed himself a rare, tight smile.

Worthington hurried back to his veranda, flinging the doors open wide.

It was barreling in fast. Too fast to stop in time.

The old Worthington Continental Railroad locomotive followed the straight track in from that useless ratty ranch in Mexico. But Worthington's big toy did not stop at the old-fashioned station he'd had constructed near the tennis courts. At eighty miles per hour, the train crashed through the barrier at the end of the line, tore a brown gash across green lawns and slammed into the east wing of Worthington's hundred-year-old mansion.

The house shook. The bedroom floor lurched under his feet. From the veranda he could see the other end of the mansion collapsing into rubble.

Two small figures jumped from the caboose.

Gunfire erupted down below. Worthington saw Remo and Chiun cut through his guards and race toward the mansion.

Hanging from the wall, Conchita's face was lit with fear mixed with hope. "What is happening?" she demanded.

Worthington wheeled from the veranda, a wild look on his

face. Racing across the room, he grabbed Conchita by the waist and lifted her off the makeshift hook. She struggled in his arms; kicking, pushing him with her bound hands.

Shoving her to the floor, Worthington dragged her by the ropes to the back of the room.

A numbered panel was affixed to the wall. With shaking hands, Worthington pressed a six-digit code. A bookcase swung away, revealing a steel-lined door and room.

Inside was a vent, cot, water and food. Worthington shoved Conchita inside his panic room and slammed the door behind them. Panting and sweating, he leaned against the door.

Conchita crawled to the rear of the small room. "It is them, isn't it?" she asked.

"Shut up," Worthington snapped. His mind raced.

Their employer could not have told them that Worthington had Conchita. There was not time. He could still bargain his way out of this. He thought of the gun he kept stashed in his desk drawer and cursed himself for not bringing it in with him. No matter. Those two would have no way of knowing he was unarmed. He could talk them away. Before she left, Rebecca Dalton had assured Worthington that the younger one, this Remo, would not want to harm his female friend. Yes, he would get rid of them. Worthington would have his country. He would get . . .

A sound outside the door. A tiny groan of metal, as if something were testing the hinges. It came and went so quickly, Worthington was not sure he had imagined it. Leaning his ear against the door, Worthington strained to hear. He jumped when a very near voice called out from the other side of the door.

"Knock-knock," Remo said.

"Who is there?" the Master of Sinanju replied.

"Dead billionaire."

"Dead billionaire who?"

"Get out of here," Worthington screamed. "I have your wetback woman with me. Leave me alone, and she lives."

For a moment he held his breath, listening for a reply.

And then the door was wrenched out in a groan of twisting metal, and Worthington was tumbling right along with it, back out into his study. He landed at the feet of the two men who had brought his great scheme to ruin.

"It's bad enough everything else," Remo complained, "but did you have to go and ruin a good knock-knock joke?"

Worthington skittered back on his rear end, one hand raised to ward off invisible blows.

"No," the billionaire said, froth forming at the corners of his mouth. "You won't stop me. I will not permit it. Don't you see? They've brought this country to ruin. Not just the Mexicans. All of them. Germans, Italians, God only knows what from Asia." He was spitting now as he spoke. "Over a hundred years of Prescott Worthingtons have seen what these filthy immigrants have done. Between them and a government that coddles these inferiors, I've seen my business brought to the verge of ruin. Well, I am going to put them to work for me now, under my rules, and they are going to lick my boots for the privilege."

Worthington was panting, back pressed against the wall. He looked from Remo to Chiun, eyes flashing in crazed fury.

"Did you hear that, Little Father?" Remo said, cupping a hand behind his ear. "I think they just called 'All aboard the WASP express.' "

A flicker of confusion crossed Worthington's face. "What?" he asked. He was distracted by something that had appeared in Chiun's hand.

The Master of Sinanju had removed from the folds of his kimono the toy engine he had taken from Worthington's office earlier in the week. The old man balanced it lightly in the palm of his right hand.

"What is that?" Worthington asked. He recognized his

train. "That is mine. You stole that, you godless Chinese thief. I demand you return it and leave my property."

The train bounced in Chiun's hand. And then the hand was up to eye level, and his hand dropped toward the wall.

The train shot from his fingertips at supersonic speed. It crossed the room in a blur, and struck Worthington in the forehead. Bone cracked. With a sucking thup, the engine buried itself halfway into Prescott Worthington's brain.

An expression of intense confusion crossed the billionaire's face, and he pitched forward onto the floor.

Remo entered the panic room and snapped Conchita's bonds. "You okay, kid?" he asked.

She nodded numbly. She was staring at Remo, a look of wonder on her face.

"You sure you're okay?" Remo asked. "You look like you've got gas or something."

"I am fine," she assured him.

He helped her over the rubble of the door and out into Worthington's study.

They were heading for the hallway when Worthington's phone buzzed. Remo fished it from the dead billionaire's pocket. He tried to open it, but couldn't.

"You are hopeless," Chiun said, shaking his head. The old Korean plucked the phone from his pupil's hand, flipped it open and answered it. "You have reached his sublime magnificence, the Master of Sinanju, unworthy though you are to hear his voice. Speak, but do not annoy."

Chiun listened for a few moments, pressing the phone to his shell-like ear in such a way that Remo could not hear who was on the other end of the line.

"Of course," Chiun said. "Yes, I am. You should be applauded for noticing, since so few do in this wretched land. Yes. Yes. I am that as well. And that. How perceptive of you. No, we will not. No, not unless you do. Yes. Of course. You are most kind. What a delightful conversation this has been." Finished, the old Asian handed the phone off to Remo. "It is for you."

"Hey, Smitty," Remo said. "If you're looking for *el Presidente,* you're going to have to yell pretty loud. Try shouting down."

But the caller was not Smith.

"Why, hello, Remo, how are you?" Rebecca Dalton asked. "I've just been having the most darling conversation with your father. Such a sweet man."

Remo shot a look at the Master of Sinanju.

The Master of Sinanju studied the ceiling. "Yeah, he gives me cavities just thinking about him," Remo said. "If you're planning on blowing up another building around us, don't bother. This one's pretty much already blowed-up."

"No," Rebecca said. "I'm done with all that. That's what I was just talking to your father about. We agreed that you'll have this part of the world. I'm moving my business elsewhere."

Remo shot a glance at the Master of Sinanju. "Did you just cut a deal with this raving loonball behind my back?"

"Of course not," Chiun sniffed. "You were facing me the entire time."

Rebecca continued as if Remo had not spoken. "I didn't think kidnapping your friend would work. But it was worth a try. Gotta reinforce the notion with my clients that I'm pulling out all the stops for them. Anyway, by the sounds of it, Prescott won't be telling anyone I sort of dropped the ball on this one, so I'm safe there. And anyway, I think I could be forgiven this tiny failure, since nothing seems to work against you. I did my best, but I know when to call it quits. Momma didn't raise no fool."

"Your momma didn't raise you at all," Remo said.

There was a slight hesitation on the other end of the line. "Water under the bridge," Rebecca said. "So anywho, I'm tearing a page out of my buddy Benson Dilkes's book and getting out of ol' Dodge. Goodbye, Remo. And please say goodbye to your dad for me. He's so darned cute."

The line went dead.

Remo spun on his teacher. "What do you think you're doing letting that batshit, crackpot nutbar just up and take off like that?"

Chiun shrugged. "I like her," the old Korean said as he padded out the door. "For a white she is much more suitable daughter-in-law material than the hussies you usually sniff after. Get my train before you leave."

"Are you nuts?" Remo shouted after him. "Get your own damned train. And I'd marry Conchita here long before I married that loony. That's what I'm going to do. I'm going to marry Conchita. What do you think about that? You can take your fine Korean maidens you're always wanting me to hook up with and cram them, you old racist."

He felt a soft touch on his forearm. He looked down into Conchita's warm brown eyes. And for a moment, he didn't think marrying her was such a bad idea at all.

"You are attractive and nice," Conchita said, "despite your best efforts to present yourself as otherwise. And you arrived at my darkest hour of need." She was thinking of her cousin and his family. Of funerals, and of extended family in Mexico, and of time she would now spend with people she had forced from her hectic life. People she could admit to herself she had thought were beneath her, but who now meant more to her than anything else in the world. She smiled sadly. "But I must decline your proposal."

Remo exhaled derisively. "Oh, believe me, sister, if I wanted you to marry me, you'd marry me. Two seconds and you'd be registering at Bloomingdale's. I have wells of charm. Deep wells."

She wrapped her arms around him, drawing him close. She did not kiss him but instead just hugged him tight, head resting on his shoulder. The tension drained from Remo's body. He hugged her back, smelling the perfume of her hair. This was something he could definitely get used to.

"You're just . . . just . . . ," Remo stammered, "lucky. Damn lucky. Prince Charming's got nothing on me."

She looked up into his eyes. "No, Remo, you are not Prince Charming," Conchita said firmly. "You are my guardian angel."

24

A tattered blue-and-white-striped canopy hung out over the front of the little wooden stall. Painted on the fringe but faded from exposure to years of sun, was the legend: LÓPEZ DE S.A. The outdoor Tijuana market bustled with activity as American tourists searched open-air kiosks for liquor, costume jewelry, souvenir sombreros and fireworks.

The little López de S.A. stall had been abandoned for several months and even before that no one paid the shabby little booth much attention, just as no one noticed the thin gringo or the ancient Asian who entered the stall and disappeared into the building behind it.

Remo and Chiun found Santa Anna hiding in a storeroom on a cot surrounded by open cases of fireworks. Worthington's great general had intended to blow himself up with bottle rockets. But that was hours ago. The book of matches he held in his shaking hands was wet from sweat and tears. When the two shadows fell across his filthy bed, the quivering man looked up in fear.

"It was not my idea, señores," Santa Anna pleaded. "Blame Prescott Worthington and his dirty money."

"Already blamed him to death," Remo said. "And Chiun here wouldn't want you to go blaming anything on money."

"That is true," the Master of Sinanju said. "The money is the only innocent in this whole affair. Not counting whatever pesos were spent to purchase your loyalty since pesos are worthless paper scraps guilty of masquerading as currency."

Santa Anna sniffled and wiped a trail of dribbling mucus onto his uniform cuff. "If you let me live, I will tell you everything of Worthington's plan."

"There's only one thing we don't know," Remo said. "Where's Rebecca Dalton?"

Santa Anna tried desperately to think of anything Worthington might have said about how he had found the woman. At that point he would have settled on a lie; anything that might extend his life. He did not realize that the look of helpless desperation in his eyes had already told Remo all he needed to know.

Santa Anna did not see the hand that ended his life, did not feel the side of Remo's hand slice sinew and bone. One moment he was sitting on his bed, frantically searching his brain for a lie, the next moment his furiously-thinking brain and the head in which it was contained were rolling off his shoulders and thumping to the grimy floor.

Chiun hefted the head by the hair.

"What are you going to do with that?" Remo asked, eyeing Santa Anna's decapitated head with concern.

"I should hang it on the gates of Fortress Folcroft as a warning to others never to attempt such a thing," Chiun replied. "There is doubtless some Canadian general right now sharpening his sword up in the frozen north, intent on leading an invasion of Smith's territory."

"We're safe from Canadian hordes, Little Father. The only things they sharpen are hockey skates. Besides, armies cost, and you're the one who's always saying how cheap Canadians are."

"That is true," the Master of Sinanju said. "Those goose herders would chop off their feet to save money on shoes." He hefted his prize, examining Santa Anna eye to eye. "This family is constantly losing parts of itself. Legs, heads. I pray to my ancestors that I will not be around to see what drops off one of them next."

They tucked the head amid some papier-mâché fright masks on a corner rack in the stall out front.

Chiun hung a tag which read TWO PESOS OR BEST OFFER from the nose. Remo said it was overpriced.

25

Two days later, Remo answered the phone in the kitchen of his Connecticut condominium. It was Smith.

"The entire scheme has collapsed," the CURE director said. "Mexico has arrested General Pichardo. It seems that he is the highest-level official that Santa Anna reached. In exchange for leniency, he is naming names of other Mexican officials involved in the scheme. It seems that with Worthington and Santa Anna dead, so too is their plan. Our president and the president of Mexico are right now in talks to make sure nothing like this happens again."

"Yippee yi-o ki-ay," Remo said. "So what about the problem of border security?"

"I suspect there will be much posturing over the issue. There will be talk of building fences, and permanently deploying the National Guard. But with ten percent of Mex-

ico's population already living here in the United States, I
doubt very much will change."

"The status quo," Remo said. "I can live with that."

"That does not mean CURE will not be vigilant. While
the politicians argue over what must be done, there are still
enemies such as the Elite Incursion Martyrdom Brigade
who will attempt to exploit our openness."

Remo grunted. In all the blather and shouting, this was
the coldest reality of border security and the one that
seemed totally ignored.

"When you find someone who needs stepping on, just
point me at them," Remo said. "I just bought new squashing shoes."

"Speaking of which, there was one tragic incident during the bedlam at the border," Smith said. "Apparently
Senators Clancy and Muldoon were caught in a stampede."

"What, did that rum-pot Clancy try to fondle a cow?"

"No, it was not cattle," Smith said. "It was at the height
of the insanity two days ago. The senators were at a joint
appearance welcoming a multitude into New Mexico. Apparently the crowd was more interested in getting in than it
was in hearing political speeches. The two senators were
trampled underfoot."

Remo pictured a wild unruly crowd of taco vendors,
cockfight impresarios and mariachi bands stomping the
two United States senators to paste. The image brought a
smile to his lips and a song to his heart.

"Two down, ninety-eight to go," Remo said. He hung up
the phone.

In the living room, the Master of Sinanju sat cross-
legged on the floor before the big-screen TV. The old Korean was watching a Mexican soap opera.

Even with the volume turned down, Remo would have
been able to tell it was not an American soap opera. On Mexican soap operas, the woman wore more makeup than their
American counterparts and the men were less effeminate.

The volume was not turned down. It was pushed so far up the rafters shook. Chiun had nudged the sound up as soon as the phone rang.

When a Spanish-language Pepsi commercial came on, the Master of Sinanju hit the mute button.

"That was Smith," Remo said.

"Did you tell him it was too late, and that Santa Anna's head has probably sold by now?"

"You know, it didn't come up," Remo said.

The old Korean offered a hum of disbelief. "Knowing the Mexicans, they have probably filled it with candy and hung it from a tree. Filthy urchins in rags are no doubt pummeling Smith's prize with sticks right now." Chiun sniffed. "It is Smith's loss, and he cannot blame our House."

"He's not blaming anyone. He actually sounded kind of happy." He considered his own words. "Well, happy for Smith, anyway. And you know what, Little Father? I'm kind of happy too."

"Bully for you and Smith," Chiun said. "The two of you may take adjoining padded rooms in his lunatic facility. You may spend your days happily gluing macaroni to cardboard."

The commercials ended. Chiun nudged the volume back up.

Remo watched his teacher watch television, the age-speckled scalp nodding contentedly at certain lines, shaking angrily at others.

For so many reasons, the past few years seemed a blur to Remo, as if someone else had been living his life. But the world was now coming back into focus. Finally.

He watched his teacher for a few minutes longer.

Another commercial. A long fingernail reached out and stabbed the MUTE button.

"What are you staring at?" Chiun asked without turning, annoyance straining his sing-song voice.

Remo smiled. "Perfection, Little Father."

The old man's shoulders straightened. His twinkling hazel eyes remained locked on the TV.

"And don't you forget it, Remo Williams."

Remo and Chiun return in

THE NEW DESTROYER:

CHOKE HOLD

(0-7653-5760-7)

by WARREN MURPHY and JAMES MULLANEY

Coming in September 2007

Remo was already running back toward the burning field. He had taken only three strides when the wall of flame belched out unexpectedly and he had to jump back to keep from getting burned. The fire receded, but Remo stopped at its edge, rotating his wrists in frustration. The heat was too intense, the smoke too dangerous. The longer his body fought to keep it out, the more he could feel his strength ebb.

He had been lucky. Nearness to the road had saved him. But Chiun had been farther out than Remo; too far out to make it back to the road before the flames became a force too great for even a Sinanju-trained body to ignore.

Helpless to act, intense heat drying his tears the instant they formed, Remo backed away from the flames. He dealt in death and now it had come to him.

Chiun, his teacher, father, the only family he had ever had on this earth, was dead.

And in his grief and weakened condition Remo almost did not feel the pressure waves of the object flying at his back until the instant before metal touched flesh.

Slower than a bullet. Sharper than an ordinary knife blade. Unseeing, he yet understood what it was, recognized it as an opportunity to channel his pain and anger.

Without missing a step, Remo pivoted on his hip. It was a move impossible to follow with the normal human eye. One moment he was facing one direction, the next, as if his hips could swivel 180 degrees, he was flying back in the direction he had come, his torso whirling around moments after his legs.

As he ran, Remo snatched from the air the silver throwing star that had been flung at his wide open back.

The band of masked killers had concealed themselves behind tree and stone wall. Somehow, they must have slowed their body rhythms to near death, for neither Remo nor Chiun had sensed their presence.

With a snap, the star left Remo's fingertips. But even as he threw it, he knew his body rhythms were off.

The star should have struck its owner mid-forehead, splitting the skull in two. Instead, it buried itself in the killer's left eye. In place of the neat death Remo had come to expect was a sloppy mess of blood and screaming.

Another killer ended the life of his writhing comrade with the end of a merciful blade.

Rage propelled Remo forward, and a hail of throwing stars filled the air around him. Harvesting them as he ran, Remo sent them flying back across the field. With fatal, distant screams, the nearest men dropped one by one. Most of the blows were fatal, but some were not. Stars struck legs and backs. Men screamed. Some scrambled to safety and disappeared into woods. Remo did not care.

And then he was among them.

A blade slid at his gut. Remo grabbed the wrist, guiding the knife into the belly of another of the masked assassins.

Remo felt a great weariness in his limbs. Behind him, the wind shifted. The first leading edge of the wispy black smoke cloud passed over and around him.

Another masked man drew two swords from scabbards at his back. Grunting, whizzing blades slicing air, he attacked. A dozen, two dozen rapid-fire slashes, meant to disorient a target before the fatal blow.

Remo snatched one of the falling swords, flipped it up onto his elbow, and with a slap of his palm, plunged it straight through the hearts of two of the killers. Joined on a skewer in death, the men collapsed.

Another blade plunged at Remo's back, and he spun to face his attacker . . .

. . . and tripped over the two skewered men.

Remo fell hard to the ground. His breath was gone, yet the killers continued to move with confidence. And, Remo realized, he was facing the great Achilles' heel of his discipline. At its core, Sinanju was about breathing, permitting its practitioners to ascend to a level unmatched by other mortals. Yet robbed of breath, unable to draw fresh oxygen into his lungs, Remo could feel the power within him ebbing.

A blow with a lashing staff landed on the meaty part of his upper back. Remo let out a reflexive grunt, which depleted the already dwindling supply of oxygen in his lungs.

One came at him with hands, launching a power fist blow at the center of Remo's chest.

In slow-motion Remo saw the hand come in, fingers curled, palm flat. A killing blow. But in the moment before the fatal blow struck, a single word rose from deep within the throat of the last living Master of Sinanju.

And that word was, "No."

Remo would not shame his father by permitting his life to be ended by these thieving offspring of the Sun Source.

Remo's hand shot out.